Three novellas from a man the *Sunday Times* has described as 'one of the most amusing writers in English'. Yet in each of these, the sound and the fury of Gwyn Thomas, writing about his native Welsh mining villages, trumpets alongside his delightfully wry, sardonic humour; *The Sky of Our Lives* is full of rage and passion as well as wit.

'Written with funny, Runyonesque formality, the case of the employed against the employer is put . . . with lovely eloquence. He does not feel sympathy with the oppressed, he feels and expresses identification. Not shrill, but hard and funny' – *The Guardian*

Gwyn Thomas was born in Rhondda, Glamorgan, in 1913, the son of a miner, youngest of twelve children. He had his first novel published in 1946 and has since written many more, plus volumes of short stories, non-fiction, and plays. He is well known as a television performer, magazine contributor, playwright and broadcaster.

ALSO BY GWYN THOMAS

Fiction

Where did I put my pity?
The alone to the alone
The world cannot hear you
Frost on my frolic
Point of order
The love man
All things betray thee
Now lead us home
The stranger at my side
Gazooka
Ring Delirium 123
The lust Lobby

Non-fiction

A Welsh eye
A few selected exits

Plays

The keep
Land organs
Jackie the jumper

THE SKY OF OUR LIVES

GWYN THOMAS

QUARTET BOOKS LONDON

Published by Quartet Books Limited 1973
27 Goodge Street, London W1P 1FD

First published in Great Britain by Hutchinson & Co Ltd, 1972

ISBN 0 704 31045 7

Printed in Great Britain by
Hunt Barnard Printing Ltd, Aylesbury, Bucks

Novellas

OSCAR

Rainwater streamed down the walls of the 'Harp'. It had rained for a week. There was nothing of the many things I could feel around me in the dark that was not soaked. I wore a waterproof jacket. That jacket was thick and good. It had belonged to an uncle of mine. I took it from his house without telling anybody, just after he died. The rain did not bother him any more. It bothered me.

I leaned with the full weight of my shoulders against the walls of the 'Harp'. I was standing in the yard of that pub. The rain bounced down from the chutes about six inches from where I stood. Besides me was a lighted window, small. The light from that window was very yellow and had a taste. Behind that window were about a dozen drunks, singing. Among those drunks was Oscar. I could tell that Oscar's voice if I was deaf. There was a feel about it, a slow greasy feel.

Oscar was a hog. I knew him well. I worked for Oscar. I was Oscar's boy. It was for Oscar I was waiting in that streaming, smelling yard of the 'Harp', pressing my shoulders against those walls that were as wet and cold as the soil of the churchyard that stood across the road.

The wind blew a kite's tail of the falling water from the chute across my mouth. I licked in the water and cursed Oscar, called him a hog seven times. I did not speak under my breath but out loud. No one could hear me in that empty yard. If anyone had heard me and if he did not know Oscar he would have said I was mad, shouting in that fashion. If he knew Oscar he would have said I was quite right. Everybody in the valley knew Oscar was a very dirty element.

I stared at the tall railings that the Council had planted on the wall of the churchyard opposite. I tried to count the number of spikes in those railings and gave up that job with the thought that they were many. I wondered whether those tall railings were to keep the dead voters in or the live voters out. There were many things done by that Council that I did not understand. But I was young. That I was working for a hog who spent less than one day in a hundred sober meant that I must have been very dense as well. The only bright thing I ever remember doing was to take that waterproof jacket from the house of my uncle who had just died.

I sang a bit of the song the drunks were singing. It was a song called 'Roll me Home', and the voters behind the curtain were singing it to some words that were coated with dirt that they had no doubt made up for themselves to work up a heat. There were maidens' voices too behind that curtain and I thought it was funny that maidens should have the chance or the time to do any such thing as sing with such a great, busy ram as Oscar in the same room. I sang in a light tenor voice that sounded very well in that enclosed yard. I used to be a boy soprano. I used to sing very sweetly and on a sad song I could make as many people cry as death. If it had not broken so soon I would have taken that soprano voice around the place singing for money, and perhaps I would have made so much out of it I would not have had to take that job with Oscar when I found there were no jobs in pits or shops for youths like me.

I glanced at the hills around. The hills of the valley were close together around the 'Harp'. The houses of the valley were thickest at this point. They were built around a colliery and the 'Harp'. The local voters did a lot of work in the colliery, and some of them did a lot of drinking at the 'Harp', not as much as Oscar did, but there was nothing ordinary about him. Behind the 'Harp' to the north was the broad mountain that Oscar owned. It was his. I always thought it queer that a man could point to a thing like a mountain and say, 'That's mine,' just as you would with a shirt or a woman or a pot. But that is what Oscar could do with this mountain.

He got it from his father. I never knew his father and I never knew where he got this mountain from. Stole it, as like as not, from sheep or from some people who were dafter than sheep. And on top of this mountain a colliery company had built its tip, its dump, the stuff that had to be got out from underground to let the elements that work there get at the coal. Oscar owned that tip too. He owned the mountain and the huge cake of black refuse that the pit people had tossed on to it. So Oscar owned a lot of dirt.

He owned me too, I suppose, or I would not have been such a dense crap as to stand there in pouring rain waiting for him to fill his guts to a point where I would have to undo his buttons for him. So, for a hog, Oscar did very well out of being a man. Nobody liked him in the valley. The elements who went to chapel thought he was on a par with the god Pan, who was half a goat. The elements who did not go to chapel thought he was all Pan or all goat, or they were red revolutionary elements who thought that all such subjects as Oscar, who got fat out of stolen land, should have a layer of this land fixed over them in such a way as to stop their breathing.

And a lot of this dislike for Oscar which was felt by the local voters was felt for me too. I worked for him and was, as they saw it, part of him. Lads who in the old days would always say, 'Hullo, Lewis,' when I passed, in a very friendly way, grew either to saying just 'Hullo', or nothing at all, and these habits came to hurt me in a deep sensitive part of me. All because Oscar was a hog and owned a mountain.

All I said in answer to the voters, who claimed I ought to be hanging my head in shame for getting pay from such an element, was that I spent much time looking for jobs that were not there or ran to cover whenever I was around, and when a youth has spent much time in such a search he will get desperate and unparticular and will take a job even from Satan if he finds Satan. I did not find him but I found Oscar, who was the next worse thing. And there we are. In Clay Street, a dark thoroughfare, where the feet get in deeper and stickier with every forward step we take.

A small cart came rolling down the road. It stopped outside

the entrance to the yard where I stood. I could hear the driver of the cart clicking his tongue at the horse. He kept clicking his tongue for a whole minute after the horse had stopped, and that made me think that the horse had a lot more sense than the driver. I knew this driver well. He was a small man by the name of Waldo Williamson, who sold vegetables from a cart about the streets and made some sort of a living in this way because his horse was nearly as daft as Waldo and allowed itself to be driven up steep slopes that no other carter would touch, to serve voters who liked living in high places.

Waldo's wife and kids did not see much of this living that he made, for this element Waldo Williamson was a man who greatly feared rheumatism and went around all the year wearing heavy oilskins, and went into every pub he passed to get cool from the heat he worked up from wearing such a load of leggings and capes. So this Waldo was nearly always drunk and broke, and only his wife, who had to sleep with him off and on, knew what he looked like without all this waterproof.

She would not tell because she was not interested enough in this Waldo to talk about him, and I always felt she was right in that, because this Waldo could not have been much of a man to live with or sleep with, and his wife, no doubt, would have slept elsewhere if she could have found another bed, which was difficult in a crowded, poor place like that valley.

Waldo came into the yard eating a piece of swede, and I could hear him groaning softly because he was getting on in age and his teeth could not have been strong, not strong enough to cope with so hard an item as a swede. He stopped in front of me, right beneath the shower from the chutes. It shows what sort of a man this Waldo was to stand there still as a mummy and get a drenching.

'You're getting wet,' I said.

'Who are you?' he asked, his voice indistinct and distant with swede-eating.

'You know me, Waldo. I'm Lewis. You're drunk as a wheel.'

'Always drunk, boy. You're Lewis. Hullo, Lew. You're Oscar's boy.' He started to laugh, rocking about in his oilskins and making a rustle like wind in a wood and his breath was right in my face. 'He got sick of women, did he, Lewis boy, and now he's got you instead.'

I drove my open hand into his face and he went down into a puddle. He laughed at that, too. Dressed like that, Waldo could have lived in puddles like a duck and not seen much difference. He looked altogether like a duck as he sat there, his lips stuck outwards like the beginnings of a beak, and wondering how the hell he got down there so near the ground with waves all around him. I jerked him to his feet, swiftly, proud of my strength, which could have jerked twelve Waldos, oilskins and all, to their feet.

He waddled into the side door of the 'Harp'. He was a well-known drinker at the 'Harp' and he never went in by the front way. His father, who was still alive and very old, was a Rechabite, and did not like the notion of his son Waldo entering pubs the front way. So Waldo used the side doors of as many as fourteen pubs in one day to please his old man. It baffled me to know how an element as old as Waldo's old man could have wit enough left to be a Rechabite or anything else; also, how it could have escaped the attention of Waldo's old man that the best and shortest cut to solving such a problem as Waldo's drinking was to get rid of Waldo, who was of no use that I could see.

At the side door, through which Waldo had gone, appeared Clarisse, one of the girls who worked at the 'Harp'. Clarisse was wearing a red blouse and the strong light from the passageway shone hard upon this blouse, and it was smooth red and had an effect on me. Clarisse was a stoutish girl with black hair, black as mine, which was very black, and her lips were thick and red like good chops of meat. Most of the young elements in the valley had chased Clarisse at some time or the other, and when they got tired Clarisse chased them, because she lived well at the 'Harp', slept soundly and had plenty of strength left over from serving up the malt and dusting around the furniture for such activities as love.

I always kept away from Clarisse, although I knew she could never have kept ahead of me if I started chasing. I did not want to give the local voters any idea that I was as mad for the maidens as Oscar was, and if I fooled around with Clarisse I knew I would be mad. I was always like a kettle on the boil with nobody to take it off or turn the gas down whenever that Clarisse came within a yard of me. So I kept away from her and lived a life that was cleaner than my linen.

'Come on in here,' said Clarisse.

I made no answer. I pressed closer to the wall.

'Don't be so daft, Lewis. Come on in here. I got tea made. You'll like that. There's nobody in here.'

When she said that about nobody being in there my body twitched a little and I had the old spots in front of my eyes. My eyes rested on the smooth, scarlet shine of her blouse, and I thought of what my father had told me once, after he had had a few pots, not long before he passed over with the lung trouble he got in the pits.

'You're like me, Lewis. Just like me, boyo. You're a good-for-nothing bloody nuisance. It's stamped all over your face like it's stamped all over the inside of me. You won't do yourself any good by trying to be any different.'

A nice man, my father, but given to saying dark, moody things like the one you have just heard. I did not agree with him. An element does not have to be like his old man. An element does not have to be like the element he works for. He grows up the way the world lets him, and if he does not want to be like any element whatever, he can always pass over and be like nobody. I wanted to show people that I could be clean and good like these elements who go to chapels and boast a lot about being good and clean, without, very often, being so, except when they are actually inside the chapels where a voter is very limited in his choice of what he would like to do. So I made no answer to this Clarisse who stood there in the lighted passageway asking me to come inside and drink tea and so on. I drank in the smooth redness of her blouse as if it were a glass of hot cordial you get at a penny a glass in the Italian refreshment shops.

'There's nobody in here,' said Clarisse again.

'I'm waiting for Oscar. I got to wait here for Oscar. Got to take him home.'

'Don't worry about him. He's well away. He's got one of those Macnaffy girls from Brimstone Terrace and he'll be a long time with her.'

'Got to wait for him. So long, Clarisse.'

She put her hands over her head and ran out into the rain towards me. She stood by my side. I stuck my lips hard into hers. I could not help doing that, as you could not help sticking your head into a soft pillow if you were in a bed and very tired. Her whole body came at me in a rush and burned mine. The steam was whistling through my ears.

'You're big and dark and strong,' she glugged, and it was this glugging sound which Clarisse seemed to have picked up from the pictures or the chickens that gave me the strength to remain like my linen, clean. What she told me was nothing new. I knew I was big and dark and strong. I was big because my father had been like that. I was dark because my mother's hair is raven and her skin the softest brown you ever saw. I was strong because all the work I had done as a kid, such as carrying loads of coal, furniture and God knows what, for voters who could not afford to pay somebody grown-up to do this carrying, could not have been done by anybody weak.

'You talk a lot of nonsense,' I said to Clarisse.

'You're dark and strong, Lewis, like a man in the book I'm reading.'

I did not know that Clarisse could read. We had been at school together and I remembered she had worn out three teachers because these three elements had vanished after a few months of trying to put some knowledge into Clarisse. I supposed she must have picked up a bit of culture from the softer-spoken customers at the 'Harp' who were clerks. I was very pleased to find that she could read books as well as spend her time bringing young, sensitive elements like me to the boil at a speed that nearly drove us forward like engines.

'What is the name of this book you are reading, Clarisse?' I asked, thinking a serious question of this type would cool her down straightaway.

'It's called *Four Green Eyes.*'

'Who's the element who's got four green eyes?'

'Two. With two green eyes each. Green with being jealous, see?'

'That's fair enough.'

'I'm jealous about you, Lewis. I'm green for you, like that book says. Why don't you ever go with girls, Lew?'

'I've got enough to do with Oscar. I haven't got the time. I haven't got the fancy.'

'Nor the strength,' she snapped, a bit angry, but I only laughed when she said that, because I knew I had the strength to lift her over the building.

'That Oscar is a hog,' she said, and I thought that if a girl like Clarisse, who was not bright at anything except making shapes at men and giving off waves of heat like a furnace, could reel off this slogan pat like that, it must be a very well-established slogan.

'He is that, twice over,' I said. 'And tell him when you get back in that I'm getting wet and cold out here. Tell him to hurry up with that element from Brimstone Terrace, Mactaffy or Macnaffy or whatever the hell her name is. Tell him I'll be too stiff to lead him and his bloody horse home over the mountain if he keeps me hanging about this yard much longer.'

'It'll be dark on that mountain, Lewis.'

'Like pitch. But me and that horse could do the journey blindfold and Oscar does it blind. So the dark doesn't matter much.'

'Why don't you get a decent job, Lewis?'

'I got one.'

'You don't call being with Oscar a decent job. I mean a good, useful job where you could get married or something.'

'Because,' I said and my voice was deep and steady and grown-up, 'because Oscar gave me a job when no one else would give me one, and as for being married, I keep my mother.'

'Oh . . . well, so long Lewis. See you again. I'll tell Oscar to put a move on.'

Her lips pushed on mine again. As she went from me my mind went along in large circles, slowly, sadly, as I thought there was not much shape on my life at all. That did not hurt me as badly as it might have, for I could not guess what alternative shape it might have had. But I felt it to be ugly and unpleasant, overweighed with as large a cake of black refuse as Oscar's mountain, but not bringing in the same kind of income. It struck me that Clarisse's mind might have come into a good patch when she had told me to get away from Oscar.

I noticed that the elements behind the lighted window had now stopped singing 'Roll me Home'. They were belting up great volume on the hymn 'Bring forth the Royal Diadem' and singing the words right out as if they had the diadem right there. This was a strange item to be hearing from such elements, but I joined in all the same because it is a hymn that goes with a great swing, and I wanted something to keep my mouth busy.

Another voice hailed me from the side door. This time it was Mrs Wilson, the landlady of the 'Harp'. She was a woman about fifty, dressed in brown; seeing her in that doorway after Clarisse was like looking at a grate from which the fire has been scraped out. But she was a clean, healthy woman, like the woman you see on the self-raising flour advertisement, and better to look at than a lot of the women in the valley who were short of food and reasons for living. 'Come and get him,' said Mrs Wilson. 'He's in the little room down there on the left.'

I knew the room. I had fished Oscar out of it more than once. It was where he went when he was with a woman, or when he wanted to talk to himself, and when Oscar was not with a woman he always felt so odd he did a lot of talking to himself, so he spent a good deal of his time in the small room on the left-hand side of the main passageway of the 'Harp'.

I pushed open the door. The Macnaffy element, from Brimstone Terrace, was sitting on a chair, her legs, in dark brown stockings, stuck on the low mantelshelf above the gas fire which was full on. The air was warm, dry, nasty, a mixture of heat and maiden and landowner. The girl was sucking at a cigarette. She was pushing it far into her mouth and there was wet halfway up the barrel. The finger-tips of her left hand were caressing the bulging calf of her right leg, hot from the gas fire, as if this bulging calf were a good friend. Her face was tired, thin and savage. I could imagine her coming from a place called Brimstone Terrace. I had never heard of a street of that name in the valley. She might have made Clarisse think of brimstone, scorching stuff which catches at the nostrils, and I do not blame Clarisse for that. She was the sort of element who has been steadily preached against ever since preaching started, which was a long time ago, but the preaching does not seem to have done much in the way of cooling elements like Macnaffy.

Oscar was sitting by the table, his head right down on the table boards. His huge, fat body poured over the sides of the chair on which he sat. His very weight gave him some kind of balance or he would have been on the floor, or under the floor where he deserved to be, a long way under the floor, a thick stone floor. I took hold of his head by the hair and the ear. I lifted it a foot. The table boards beneath were dull and steamy from the heat of him. His jacket and waistcoat hung open and there were dark finger-marks all the way up his white shirt, pulled up crumpled. If these finger-marks were the finger-marks of the savage-looking Macnaffy, I thought she must have been playing on Oscar like a piano. I wondered what kind of music would come out of a hog. Brief, dirty, snorting little tunes. I dropped his head back on to the table and even the sharp bang he got from that did not make him any wider awake.

The girl sitting by the fire grinned at me, as if she were trying to be friendly. I was strong and lean and must have been a great and pleasant change for her eyes after a session with Oscar in so close a room. I looked back at her, without smiling. She was no change for my eyes.

'What a bloody weight,' she said, jerking her head at Oscar. Her voice was soft and dark, which was a great feature of most women in the valley, even women who looked as if they were going to rip you open like this Macnaffy. Voices, like cats' backs, the velvet of skin and purr.

'He's big,' I said, sticking my knee into the blue-serged overflow of Oscar's flesh to give a leverage.

'How the hell do you feed him up to that size?' The girl's face was angrier and more savage as she asked that as if she herself had never had anywhere near enough food, and disliked the idea of Oscar wolfing more in a day than she had to get through in a lifetime in Brimstone Terrace, or wherever it was she lived. 'What do you feed him on?'

'Acorns. And twice a year I bathe him in swill.'

'Looks like it. How do you get him home?'

'First I drag him. Then I get him on a horse.'

'That doesn't sound like much of a job to me. Why don't you get fixed up as a waiter or a welder or something?'

'Dragging Oscar was a hard enough job to get.'

I put my hands beneath Oscar's armpits and tried to lift him. He budged only a little, only such a little as caused him nearly to tip off his chair. The eyes of the Macnaffy girl were fiercer as they glared at the still, sodden Oscar. Her face was like chalk writing something on the air. She did not have the body to cope with a man like Oscar. She flicked a burning chunk of tobacco from her cigarette which had started to burn unevenly.

'What gives him the right to think he can go around expecting girls to lie at his feet like mats to be jumped on?'

'Did he jump on you?' I dropped Oscar to ask the question clearly. I was interested in Oscar's antics.

'Near as hell to jumping. First he got me a bit drunk. Then he got me in here. Next thing I know I think the whole bloody roof has come down on me. What gives him the right? That's what I'd like to know.'

'He owns a mountain. He can jump on that and he thinks there's nobody as important as a mountain.'

'Owns a mountain? What sort of god does that make him?'

'Anybody who owns a mountain can jump anywhere. There is also a big coal-tip on top of Oscar's mountain and he owns that too. And there are twenty or thirty people who work on that tip picking up bits of coal and putting them into sacks for Oscar. He sells those sacks of coal. So he's got a lot of money as well as a lot of mountain. As far as Oscar goes, there's nobody bigger than Oscar.'

'You know a lot for a kid. How old are you?'

'Past nineteen.'

'You know all about life?'

'I know all about Oscar.'

'He's most of it. What a bloody weight.'

'What a bloody life.'

'It strikes me like that, too. So long, boyo. What's your name?

'Lewis.'

'So long, Lewis.' And the Macnaffy element pushed her hat down on to her hair, which was black and flat and glossy, and looked as hard and full of thoughts as the skull underneath. She walked out of the room into the passageway. She heeled over on a sliding mat outside the door and rubbed her face against the rough plasterwork of the wall. She cursed in a streaming fashion that made me certain Clarisse was right about the name of the street this element lived in.

Mr Wilson, the landlord, came out from a back room and said there were plenty of words in the language to draw on without needing to stray into the black pastures where the Macnaffy girl seemed to do most of her talking. She opened the front door and banged it behind her. From outside I could hear her talking still. She was probably telling Wilson to go to hell.

Wilson, up the corridor, went on with his speech against strong language, using a throaty, solemn voice as if he were some kind of apostle who had got himself landed in a pub by some mistake about buses. I decided that Wilson would be giving everybody a lot more pleasure if he shut up and came to give me a hand with Oscar. I shouted on him.

Wilson came into the room where I stood alongside Oscar, wondering whether to kick the chair from under him or wait for a crane. Wilson was eager to help. He wanted to get Oscar out of the building. It was getting late, and, in any case, no building with decent stone in the walls and clean wood in the beams would want Oscar in it for long.

'He's all right as long as he keeps on singing,' said Wilson.

'Then why don't you keep on singing?'

'About quarter to ten the boys always start on hymns. Then Oscar loses interest and comes in here. Is he a pagan?'

'God knows what he is. Never asked him and he never tells me. Jack him up there, Mr Wilson. We can carry him between us.'

And between us we got Oscar to the side door.

'You prop him up there, Mr Wilson, while I go and get the horse.'

Wilson tilted his body hard against Oscar and kept him upright that way. He was a stout man, Wilson, but nowhere near Oscar's class. He was clean-looking, too, but nowhere near his wife's class.

I got Oscar's horse from the outhouse in the yard where we stabled it. There were chinks in the roof of that outhouse. The horse was wet and miserable and whinnied when I touched it. It was a brown mare, strong, and never had a thought. It always did as it was told and, just because it did that, would die, before its time, of weakness, like most of the voters who lived in that valley. This horse did not even have savage thoughts about Oscar to warm the inside of its head when living made it icy, so I felt very sorry for that horse.

The rain had slackened, sick of itself. The water still came down in stutters from the chute. Wilson helped me to get Oscar out into the yard and we stood him under the falling water. After two minutes of that Oscar was soaked and half awake. Wilson said Oscar would probably get pneumonia after that treatment.

'If he gets that,' I said, 'it'll keep him off the booze for a spell and I'll get some peace. But if the pneumonia feels like me it'll keep away from him and he won't get it.'

'You're very fierce.'

I made no answer to that, because I knew Wilson for a man who would get stuck in an argument about human nature the second you showed an interest in this subject. I wiped Oscar's mouth and eyes with my sleeve, which was thick and rough and made him grunt.

'Your father was a very fierce man, too,' said Wilson. 'I remember him. He was a great man for strikes.'

'He spent most of his time not working. Get the horse against that wall. Then we'll get Oscar up. Lot to be said for my old man's views on work.'

It took us five minutes to get Oscar settled in the saddle. The struggle winded Wilson and for a while he was in no way to talk about human nature or anything else. I told Oscar to hang on to the saddle with both hands, and, mumbling some words which I did not understand, except two, gas and fire, he did that.

I wheeled the horse around. I said so long to Wilson. He was asking himself aloud how long Oscar could keep up this pace.

'He'll never fill,' I said. 'If it was water that Oscar drank, he'd be full of fish.'

I led the horse out of the yard. I bawled to Oscar the whole time that if his hands slipped off the saddle and he fell off he could stay off as far as I and the horse were concerned. The horse was whinnying again. It must have felt as if somebody had just dumped the earth on to its back and I was sorrier for it than ever.

I heard Wilson say that horses were just like human beings, after all, and I thought to myself that keeping the 'Harp' had not done much in the way of gingering up Wilson's wits. Clarisse came to the side door, too, and said she would be seeing me again soon. I looked back as we got on to the main road. I could see Clarisse against the strong, white light of the passageway. She was rubbing her head against Wilson's shoulder. That is how Clarisse was. If she saw anything, she would rub some part of herself against it. Ready, eager, kind, too much and too often to be wise.

The main road took us upward for ten minutes. I kept one hand on Oscar and the other on the bridle. The houses on either side of us were low, grey, poor, alike. They were different from the churchyard we had passed only in that rents on the houses were steadier and the rain more of a nuisance. We came to a corner where two large chapels faced each other from opposite sides of the street. They were ugly, flat-faced buildings and even in all that dark they seemed to be scowling at each other. They had that mean, grey look and the windows were thin, peeping slits. One was Baptist and what the other was I never did know. It must have been something different or they would not have been so near. Or would they?

We continued upwards. We came to a pair of iron gates. They had been torn half off their hinges and had sagged heavily into the earth. They did not move any more. On both sides of the gates extended a tall wall, built to last. Inside the enclosure was what the wall had been built to protect, a disused air-fan, a knocked-in building, from which most of the machinery had been stolen or sold as scrap. The fan had once driven air into a surface colliery working, a level, as it was called, from which soft coal was swiftly and easily dug. It had made a lot of money and been bad to work in. It had killed many men, so many they had to close it up at last, and then needed no more air from that fan which stood alongside those gates that were rusting and unmoving, needed no more air than the men it had put away.

Through the gates we passed to approach the base of the mountain that Oscar owned. Up the mountain, with its vast black cap of coal-tip, we followed a broad, winding path. We skirted a wood that had been made thin by the axes of voters who had chopped down many of these trees for firewood during strikes.

Oscar had brought up policemen to defend these trees, which he said were his. But those voters, who were savage in their ways of thinking and doing, even when they had firewood and no axes, were even more savage when they had axes and no firewood. So the policemen had had to leave them alone, and they told Oscar that if he had any sense he would leave them alone, too, or the axe-bearing voters might get him mixed up with a tree and start lopping bits off him.

The tip stretched up to a sharp peak and to the left of that peak was a grassy plateau they had not yet thought of covering with tip. The path across this plateau took us close to the lip of a deep quarry. The wind was blowing in strongly from the direction of the sea. I had to watch the horse carefully at this point to see that it did not stumble on the sodden path. There was always a wind blowing across the plateau. Perhaps it was always there, did not come from anywhere, did not go anywhere, and that would belong to Oscar, too. The cold of it caught Oscar on the face and he rolled his head and made noises in his throat to show that he was now taking more notice of things.

He took up a part of that song they had been singing in the 'Harp'. 'Roll Me Home to where the Good Old Wife Is Waiting', a song especially made for weak-headed elements who have been warned off thinking. Oscar always woke up at that point of the ride home. I was always glad to hear the sound of his singing. His mumbling kept me company and it meant, too, that he was getting sober enough to keep himself on the mare, and that saved me all the bother of having to jerk him back on when he started to slip in his sleep.

The lip of the quarry we were skirting was jagged and bitten at parts, and was dangerous to all those who did not know the path and had no wish to leave the path by way of the quarry. Oscar had tried stringing a wire fence across the lip, but some voters had kicked the fence down because they did not like the idea of Oscar covering the mountain with wire as well as owning it. A few sheep had walked over this quarry and got themselves killed. One man, too, had thrown himself over and broken his neck. But this man had been walking around the mountain for months before preaching on a high note to molehills and ferns and other such things that cannot hear and do not take to preaching; so everybody thought that it was not exactly the quarry's fault if this element had broken his neck at the bottom of it.

The plateau ended and we passed down into a shallow ravine where the path was stony and flanked a fierce, yellow stream. On our right was the northern slope of the tip. This was the place where all the tipping was done and the only place where the tip continued to grow. This was the place where those people, poor elements from some streets called the Terraces, picked coal for

Oscar at fivepence a bag and Oscar sold each bag for one and sevenpence. Those elements must have been very poor indeed, lower down even than the dole, I supposed, to be spending their time bending down, skipping out of the way of big lumps of stone that came hurtling out of the trams which were emptied at the top of the tip and picking coal for Oscar at so little profit to themselves and at so great a profit to him.

We came to a clump of trees. Behind this clump was Oscar's house. It was a bigger house than most in all that valley. It was not much to look at, but it was quite big, with a stone yard in front and a lot of windows. If jails were built smaller this house would have looked just like a jail. As I helped Oscar from his horse, I could hear from beneath us the swish of buses making their way along the main road of the valley. Using one of those buses Oscar could have got more quickly to and from the 'Harp'. But he did not like using the buses. He liked crossing the mountain. It was his.

We entered the kitchen of the house. It was a big room, half stone-flagged, half lino-covered, with about six square feet in front of the hearth covered by three odd-coloured mats, which I had bought without Oscar knowing because the place was so cold. There was a light showing from beneath the pantry door and I could hear the sound of a saw-knife going through the crust of a loaf.

I lit the gas and led Oscar to sit in a further corner, far away from the fire, a corner cold enough to keep him awake so that he could have his supper and not keep me waiting. Oscar sat quietly in his chair, his huge face hanging low, staring at the odd coloured mats in front of the hearth as if he were wondering how they could have grown there. When his eyes grew weary of the mats he stared at the piled-up fire as if wondering what it was for. He looked more tired, dafter than I had ever seen him before. I thought his brain might be starting to dissolve or swim about in his head as a result of all the stuff he drank. I reminded myself to explain about the mats to Oscar one night to save him the bother of going crazy through trying to puzzle how they had come to be there.

Out of the pantry came Meg. Meg was about thirty and big in the body, with a face that was dark and solemn, that had lost most of its shape and all its laughter. Alone, Meg and I would talk all right together, talk about pictures we had seen and sometimes sing songs we had learned from the gramophone or picked up as kids from the chapel, sing in harmony, nicely, too, for Meg had a low contralto to put a soft frame around my tenor. But if Oscar was with us that dark, solemn look, that was like the butt-end of a long funeral, stayed on Meg's face as if it were nailed there.

At one time Meg had been one of the elements who had picked coal for Oscar on his tip. She and a brother of hers had been together as pickers. Oscar had fancied the look of her and taken her into his house to get meals ready. Then the brother found that Meg was preparing meals in Oscar's bed, and even years of stooping down for Oscar had not made this brother so simple as to believe that there was any cooking to be done in that quarter of Oscar's house. So he made a dive at Oscar one day when Oscar was riding around the tip helping me to keep the pickers up to the mark.

Oscar beat Meg's brother with his whip and his boots and got him put in jail for assault. Meg always said that her brother deserved to go to jail for being silly enough to think that being a home comfort to Oscar was any worse than picking coal at fivepence a bag on that bloody tip. So, she had stayed on with Oscar, his cook, his cleaner and his stand-by in the nights, and around her face the time was nearly always night-time.

Meg laid the food on the table and made our tea in a six-pint teapot on the deep polished hob.

'It's ready,' she said.

'Don't want any,' said Oscar, and he shook his great, fat head stupidly from side to side.

'He doesn't want any,' I said, surprised, because one of the notable things about this Oscar was that he hardly ever stopped eating. He ate like a goat.

'What's the matter with him?' asked Meg. 'He must be going to die if he won't eat.'

'He's tired.'

'Who's he been with?'

'Somebody from Brimstone Terrace. Macnaffy. Funny name like that. Looked like a bag. She didn't like Oscar much.'

Meg said 'Oh', as if she could read right into the mind of that Macnaffy element, and thought it was a good mind to have had those thoughts about Oscar. Then, after she had said 'Oh', Meg took a good long stare at Oscar, uttered a short little groan and began slowly to strip off the clothes from the top part of her body. She stood half naked about a yard away from me, and, to take my mind off this exhibition, I lit a cigarette and watched her. Her breasts were big and feeble-looking, but her waist still seemed slender and firm, although I knew not much of such items.

She dragged a hard, wooden chair from against one of the walls and placed it with its back to the fire. She sat down on it facing Oscar. That was part of Meg's job. It might sound funny, but that is what Meg had to do whenever Oscar came home at nights weary and stupid and listless after a long session of drinking and chasing. She would half strip in that fashion and sit there facing him. Oscar would look at her and before very long he, being a hog and a bit crazy from owning that mountain, the sight of her flesh, which was very white and soft, would coax all his snoring desires from their rat-holes and he would come lunging to his feet like some element who has just been brought back from the dead, a solid sheet of flame with all his appetites barking like dogs from him, hungry for food and Meg and Christ knows what.

But that night he just kept staring at Meg as if she were no more than a dead person wearing a double layer of clothes than usual to celebrate the coming of the final frost. Meg fidgeted a bit on the hard seat of her chair. Not an eyelid of Oscar's batted. Meg's head drooped suddenly until she was bent almost double. She pushed her fingers through her hair. A thick belt of redness showed on her neck and the top part of her back. I thought she was going to cry. My mind was reddish, too, and I tried to match up the shade of it with the flush on Meg's back. I was sorry for her, in a raw, hesitating way, as I had felt sorry for Oscar's horse.

'Get your clothes on, Meg,' I said. 'Nothing will stir him much before Christmas. Go to bed.'

Meg pulled her clothes on and stood against the fire. I handed her what was left of my cigarette. She liked smoking my stumps. She nodded her head at Oscar.

'You can do away with cats, dogs,' she said, 'and nobody bothers you. But you can't do away with him. If you did that, there'd be a hell of a howl.'

'Don't you try doing it, Meg,' I said. 'It's not worth getting into trouble for something you do to Oscar.'

'You're right, Lewis. I think you're right.'

Oscar's eyes brightened a shade. He flung his right arm out towards us.

'You two,' he said. 'Get out of my house. Get right out of my bloody sight.'

Meg went through the door that led to the stairs. Most often I slept in Oscar's house, too. But that night I wanted more than anything to sleep somewhere else. So I made my way towards the house in the Terraces, those rows of houses that stretched along the mountainside, where my mother lived. I shouted to Oscar as I went through the front door that I would be back up at his house at eight o'clock the next morning. I got no answer back from him. I did not want an answer. Oscar could not see into the future as far as eight o'clock the next day. It would have pleased me if he had not been able to see at all. He was a hog.

Outside, the night had become still and clear. Somewhere in the sky the moon must have come out, but I could not see it and had no wish to jerk my neck around looking for it. Above the tops of the trees that surrounded Oscar's house I could see the tall tipping equipment standing out against the sky on the peak of Oscar's tip. I stood quite still for a minute in that stone-flagged yard. I thought of the faces of Meg and the Macnaffy element. I cursed that tipping equipment because it was ugly and noisy and dangerous, and because the stuff it shot down the tip's side often hurt the limbs of the people who stood waiting to pick up the scraps of coal that went to fill Oscar's bags and Oscar's pockets.

It struck me as odd that I should think one second about Meg and Macnaffy and the next about elements who had picked the coal on Oscar's tip. It was because, some time or another, I had seen the same look on all their faces, the look of people who are being fed in parts through a mangle. And at the handle of the mangle, turning away like blue hell in case anybody should have a little less pain than he paid rent on, stood Oscar. Every way I looked, down, up, sideways, I could see Oscar. He was a big figure, planted there on his mountain.

I followed the course of the small, yellow stream that cut into the ravine's bed and soon I reached the top Terrace where my mother lived. My mother's house was one of a hundred in a row and it was just like the other ninety-nine. Even the smells were the same, a mixture of cabbage and onion which came from the damp, and another smell that arose from rent that had gone high. Oscar owned a lot of these houses and I loved him no more deeply for that.

I did not bother to go around the front way to the house. That would have added minutes to my journey and it was getting late. The back wall looked out on to the mountain. There was a door let into this wall. It was bolted from the inside. I climbed the wall. I knew exactly where to put my hands and feet. I had done the climb a thousand times in dark and light. A cat could have done it no better. As I straddled the top of the wall, a policeman passed, flashed his lamp and asked me what I was up to. I said it was my house and what of it. He recognized me as Oscar's boy and passed on. The policemen never bothered you in the Terraces if they knew you were connected with some such character as Oscar.

My mother was in bed and the fire out. I never saw much of her. She had greyed off into a fixed quietness since my father died. She said my job with Oscar was not respectable and she had not liked me for taking it. So, even when I saw her, she just looked at me, offered me what bit of food happened to be going, never said very much, looked as if she were very far away in some place where the air was sweeter and the rates were lower, as if she thought everything around was cruel and dirty, which, no doubt it was.

There was a light shining in the kitchen of the house next door. This was the house where my friend Danny and his wife Hannah lived. Danny was older than I. He would have been about thirty-five, but he was a nice element, as was his wife Hannah. He had been a friend of my father and he was my friend, too. I decided to go in and have a chat with them before going to bed. I told myself that it was a good thing to talk once in a while with people like Danny, who did not own mountains, and to people like Hannah, who were not whores. I told myself that I would discover boils breaking out all over my brain if I spent my time talking only to elements like Oscar, Meg, Clarisse, and that girl from Brimstone Terrace who looked savage and sucked at a wet cigarette.

The wall between my mother's house and Danny's was so low I could step over it. The voters in the Terraces had nothing of such value as to make it worth their while to build high walls to keep other voters away from it. From the small back paving of

Danny's house, I could look through the uncertained window of his kitchen. Through the window I could see Danny and Hannah sitting in silence by the fireplace.

I went in. They were glad to see me, as if they had been sitting for too long in silence. They smiled as they dragged a third chair up to the fire for me to sit on. There were only three chairs in the room. Danny was a short, frail, unhealthy-looking man with a gentle, musical voice that went up and down, as if it were searching for something, as it might have been, for there were a lot of things that Danny did not have.

He wore a flannel shirt, open at the neck, and having that shirt hanging loose over his chest only made him look frailer. Hannah was stronger-looking, dark, with the loveliest face that was ever seen in all the valley. I, as I sat between them, knowing little about such things, thought that if it was Oscar who was married to Hannah and the deep loveliness she had he would not have been sitting up as late as Danny crouching over an almost dead hearth. But Danny had not worked for nine years and his body was weak, so that must have made a great difference.

'I'll go and get a bit of coal for this fire,' said Danny. 'I'm not sure I'll be able to find any, but I'll try. There's been a spell on that fire ever since I tried burning that old boot mixed up with the cokes. God, we got to have some brightness now and then.'

'Brightness is all right,' I said. It was not much of a remark to make. But there was a sad sound in Danny's voice that had started pumping up the old sorrow in me again, and you cannot think of anything smart to say when you are being pumped like that.

Danny went outside. Hannah turned in her chair and looked full into my face. What I felt when she did that was what I cannot describe. It was something I could never have felt even after a hundred years of being chained up and stared at by Meg or Clarisse. It went to my roots and stuck there, tingling. Her face was sad, like a mountain under long-falling rain. She glanced at the door through which Danny had gone, and I could sense a whole river of words inside her, dyked-up, wanting to come out to where somebody but her could hear them.

'Oh Christ, Lewis,' she said, suddenly, and in a whisper: 'I get fed up sometimes, fed up so I can't stand it.'

'You wait, Hannah,' I said. 'You wait until Danny gets work and then things will be fine.' I never remembered Danny working and never thought he would work again, but I had always heard people in the Terraces saying that when so-and-so was working again everything would be fine. So I passed it on to Hannah and hoped it made some sense to her. She looked no happier. Rather did she look as if the rain was belting a little harder on the wet mountain that she looked like. Her features came closer together in a central clump of sadness.

'He had work,' she said. 'Last week he had a job delivering coal for Simons, the coalman. He wasn't on that job for a day. The sacks were too heavy for Danny and he finished up on the pavement, so Simons told him to go home and work up some strength.'

'You just wait till he works up some strength.'

'Where the hell from?' asked Hannah. She kicked her black dull shoe-tip into the lowest bar of the grate where the powdered ash had formed into a tight, airless drift. The ash loosened and the dust came up into the air around us, making for our heads as if it were wanting to answer our questions for us, and I do not suppose that dust would have made any messier job of that than we did. Hannah wiped her shoe in her stocking. 'When'll that be, Lewis?' she asked. 'Where'll it come from, that strength?'

'I don't know. There's a lot of things I don't know. Every day there's more and more things I don't know, Hannah. I must be dim.'

'But you got strength,' she said.

I said 'Aye' and was glad I had strength, because from what I could see life was very hard in those Terraces if you did not have it, and from what I heard the whole world was just like the Terraces, only worse in parts and colder. Danny came back in with a single piece of coal on a shovel. He nodded at it.

'That's the last of it and that took some finding.' He threw it on the fire. 'There was a cat sitting on it. If I thought the cat could have hatched another lump out of it I'd have let it stay. It's dear stuff to buy when you're not working, this coal. I've had to buy every lump we've burned since Oscar got the policemen to stand guard over his tip and stop us helping ourselves to a bagful. If it gets any dearer to buy we'll have to burn it first and eat what's left to save a bit on the groceries.'

'Oscar's doing well out of that tip,' I said.

'It wasn't so bad when we could pick an odd bag off that tip, but now he's got those poor bloody half-wits picking the coal for him to sell.'

'They're very backward. They'll do anything for a few bob. They don't know any different.'

'You ought to know different. You got some sort of brain. But you work for Oscar.'

'Oh, it's a job, Danny.'

'But that Oscar's a hog. You've said that yourself, God knows how many times. Your old man would have kicked you over the roof for taking money off such a crap. Somebody'd be doing the world a kindness to put him out of the way. But you help to keep him in the way.'

'As long as he gives me pay, he can be any sort of hog he likes.'

'That's not the point,' said Danny in a high, excited voice, and I could see that something was worrying him, and that he would like a long argument with me or even a quarrel to relieve his own feelings.

Hannah jumped to her feet and her lips were small and bitter as she looked down at Danny.

'That is the point,' she said. 'Let's be glad somebody can have a job and keep it. So long, Lewis.' She pushed her chair out of the way. 'I'm going to bed.'

She left the room. Danny's mouth, which had been hanging open, closed tight and his grey skin flushed as if a brush were being drawn over it, hard.

'She meant that for me, Lewis. Last week I got a job. I waited a long time for it. There should have been an eclipse to celebrate, but there wasn't and that was just as well. It was a job carrying sacks of coal and they had to pick me off a pavement. Jesus, Lewis, I felt bad. Not just because the only job I've had in nine years finished almost before it started. I felt bad inside, too. I went and saw the doctor. He said my heart is bad. By the look of him as he said that it must be very bad. But he couldn't have looked any worse than I felt. So what are the chances of me working again? Not much now, with people knowing how I finished up on the ground after carrying one sack for Simons the coalman. I didn't tell Hannah what's supposed to be wrong with me. She'll guess that. Oh, hell, Lew, just think what kind of life she's had. That's what makes me sick. I lost my work seven months after we got married. I was healthy enough then, strong enough. I could have dug a whole mountain away if it would have helped Hannah, and if there had been a mountain that did not belong to some bastard like Oscar. That doctor said strain was my trouble. He's talking nonsense. It was plain, simple bloody worry that ate the strength out of my heart. But now I'm not worrying. What if I die. I won't lose anything by getting rid of myself, and Hannah might gain something. That's a hell of a thing for a man to be saying who's still pretty young, but I'm saying it and I mean it.'

'A hell of a thing,' I said.

'And I'm not going to be so daft as I've been.'

'What do you mean, Danny?'

'I've been afraid. Afraid of Oscar, afraid of policemen, afraid of offending anybody in case I made things bad for myself. Now nobody can make things worse for me. Funny how good that makes you feel. There's nothing worse than dying, is there? They never can do anything worse than that to you, never mind which of their ten million bloody laws you break. The pity is that I've waited and worried myself into a state where I haven't got the strength to make any kind of trouble that would warm all the coldness of me. But I suppose they'll beat me in the end, all those people who helped to push me and Hannah down into the drain. They've broken most of the spirit I ever had. You can't be afraid for years and years and then say: "To hell with fear." It's not as simple, boy. It stays, like blood or bone, part of what makes you live. So even if I studied the problems hard and fought for what I wanted like a bloody beast I could never get back a millionth of what they've taken from me. They are cruel bastards, Lewis, these people who stand above us and kick our lives into any shape that pleases them, cruel and bad and blind. They've beaten me. They'll never have any more trouble with me than they'd have with a louse. I wouldn't have the nerve to take a bite at anybody's flesh if there was no other food around. I'd be afraid of the copper who'd call around in the morning. They've sucked me as dry as a cork. They can be proud of what they've done to me and pass on to the the next life they want to make a little meat ball out of. But one thing I will do, just one thing. I'm not going to pay for any more coal. That's a wonderful bloody triumph. They tell me I'm going to die years too soon and years too late, depending on who's talking. So I stand up and defy the world. How do I defy it? I say I'm not going to pay for any more coal. That's life at its highest, that was.'

I kept my eyes on the fireplace. A lot of what Danny had said had slipped past my ears, but I had the feeling that all his words were bunches of nettles being drawn up and down the bare sides of my body.

'Where you going to get your coal then, Danny?'

'From Oscar's tip.'

'Oscar'll get you put in jail.'

'What's the difference? I'll be up there tomorrow morning.'

'Why don't you pick for Oscar, Danny? You'd get some free bags then.'

'I'd rather pick the stuff that covers my own bones.'

'You don't like Oscar.'

'I could choke him.'

'But look, Danny, how you going to carry sacks of coal down a steep mountain if you couldn't carry one along a flat pavement for Simons.'

'Well,' and Danny smiled a bit for the first time that night, 'Hannah might think I've gone beyond the stage of wanting to try. I'll show Hannah.'

After that there was not much that either Danny or I could say. I asked him if he was sleepy. He opened his eyes wide and said he did not mind if he never slept again. We went outside on to the small back-paving. We looked up at the stars, not because there was anything we wanted to find out about them, but because stars are good things to look at when you feel fierce enough to put your boot through somebody, and I was sorry for Danny in a way that made me want to do that to somebody. Then we crossed over into the kitchen of my mother's house. I made us some tea. As we drank it, we stared in silence for a while at the fireless grate. Then we hummed together. Singing, for people who live in the Terraces, is good. It puts the brain to sleep at times when it is neither wise nor useful to have the brain awake. When they sing the edges of things are not as sharp as they are usually.

'See you tomorrow then,' said Danny as he got up to go.

'All right, Danny,' I said, and hoped I would not see him,

because I knew that Oscar was savage in his ways with trespassers and all other voters whom Oscar thought were laying hands on anything that Oscar thought belonged to him. As I watched the small, stooped body of Danny make its way over the wall that separated his house from mine, it came into my head that Oscar could never be as savage as the life of this Danny had been, and, knowing Oscar, that was not saying much for the life.

The sun woke me the next morning. I could hear no stir from below or from my mother's bedroom. I got up and dressed. Downstairs I scraped the cinders from the grate and kindled a fire. I threw some sugar on the fire to make the sticks catch more quickly. My mother would have told me not to do that. She would have said sugar was to be eaten, not tossed on fires. I did not like eating sugar, so I always thought it was nice to see the fire jumping into flame after getting a handful of stuff I did not like.

I made some tea. I poured out a strong cup for my mother and took it upstairs. I knocked on her bedroom door. There was no answer. She slept well. I remembered that there was nothing in my mother's world worth getting up at a quarter to seven for. The distant look she wore showed that. She was elsewhere all the time. I could not blame her for being like that in the Terraces. That was a hard place to be in whatever kind of look you wore on your face.

I did not knock a second time on my mother's door or I might have heard her asking me what kind of new world had come into being that I should be rousing people so soon after the dawn. I drank the tea myself as I tiptoed down the stairs. A section of the wallpaper swung loose from the damp wall that led from the bottom of the stairs to the front door. I fixed that back with a nail I had in my pocket. I knew that the nail, unhammered, would soon work itself loose, but I felt pleased at having done it, because it showed that being with Oscar had not yet made a hog out of me or I would not have been doing all these kind and thoughtful things at a quarter to seven in the morning. Anybody who will go to the trouble of fixing wallpaper back to the wall in a house in the Terraces, where whole houses are liable to fall down on your head if you kick too hard against the wainscoting in passing, must be a very pure and noble kind of element.

From the pavement outside I could hear the nailed boots of workers scraping along home from work and that made me think of Danny. I swallowed some more tea and with it a chunk of bread pudding, ice-cold and smooth to the tongue, which I found in the pantry. I chewed and drank and made as great a noise in my head as I could with these activities, because I did not want to think of Danny, and any noise in the head kept up long enough is a great cure for thought. There was nothing I could do about Danny or for him. The sun could have been twice as strong and warm and heavy, the hills twice as high and green, and Danny would still be in a mess. I thought that was funny, so funny it took about half the taste from my bread pudding.

As I left the house, I called out: 'So long.' I did not think anyone would be awake to hear it, but it makes me uneasy to leave any place in silence. But as I stood by the back door throwing back the rusted bolts, another voice said: 'So long.' I turned around. Hannah was standing by her bedroom window which was a quarter open, staring across the valley in a fixed way as if she were looking for someone there. The black of her hair made a wide margin for her face. Her face was white, a kind of overwashed, lily-valley whiteness. She looked to me as if she might still be asleep, drawn to that window by a dream, but I did not think any dream, even after a cask of cheese, would be so odd as to draw an element to a bedroom window to look down over the Terraces, or to make them say 'So long' to someone like me.

I did not open the back door. I swung myself with a strong, easy upswing of arms and body and got on top of the wall for a few seconds. I was showing off before Hannah. But Hannah was not looking and that made me decide that I would never again go over a door instead of through it. It was a great waste of time and skill unless you made sure there was somebody looking.

'So long, Lewis,' said Hannah again, and her low voice, matching the smooth thickness of the sunlight, made me feel better as I jumped from the wall on to the grass of the mountain side. I made my way to the path that would lead me to Oscar's house.

On that path I came across a small voter of about fifty, very grey about the head and wearing a large, rainproof fisherman's hat which he wore pulled down towards his neck, and this hat, looking strange on a voter who had nothing to do with fish, gave him the look of something growing out of the earth, something you would think twice, and more than twice, about picking.

I knew this voter. Everybody called him No Doubt. That was because he nearly always said 'No doubt' in answer to whatever it was you said to him. This meant that conversation did not get along very fast with this element, but I did not blame him for going in for these brief answers like 'No doubt'. In the Terraces many an element has been fined or put in jail for what is called free speech, so it is useful to keep your talk limited to such phrases as nobody can put two meanings on or put you in jail for, such a phrase as 'No doubt', for example, which is quite harmless to governments and kings and bishops and so on.

I was surprised to see this voter marching up the mountain at seven o'clock in the morning. He was one of the pickers on Oscar's tip and they were not supposed to start picking until eight o'clock. True, it was a fine morning and healthier than bed, but I thought he would have seen enough of the mountain during his work without queueing up on it an hour before time. He was still limping from a crack on the leg from a rolling stone he had got on Oscar's tip a month before.

'God, it's a lovely morning,' I said.

'No doubt,' said No Doubt, taken aback a bit, because he must have thought I was addressing him as God, which he was not, being little, grey, overworked and limping.

'What are you doing up here so early,' I asked.

'No doubt,' said No Doubt, cautiously.

'That isn't an answer.'

'My leg, it hurts in the morning. So I like to come up here.'

'I'm sorry to hear about your leg, No Doubt. You'll have to take care of it. You won't get any compensation from that Oscar if it goes bad.'

'Don't want any.'

'I don't follow you there, No Doubt.'

'I'm grateful to Oscar.'

'What are you grateful to him for?'

'For giving me the chance to come up here on the mountain to work.'

'You joking?'

'I love the mountain. I don't like being down there in the

houses. I don't like the houses much at all. If I didn't have this picking to do for Oscar people would say I was funny to come up here so early in the morning and spend most of my day up here. I feel more at home on the mountains.'

'You got any kids, No Doubt?'

'I've got four kids. They've gone away now. They went away to work. The house has gone very quiet since they went. They made a lot of noise, those kids. But when I'm up here, on the mountain, I don't think about them or the house. Always very nice and peaceful up here.'

'You ought to have been a sheep, No Doubt. No offence, mind, when I say that, but I really think you ought to have been a sheep.'

'No doubt,' said No Doubt.

The path divided. To the right it went to Oscar's house. To the left it went to Oscar's tip. No Doubt went to the left and as I watched him limp away between the ferns, it seemed as if the loneliness of this little element came out from him and stuck in the air like a smell. He was like Meg and Danny and Hannah, because they, too, seemed to be going around with a rope on their necks jerking them to a halt every time they tried moving forward, and a load of old iron where their hearts should have been. This is a great waste of iron, besides being the cause of great pain to those elements who carry it about. So I felt sorry for No Doubt and thought I was doing well enough in this line of being sorry to get some pay for it, like a preacher.

In Oscar's house I found Meg in a clean, blue apron standing over a breakfast table that had not been touched. Oscar's porridge basin, which always looked to me bigger than the contraption I had had to bath in when I was a kid, stood on its usual plate, full of porridge that had gone cold.

'Where's Oscar, Meg?'

'He says he's not coming down. He's sitting up in bed. He's grey and he's trembling and he's going crazy, I think. He told me to send you up when you came in. I think he's going off his head this time and I hope he goes the whole way and chucks himself through the bloody window on to those stone slabs.'

Meg was talking out loud in a wild, singing voice and in her excitement she had let her fingers clasp the edge of Oscar's porridge bowl and her finger-tips were sliding down fast into the porridge. I nodded my head at her hand and she drew up her fingers and wiped them on her blue apron.

'He's queer. All he does is sit there and stare at himself in the mirror in the wall and mumbles a bit. The big mirror, you know, the big one with the brown frame that had the heads carved at the top, the one he looks at himself when he walks about naked in the nights.'

'I know that mirror, Meg. I know very well the one you mean.' I was a bit annoyed by the way Meg was carrying on about this mirror as if it were more important than the fact that Oscar was sitting up in his bed, going grey and gibbering and clean off his head for all I knew. Women do that. They see two things, one big, one little. If they want to take their minds or your mind off the big one they will chatter like hell about the little one. I told Meg to sit down and drink tea and not worry.

I walked up the stairs, very slowly and letting my fingers slide and jolt over the joints in the wood with which the walls of the stairway had been encased by Oscar's father, who had got hold of more wood by chopping down trees than he had known rightly what to do with. I walked slowly, because I wanted to give Oscar time to come back to normal. Once he got hungry he would be all right again. The only trouble with that man, as I saw it, was that he never saw beer without drinking it, never saw a woman without wanting her, never wanted a woman without getting her, and, most important, never wanted to get away from that big slab of earth he owned and got his wealth from.

I pushed open the bedroom door without knocking: I had become a kind of shadow to this Oscar and shadows do not knock. I found him just as Meg had described. He was sitting in the bed with his legs drawn up and, between his vast gut and his legs, looked as if he had taken another bed into bed with him to start some new fashion that only landowners could afford.

The colour had drained from his face. It might have gone lower down his body for a change, being sick of Oscar's face as I sometimes got, but his face was like the fine ash when the cinders have been riddled away. His lower lip was hanging down over his chin like a pale red sunshade. He looked daft and dazed about the mouth, but in his eyes there was still the old, bright cunning. I did not suppose there would be enough good air in the heart and mind of this Oscar to keep alive for long that part of man's sadness which causes the eyes to become for ever dark and dead looking.

I stood by the side of the bed and looked right down at him. He did not stop gazing at himself in the huge mirror on the wall opposite. He seemed afraid that his reflection would vanish and never return if he turned his eyes away from it for a second.

'What's the matter with you, Oscar?' I asked. I called him Oscar because a shadow can be as free as it pleases in its ways of talking and, anyway, I did not give a split damn whether or not I was polite to an element like Oscar. To me he was just part of a mountain.

'I feel queer, Lewis.' He upturned his head sharply to look at me.

'You look queer. You look as if you were stunned. Who stunned you?'

'No, not stunned. My head's clear, clear enough. I want a change.'

'You live all right, Oscar. You live better than most; like a prince, seems to me. What you want a change for?'

'Don't know exactly. Just want it.' He waved his hand as if he were fanning his chest, as if his hand were his tongue trying to light on some words that would make some sense to him and to me. 'I don't want to do any more drinking. Like a bloody tank. Going to give it up.'

'That'll save me a lot of trouble. That'll save me and the mare nights of trouble.'

'And women. I could be sick at the thought of them. So many, my God. Every damned one of them the same. Always the same. From now on, to hell with them.'

'That'll save the women a lot of trouble. That'll save them a lot of time and weight and trouble.'

'You're a cheeky young bastard,' said Oscar, but quite quietly. He gave me a stare with both his eyes, forgetting his reflection in the mirror now and I could see as clearly as I could see him that he had no love for me, because I was lean and young and strong, because I did not give a damn for anything he was or anything he had, because I would never draw my tongue in adoration across his toes, as a lot of other elements were willing to do, elements that misery had squeezed the guts and goodness and hope out of, like No Doubt.

'I'm only telling you, Oscar, what the women tell me. I'm just passing it on.'

'What women?'

'Macnaffy, for one. The lolly you had in the "Harp" last night. She looked as if she had been walked over by a horse. She said she felt like that, too. And Meg could do with a rest. You are a great burden on Meg.'

'Meg? Who the hell is she to . . . I'll show that Meg.'

'You can't show her. She's seen everything.' I had gingered up my tone a little and it was hard. Oscar gave me another glance.

'That's right, boy,' he said. 'I want a change.'

'Why not go away for a spell. You've got nothing much to do here.'

'I'm all right here. Never been away from here. I'm all right just where I am. I want to do something different, something I've never done before.'

'Try some work. A lot of the voters go in for that.'

'I own a mountain. I own fifty houses. And that's work.'

'Nice work.'

'I want to feel something different.'

'Try being poor. You've never tried that. A lot of voters go in for that, too.'

'Less of your bloody lip. I got money. There must be something I could do to get a new feeling. All the other feelings are old and they stink. I been drunk so often. And women, I've had them under me so often they're like part of the earth. Sit down there on the side of the bed. Don't feel quite so bloody now talking to you. Sit down for Christ's sake when I tell you to. You're standing there like a bloody judge and I know you're only a kid. I want to talk. I feel queer and when I talk I get better. You know those people that pick for me on that tip. They're mine. If it wasn't for me saying they come and pick my coal they wouldn't be there picking. When I wanted to I cleared them off the tip. That's what I can do. If I told them to get off this mountain, off they'd have to get. They'd be rotting about on their beds having more bastards like themselves. I ought to be able to do as I like to people like that. Don't know what they live for, anyway. Sometimes I've watched them. Sometimes when a stone has come rolling down the tip, I've watched them run and duck and lie on their guts full stretch to get out of the stone's way, as if they had as much to live for as a bloody king or me or somebody like that, and sometimes I've prayed, I've watched the stone and prayed that the stone would be smarter than them and smack their bloody brains out, just to teach them a lesson. I ought to be able to do as I like to them. I've often felt like that. I'd like to kill somebody, Lewis. That's the thing to make you tingle, I bet. To smash somebody into hell and to shout as you're smashing. "There you are, you poor blundering bastard. There go your dreams and your eyes and your hopes and your arms, all the bloody things you got that make you feel so grand, so proud . . ." '

Then Oscar twitched his legs down flat and threw his head back with a crack against the back of the bed. I jumped to my feet, thinking he was going to pass into a fit. I moved back a little from the bed and looked at the door. I did not wish to be in that room if Oscar was going to be taken in such a fashion. I did not know how I would handle a man with a body shaped so much like a whale, and a mind shaped so much like another man's rear.

But all Oscar did was to press his knuckles with violent force into his eyes and start to shake as if he were freezing. The room, to me, was heavily, stickily warm, and the sight of Oscar shaking as if he had long icicles sticking into him was very surprising indeed. But I told myself that if a man was going to make such speeches as the one Oscar had just made, no icicle could be made too long to be jerked into him and he deserved to tremble. I thought that if I were in Oscar's place I would have cracked my head against that bed back with such vigour I would have put an end to all temptation to make further speeches of that kind, for such speeches seemed to be opening up a pathway that would lead Oscar, at great speed, to wherever it is they take people who have dumped their wits into the early-morning ash bucket.

He uncovered his eyes and gazed at me as if he were trying to put me under a spell. His eyes were red and painful and weak, and their stare would not have affected a woodlouse.

'Even you,' he said.

'What about me?'

'Even you would come in handy if I wanted to try out my hand with that new feeling. You wouldn't be living if it wasn't for me. You're as much mine as those people who stand about on the tip up there waiting around with their sacks to pick my coal. I could try it out even on you. That would stop your bloody lip, you . . .'

And he rolled like a flash on to his side and shot his hand beneath the bed. His hand swung wildly back and fore in search for the chamber. For a second I could not see what was meant by all this activity. Then I saw he had a notion of swinging this article up from under the bed and breaking it over my head. I kicked his hand as hard as I could. The vessel shot from his grasp and landed with cracking force against a farther wall.

'You'd better not try any of those tricks with me, Oscar.' I pushed him back into the bed. He was weak as a baby now and crying and sucking his hand where I had kicked it, sucking it slowly as if he liked it, as if it were a toffee apple. 'So you'd like to kill people, would you, because your mouth's a bit stale after the beer and you're a bit worn out by the women. That's a very nice thing for you, Oscar. Owning a mountain's driving you off your head, boy. One day you'll be ordering all the people who pick your coal and pay your rent to come filing one by one into this bedroom while you brain them with the bloody jerry, like you wanted to do to me. Just to give you a few new thrills. Be careful, Oscar. You are not the only voter in these parts who feels he'd like to put somebody away. It's a very widespread feeling. I know a lot of people who feel like that. And it's just you they'd like to put away. Not anybody. Just you. And they wouldn't do it to give them a fresher outlook after Christ knows how many years on the booze and the batter on money they never worked for. They'd do it because they think you are a dirty nuisance who goes around having the same effect as an eclipse or a disease. You get a lot too much to live on, Oscar, and you get it too easy, and you live among too many people who don't get enough to live on and never get it easy, like my pal Danny. That's mad. Anybody can see that's mad. So you follow suit. You go mad, too. Nothing surprising in that, Oscar.'

I do not think he heard much of what I had said. If he had, he would probably have leaped out of bed and made a fresh start with the chamber swinging. I marched from the bedroom, leaving him to his trembling, sucking and owning.

When I got down to the kitchen, Meg cut me a slice of cold, fat pork and sandwiched it for me. I was fond of that and I ate it with a cup of tea. We looked at each other and we said all we wanted to say in that way without opening our mouths. Even if I had wanted to talk, my mouth was too full with all that pork and bread, and Meg would have had to lay her ear on my face to follow what I was saying. But there was no need for that. We both knew how the other felt to the last shiver of the last nerve.

I was glad when I left the house. The air was sweet on the face and the brush of grass and fern was fresh on my legs. I got to the tip early that morning. I walked up the tip's steep side and cursed every time my feet slipped on its crumbling surface. I cursed, too, the elements who had been daft enough to dump all those tons of black dirt on to the head of so lovely a mountain. It struck me that a character like that No Doubt, with all his talk of love for mountains, must hate that tip deeply, but the hates of a voter like No Doubt must be so deep and silent, he being poor and queer in his ways, they had probably got all tangled and did not mean anything more, bumping into one another and being battered instead of shooting outwards and battering the things he hated.

When I got to the top of the tip, I started to do my job. It was a very simple job. An idiot could have done it, only an idiot would have been too honest to put up with Oscar. All I had to do was to stand there, far enough away from the tipping machine to be out of the dust, and count the number of elements who had turned up to do the picking and count the number of sacks picked. Then I had to see that these sacks were piled up in the proper order to be taken away by the cart that came for them at the end of the afternoon.

Any job connected with counting I consider to be very easy, especially when you are doing this job within hearing and seeing distance of other elements whose jobs cause them to be scratching about bent up like monkeys for bits of coal, getting their guts turned half solid with coal dust and their limbs occasionally knocked inside out by those small rocks that came flying down from the trains emptied by the tipping machine. I would not blame any voter who told his parents that he would rather stay permanently under the bed or on the Insurance if he could not find some job connected with counting.

I liked being on top of that tip. It was high. Even the wind in winter when it was high and seemed in a mood to toss me about two miles, I did not dislike it, for I dislike only those people and things that harm me and know they harm. From this summit I could see for great distances. To the south ran the fat green plain, full of plants and farmers and other voters I knew little of, and that plain finished with the sea. The sea did not interest me because the urge to fish was never in my family, and there were plenty of places to drown in inside the hills.

To the north ran ranges of hills till the eye lost them. On each new hill there would most likely be some element like Oscar owning it, and between the hills, on the valley sides, elements like Danny getting it in the neck and going black in the face because of it. It all seemed very endless and unsweet, and I never felt that I would like to leave the mountain on which I stood and travel over the mountains I could see to the farthest distance. There was no mystery in them. I knew and did not love the life that crawled between the cracks.

About two hours after the picking started, the tipping machine broke down. This machine was often breaking down, and it made such a lot of dirt and noise when it was not, you liked it much better when this breaking down took place. Job Hicks, a fair-haired voter, who was in charge of this contraption, and whose hair was never fair for much longer than ten minutes after jerking the thing into life, came up to me and said there was a very serious break this time. A crankshaft had gone, said Job, and from the solemn tone in which he said that, I understood that this crankshaft was as important to this tipping contraption as rent to a landlord or breath to an ordinary voter, or God to some element at prayer.

'All right, Job,' I said. 'It's not our loss. It doesn't grieve me at all. I'll go and ask Oscar if he wants to send the pickers home.'

I raced down the tip. I could go down that tip fast as the wind, picking out places for my feet to land where they would not double up under me and never once did I choose a wrong place. The speed I gathered carried me at a gallop about fifty feet from the base of the tip.

I found Oscar sitting in front of the kitchen, stroking the barrel of a heavy sporting gun which he had laid across his knees. All his trembling and greyness had gone. He was merry again and chewing great slices of meat from a plate which Meg had arranged for him on the hob. He looked as if he might have just used the gun to kill the very animal he was eating.

'Hullo, Lewis,' he said, smiling, as if he had never even dreamed of opening the top of my skull with the bedroom vessel. It was getting difficult to follow the changes in this man.

'The machine's broken down,' I said, when I saw that his jaws were quiet enough to let him hear something. 'There'll be no more picking today. What about the pickers? Shall I send them home?'

'Send them home, boy. When the tipper's not sending any fresh stuff down there's so little coal there to pick they start fighting about who's to have it. And they haven't got so much strength they can afford to throw it away on fighting.' And he started to laugh, stuffing his mouth with meat at the same time, as if he had just let off the joke of the month and was refuelling to work up steam for the next one.

'All right. I'll tell them that.' I took the top thick slice of buttered toast that Meg was bringing from the table to the fireplace. My eyes must have brightened as my teeth sank into it because Meg smiled at me as she passed. She probably saw something clean about the great hunger of an element like me as compared with Oscar.

Back at the tip, I gathered the pickers together, about twenty of them, and told them there would be no more picking that day; they could go home. Most of them laughed. All the younger ones did and I was glad to see that, because it is a very strange thing to see voters who are too earnest about their work, especially such work as brings in little more than sunburn and backache.

They arranged their full, half-full or empty sacks in a tidy heap on the side and in the little red book I used to note down the results of my counting, I made a record of how much each had done. As I wrote small knots of the pickers took turns at peering over my shoulder to make sure that I was not doing my duty to Oscar by cheating them. The old man called No Doubt lingered behind after the others and asked me if he could stay on and do some quiet picking on his own. The old man looked very weary and was more stooped than he had been when I met him on the mountain path earlier that morning. His hand kept wandering down to his hurt leg and stroking it as if the pain kept calling to his fingers.

'You go home, No Doubt,' I said. 'Go home and lie down and rest.'

'Don't want to go home. It's quiet there. Too quiet.'

'That's all the better for sleep. That's what you want, boy, sleep. Go on down now and for Christ's sake don't be so anxious about making profit for Oscar.'

He went off, muttering something about that not being what he was anxious about. As I watched him go, I hoped he would go home and sleep, sleep for a long time and have a whole procession of dreams, good dreams that would make him laugh and pass on the time for him more quickly than waking, dreams of some place where no tips crowned the mountains, where all the kids a man had were not obliged to leave their homes and go to work elsewhere.

I thought maybe that the brain of this No Doubt might have shrunk with sadness to a size so small there was no room left in it any more for such items as dreams, and that when he lay down the only thing he felt were ancient aches that stamped across his body like voters on the march, and that when he woke again he would count, by his bruises, the hours he had slept.

I wondered how the kids of this No Doubt could have felt when they left him like that, in a body, to walk about in an empty house where the joy went out of the window as the rain came through the roof, driven to find his minutes of peace in the tread of his feet on a mountain that for him was not much more than a bulging grave . . . No Doubt vanished from sight over the breast.

I wandered to the further side of the mountain, away from Oscar's house, away from the tip. I did not want to see Oscar again for a spell. On the mountain's lip were two small crags, and between them, a natural seat, a flat slab of rock. I liked sitting there, on the sun-warmed rock, staring down into the narrow valley, at the untidy straggle of houses that mounted it. I picked out the cream-washed house standing apart from the others on the edge of an allotment in which Clarisse lived.

It was nice to sit there with the sun passing from the rock into my body, warming it, and thinking of Clarisse, who seemed to have plenty of warmth, whether the sun was about or not. There was a man digging in the allotment that bordered Clarisse's dwelling. I wondered if that element had enough interest left over from digging and growing things to take any interest in the shapes that Clarisse made, or to have the same kind of thoughts about Clarisse as I had.

I got tired of looking at those houses in their formless journey to the summit of the hill that divided the valley from the plain. I got tired of looking at the cream-washed walls of the house where Clarisse lived. Looking at walls was not the same as looking at Clarisse. They were of different colours, and after a while said different things to my senses. So I slewed my body away from the valley and looked back over the mountain.

I saw a man's figure walking up from the direction of the Terraces towards the tip. It looked like Danny because the figure had a small, stooped way of walking, and there was something that looked like an empty sack thrown over his shoulder. As the man came to the foot of the tip I saw that it was Danny. He walked up the tip about six feet and bent down as he started to pick. There would be but little there for him to pick, but I could not expect Danny to know that.

My eyes moved towards Oscar's house. Oscar was riding his horse at walking pace towards the tip. Even from that distance I could see the slight sway of his body always as he rode. He was such a big element, that Oscar. You could have seen him half a world away. I knew he would play hell with Danny if he found him picking coal on his tip. I did not want Danny played hell with. He was my friend and my father's friend, and he had plenty on his plate without being chivvied around by Oscar. So I stood up and started signalling to Danny to get away. I shouted, too, to help out the signalling. Danny turned his head to face the spot from which I was shouting, but he made no sense of the words that came from me or of the tricks I was doing with my waving arms. I started to run, hoping I could reach Danny before Oscar and strife did. But Oscar had already seen Danny and was bawling in a way that even I, far off, could hear.

'Get off that tip, you dirty bastard.' He must have shouted that a dozen times, shouted it up in a huge voice from a stomach that had the size and quality of a big drum, so that the grass and ferns and Danny and me could not help having a clear idea of what Oscar thought of Danny and what he expected Danny to do.

I stopped running. There was no point in running any more. I walked as slowly as I could, my eyes fixed, not on Oscar, but on Danny. Danny was not moving, just standing there, his sack dangling in his hand, the other hand keeping the mouth of the sack open to admit the ribblings of coal he picked up. Oscar had dug his horse into a gallop now, and, almost in the time it took me to get a mouthful of spittle and swallow it, he had brought his horse to a halt about ten yards from where Danny stood, his face brownish with rage, a colour not much different from the horse's. Oscar had his sporting gun slipped into two clips he had fixed on to his saddle. I was quite close to them now, but neither of them seemed to notice me. Danny had his head lowered and his face was fuller of anger even than Oscar's. And it was white, white as lime against the surface of that tip. He looked as if he were so frozen and quiet inside, all his fear had gone asleep or died.

'Who's a dirty bastard?' asked Danny, not loudly or defiantly, but as if he were asking the time.

'You are,' said Oscar, and he smacked his little whip against the side of his brown riding boots. 'Get off this mountain before I kick you off.'

'Look, brother,' said Danny, 'last night I had a dream. In this dream I saw God. And God said: "I've washed my hands of those landowners. They're a worse plague than frogs or boils and I wash my hands of them." So you can go to hell, Oscar.'

Oscar spurred his horse at him, leaned forward as he lunged out at Danny. The tip of the whip skimmed Danny's forehead. Danny crouched and sprang forward like a bullet. He got his fingers fastened tight into Oscar's shirt-front, and at first I thought he was going to choke Oscar, and I was very interested. Danny gave a great tug and it was his whole mind and heart that seemed to be tugging and not just the muscles and strength part, which could not have been very great in Danny. Oscar came tumbling down from his horse and if he had landed upon Danny, Danny would have died. But Danny had skipped out of the way and was standing over Oscar with the sole of his boot planted on Oscar's mouth. Oscar had landed on his back on the softish gravel of the tip, the breath knocked out of him, but not hurt.

Danny picked up a stone the size of his own head. He held this above Oscar's eyes.

'If I had any sense,' he said. 'I'd bring this down over your head and if I did that, I'd have the feeling I'd done one useful thing on earth. But I don't like giving pain. People of my sort don't as a rule. We just get it, get it till we can't hold any more, and we pass over the feeling how the hell we stood it for so long. It's boys of your stripe who like giving out the pain, and, holy Christ, you always get away with it. We've put up with enough from the people we can't see, who live far away, who make a mess of our lives without ever clapping their eyes on us. But you live on our doorsteps and we're going to deal with you. If I want free coal from this tip, I'll get it.'

And Danny turned away from him, climbed back up the tip to a point farther than where he had been standing before. Oscar jacked himself up from the ground, twitching and groaning and moving slowly, so slowly you would have said he had made a bet to move more slowly than anybody else. It seemed like a year before he got himself straight. His stomach sagged down, because all the breath had not come back into his body, and he seemed to need this breath to keep it up.

He wiped his sleeve hard across his mouth to wipe away the black scraps of earth Danny's boots had left there. He had the expression on his face of one who had just had an experience which he finds very new, very bad. He did not look at me. Nor did he turn around to look at Danny. His hand found the bridle of his horse and he led it away.

Danny was bent low over the side of the tip, searching for the scraps left over by Oscar's pickers. Once I saw his hand tremble as it touched the tip's surface and a thin, black dust rose around his arm. I watched Danny, I followed with my ears the clomp of Oscar and his mare through the tall, dry grass. Then the clomping stopped. I turned my head towards Oscar. He was standing beside his horse, his gun levelled at Danny.

'Watch out, Danny,' I shouted, and I did not feel I could do any more than that. I fixed my eyes on the ground, expecting a great noise when the gun went off. It went off. The noise was not as great as my promise of it. The zip of it passing dragged my eyes to the tip. I saw the earth a yard to the right of Danny shoot up. Startled, Danny swung around, his arms above him in the air, off balance. His legs shot from beneath him and he came plunging down, somersaulting. He slithered the last two feet and his head came to a stop against one of the large stones that littered the tip at its extreme edge. The stone moved with the force of Danny's body against it. But Danny did not move. I began shouting at Oscar, but he was on his horse and galloping away by the time I had got ten words from my mouth.

I sat down beside Danny. I did not touch him. His face seemed to be all on a slant. I knew little about such things as death, but I knew that Danny was dead, because I could not feel that he was anything else but that. I sat by his side, not wanting to move, because he moved not at all. I wondered at that slant of his head and the wide, senseless openness of his mouth. I sat there for fifteen minutes and never have I done less thinking than I did then. I was blank, part of the mountain, part of Danny, and both these things, as I saw it, were dead. I sat on a stone, quite near him, crouched over him like a kid, as if I wanted to stand between him and the cold I knew would soon be coming. My body got cramped, cramped as my brain, sitting in that position. I got to my feet with a jump and walked quickly back to Oscar's house.

Oscar was sitting by the fire when I went in. As I pushed the door open, he turned around quickly and he seemed glad to see that it was me.

'All right, Oscar,' I said. 'You got your new feeling. He's dead. How does it feel?'

'Say you didn't see me, Lewis. Say you didn't see me,' like a song, with a soft, blubbering, sliding tune. 'Say you didn't see me, Lewis.'

'All right. I'll say what you want me to say. I got a job with you. The truth is nothing up against that. Anything you want, I'll say. But all the same, he's dead.'

'Oh Christ.'

'He died of fright.'

'Fright?'

'Your bullet didn't hit him. He wasn't hit by that at all. He was frightened and he fell. He thought he'd got away from his fear. He thought he'd be brave for a change. But in the end the fear caught up with him again. It must travel very fast and stick like hell, this fear.'

'What you talking about? Speak clear, for God's sake. I don't know what you're talking about. So I didn't hit him? So I . . . '

'But you fired at him.' I threw that at Oscar, because I could see he was getting less pale, less afraid.

'Say you didn't see me, Lewis.' He got up and searched in one of the drawers of the big chest against the wall. He found a wallet and from one of the inner flaps he took some notes, about ten. He handed them to me.

'I don't want them,' I said. 'But I'll take them and I'll say anything you want.'

He sat down again and I could see he was very frightened, as frightened as Danny had been when he started somersaulting down that tip. But I knew Oscar. I knew his fright would pass as soon as he had had some food to eat, some drink and time to feel that he was in no danger. And he would be glad, too, glad he had killed somebody, somebody who had been on his mountain without the right to be there, somebody poorer than he was, somebody who had been on the same earth as Oscar without the right to be there either. And I felt my hatred of Oscar boiling down into a solid lump with a hard, biting point. He shouted on Meg to bring him something to eat. I knew as I looked at him that I could say anything to him and he would not answer back.

'In any case,' I said, 'nobody'd believe me. If you were to say you had seen forty bullets put into the bloke and they couldn't find either the bullets or the bloke, they'd still believe you. You're a great figure in these parts, Oscar, what with owning a mountain and about a hundred bloody houses. I live in one of those houses. I help my mother to pay the rent on it. So that would make me out to be a liar from the beginning. That fellow who's dead out there, name's Danny, friend of mine. He lived in one of your houses, too. Never thought much of it. Damp, draughty, bloody hole he said it was. Always reckoned he'd have done better in the shelter line if he'd been born a rabbit. His life was just like this house. Damp and draughty. Not sorry to get out of it, from what he was telling me. Nice chap, very quiet, and, Christ, he's got a pretty wife, Oscar. You ought to see her, Oscar. She's the prettiest woman I ever saw, but you've never seen her because she wouldn't be seen dead in the knocking shops you call at. But if you had seen her, you'd have killed Danny just for sake of getting her. Honest to God.'

He looked at me, his eyes made small by the task of trying to eat too much at once, and his look said that he could not make up his mind whether to smile at me or kick me in the chin. But he said nothing and just watched Meg bringing in more food.

'And now,' I said, 'I'd better go down into the valley and tell whoever ought to be told that somebody's dropped dead on Oscar's tip.'

It was very early afternoon two days later when an inquest was held on Danny. This event took place in a vestry, the vestry of one of those two chapels that snarled at each other across a road on the hill that led up to the disused air-fan at the foot of the mountain. I thought as I took my place on one of the benches in this small room that Danny would not have liked having his business discussed in such a place, for he had never been a great friend of vestries and chapels.

He had told me often that his only notion of a sound religion was a tank to be used as protection for the skull from the many elements who seemed eager to take a whack at it. He had surprised me that day on the tip when he spoke to Oscar of having heard God in a dream delivering a very sensible statement on landowners. I had never heard Danny mention God before and either he had eaten an odd supper to have such mixed company in his dreams, or he had been making the whole thing up like a story for the benefit of Oscar. But there was not much that Danny could do now to protest against being talked about in a vestry. He was even more under people's thumbs now than he had been before, and it made me sad to consider that not even dying seemed to make any improvement for the voters in this respect.

The vestry started to fill up with various elements. Most of them were very important looking and were not known to me at all. They seemed to have something to do with the law which seems to breed many elements who have a knack of dressing up to look a lot more important than they are. As I waited for these voters to stop shaking hands and settle down, I remembered that I had done some singing in that vestry a long time before.

It was as one of a choir in a cantata called 'Rainbow Tints'. In this cantata the young elements who did the singing were dressed up in a lot of coloured stuff like chintz, and the aim of all these colours was to show how joyful they were about being Christians. There was not much plot to that cantata, and the most I remember of it was crouching down behind a big alto called Wilkinson James and wearing a kind of red shirt made from a bedspread, my tint being scarlet.

I told myself that that vestry must be leading a very interesting life to house two such events as that cantata and an inquest on Danny. I wondered what the composer of 'Rainbow Tints', a happy man, no doubt, would have thought of the darkly dressed collection of voters who had gathered in the vestry that afternoon to decide why a man should die while picking a bag of coal on a tip where he had no business to be, according to what they took to be the law. If he looked closely enough, it would certainly broaden his rainbow.

Oscar came and sat beside me. He had taken off his brown riding boots for once and was wearing a blue-serge suit, very tight on him, because Oscar put on weight as easily as other people take on breath.

Hannah took a seat on a bench opposite ours. She looked dazed, like a person would look listening to a lot of nonsense in foreign tongues. It was not that the idea of Danny being dead had not sunk into her yet. It had probably sunk in too far. There is a region beyond understanding that contains a lot of pain. Hannah was wearing a grey top-coat that hung loosely from her shoulders. She could not have had the money to get fitted up with black yet. The insurance elements were most likely waiting the usual three days before being sure that Danny would not go in for miracles and start rubbing his eyes.

As soon as Hannah sat down, Oscar began staring at her, and after a while I noticed that he was rubbing his left knee-cap with his right hand, which is what he always did when he got excited. I knew he would do that as soon as he saw Hannah. I had never seen anybody quite like Hannah. Nor, for that matter, had I seen anybody quite like that Oscar. The grief in Hannah's face was the purest whitest mid-winter and would have moved most men to a bitter prayer for the past and future of our race. But not Oscar. The animals learned from him. From the promise of him, a long time ago, the apes came, must have come. I reminded myself to give Hannah a half of the money I had got from Oscar.

Silence fell as the coroner took his seat, and this man looked like a part of silence. He had lost a lot of hair and I supposed that was only right, because it must be very difficult to keep a check on death and your hair at the same time. He had a mumbling way of speaking, as if he were throwing his voice and it never quite landed, and I did not catch much of what he was saying.

The next man to talk was a lot clearer, too clear. His tongue seemed to go bouncing about the room. He wore a come-to-Jesus collar, which is a collar that has two wings sticking out of it instead of going down flat. I have noticed that something is always bouncing about the room when an element wearing a collar of this type is present. The sharp wings must stab them into making a stir. This element was a solicitor and strongly in favour of Oscar. If he had not been so young and thin I would have said he was Oscar's father, so highly did he think of Oscar. He made sure that everyone knew that Danny had had a seizure on a tip that was private property on which he had been trespassing and picking coal, which amounted to thieving, and he repeated this rigmarole so often I got to the point of thinking that this element was such a firm believer in the law he even believed that everybody who took to trespassing and thieving on a tip that did not belong to him just got a seizure as a matter of course, the law keeping a stock of these seizures in reserve to be bolted out every time the police got a notion there was trespassing going on.

Then a doctor, who looked sleepy, got up and said things about Danny's heart in a peevish way, as if it was thinking about this heart that had made him sleepy. He sounded altogether as if he found the subject very dull and not likely to ginger him up at all. The element with the wings on his collar kept smiling at Oscar and shaking his head in agreement with every word the doctor said, and he got such a great roll into this head-shaking it would not have surprised me to see the wings suddenly outspreading and this element whirring his way through the ceiling.

Following the doctor was Simons, the coal merchant. He wore a bow-tie and a long, new, black overcoat, in which he looked very impressive, and all this splendour of Simons' outfit seemed to mean that either Simons considered this inquest to be a very high-class event, or that Simons was doing very well out of the coal trade.

At first I could not understand why Simons should be there at all, unless he had applied for the chance of showing himself off. Then I remembered he had employed Danny for about two hours and as Danny had done no more than those two hours of work in about nine years, that made Simons a great figure in Danny's life, so great that if Danny had had kids instead of his other troubles, some of these kids would have been called after this Simons. He was nervous and I had noticed him bobbing to his feet several times, thinking it was his turn before his turn actually came round. No doubt, Simons had never before seen so much law in one room in one afternoon in all his life.

He said how he had engaged Danny, and he said he had done this largely because Danny was such a poor and haggard-looking element. Then he spoke of finding Danny flat on a pavement with a sack of coal across his back. Some of the coal, said Simons, had spilled out of the sack and had rolled off into a gutter where kids had picked it up, showing how careful you had to be to engage only elements who could stand up straight when carrying sacks of coal. Simons got sort of fixed in his description of Danny lying on that pavement with the sack above him, as if Danny had got into that position right at the beginning of the day and had waited for somebody to place the sack across him.

Then they called me and I spoke up steadily and without nerves, because I had a strong feeling that I was not the daftest person present, not in competition with Simons, who was too dressed-up to think; Oscar, who was too dirty about the mind to think; Hannah, who was too beaten about by grief to think .... Compared with those elements, I felt very bright indeed.

I told them I had been standing about a hundred yards from the tip when I saw Danny picking above on the tip. I said I had heard him shout as if in pain, had seen him spin around and come tumbling down until his head came to rest against one of those large stones. The coroner asked me if there was any sign of life in him when I reached him. I was silent for a while. I was thinking of those long, blank peculiar minutes I had spent at Danny's side. I said no, there was no sign of any life.

After that they seemed to have had enough and I was not sorry. The sight of Oscar there fixing his hot little eyes on Hannah, and squirting his desire from them like a hose, was making me wild.

I knew that all I had to do to slap his face into the yellowest colour of clay, and to make his fat body tremble in a way that would make the vestry rock, was to mention that I had seen him point his gun at Danny, that he would have put a bullet clean through Danny if he could have kept his aim steady enough.

But I said nothing about that. I felt no sense of shame or dirtiness at keeping my tongue silent about such things. Living in a place like the Terraces gives you very peculiar feelings about items like truth and honesty, and on top of that my spell with Oscar had done something to my conscience, covered it with ice or corns. Anyway there was very little feeling in it. Maybe I had never had much. Maybe my mother was never able to afford the kind of food that makes for conscience. All I know is that if I have one it might have well been dead for all movement I got out of it as I stood up and spoke my piece for those voters in the vestry, and I have always thought that as long as men keep on behaving so much like monkeys off the leash, that was just as well.

The air in the vestry became warm. The windows in such places as vestries are not opened any too often. And listening to the slowly told tale of how death came to a man you have known well, with no great pity shown by the tellers, is like sitting in a room in which a damp fire burns with much smoke and no flame. Most of the elements present began to stir about in their seats. We heard the coroner give out that Danny's death was natural. We were glad to hear that, although there were some of us who would have liked to hear the coroner pass a verdict on nature as well.

Hannah was the first to leave the room at the finish. Oscar and I followed her out. We stood on the kerb and watched her mount a bus. Oscar craned his body to be able to watch her as she made her way down the aisle of the bus. He said nothing. His lust, I supposed, was right beneath his tongue, swelling, fierce, jamming it hard against his palate, making him dumb.

'We'll go to the "Harp",' said Oscar. 'We'll go there now and have something to eat, and I could do with a drink.'

'On Tuesday you said you weren't going to drink any more.'

'What Tuesday? I couldn't have said anything like that. I must have been daft to say anything like that.'

'You said it. You were in bed. I heard you saying it.'

'Must have been joking.'

'Nobody laughed.'

I looked at him. His face was red, eager, thoughtful. It did not seem as if he remembered about the spasm on the bed. I thought Oscar was lucky indeed to be able to clear out of his head things he had said and done no more than two days before. If you have the courage that comes from never being slapped down, cheated or made hungry, you can perform this cleaning-out process and think nothing of it.

Only those whose poverty seems to have existed from the earth's beginning have to put up with being dragged below the surface by the dead chains of past years, past days. The poor hug to their hearts all the yesterdays they know have not been lived and the burden is a heavy one. But Oscar was free. He could cut afresh the tape of each new morning, and the day he marched through was a road in itself, whole and complete, attached to no navel string of before or after. Yesterday meant no more to Oscar than the past life of the farthest star to me. It was all right, for Oscar.

The 'Harp' had not opened its doors for the evening session when we got there. We went around the side and knocked. Wilson came to the door with his waistcoat open and a newspaper in his hand. He looked twice at Oscar to make sure that Oscar was not riding a horse, then asked why Oscar was not riding a horse. He could not get over this and seemed surprised at Oscar's blue-serge suit, and buttoned up his own waistcoat as if in tribute to this new neatness that he saw in Oscar.

'A chap died on my tip,' said Oscar. 'So I had to dress up for the inquest. A bloody nuisance, some of these chaps.'

'Same as I think,' said Wilson, letting us in and shaking his paper in our faces as if we were a pair of wasps. 'And this paper says the same. It says the world is losing its moral sense.'

'Its what?

'Its moral sense. You know that thing.'

Oscar did not know at all what it was, judging by the blank look he wore, but he told Wilson in a low voice that it was a pity the world was losing it, just to be on the safe side.

'I don't know where the world is going to be without a moral sense,' said Wilson, upon whom this item had obviously made a deep impression, and who seemed to be worrying about it as if the moral sense were the tail of his only shirt and he was standing in a draught.

I did not see why Wilson should worry his guts out in this fashion about the moral sense. From what I knew of the 'Harp' and the capers of such customers as Oscar, the cellar and attic of the place must have been full of moral sense that had gone mouldy and been pushed out of the way because nobody could find any use for it except to stuff chairs.

'Bring us something to eat in the little room, Wilson,' said Oscar.

'The usual? Bacon, sausage, kidneys, liver?'

'That'll do. And three pints.'

Wilson led us into the small room where Oscar had taken the Macnaffy girl. He lit the gas fire and handed his newspaper to Oscar. Oscar looked at it for just over a minute, took in the pictures, giggled a bit over a photograph of two old chimpanzees scratching a young chimpanzee, then gave the paper to me.

He closed his eyes and leaned back on his chair. He had no interest in print. As far as he was concerned, reading had no point. There was nothing in life he wanted to read about. He was doing all right. There was nothing to be said about that. He was all the comment that was needed. Mountains and tips and houses are very solid things and not likely to be washed away by words. So words contained not even the attraction of terror for Oscar.

I read an article about God in the middle of the paper, and the element who wrote this article was making it his business to bring back to the world that moral sense which, according to Wilson, had got itself lost. After reading the article I did not see that it made much difference to the situation at all.

Clarisse brought in the food and drink. Seeing me in a clean collar and tie made her treat me with more respect than usual. She did not often see me in a tie and the one I wore then was green with red stripes and was very prominent, like a flag. At the sight of that tie Clarisse must have felt like saluting as well as showing me respect, which took the form of keeping quiet instead of praising the shape of my body, her usual approach. But all she did was rub her leg against mine. She did that with Oscar's leg, too, which made me think that if there had been eighty or so legs in that room instead of just four Clarisse would have rubbed part of her own leg right away before she got out into the fresh air again. In all that valley Clarisse was the fullest answer to a cold climate I ever came across.

Oscar cleaned his plate minutes ahead of me. I was keeping my bacon and kidneys until the last, because I considered these items very tasty and not to be rushed. Before I could get to them Oscar took hold of my plate and ate them for me. I asked him whether I had kept them in just the right condition for him, and whether he would not like all his food served by way of my plate, but he was too busy eating to pay any attention to all this wit.

'And you can take the beer you brought for me, too,' I said. 'You know I don't like it.'

'More for me. More for me. More for me,' he started to shout in a high, childish voice, which sounded odd coming from an element with so tremendous a body as Oscar, an element whose own childhood was so deeply buried beneath the thick hogdirt of sodden lusting. He was very excited about something. I had seen that from the way his hands kept playing about in the vestry, and this high, childish voice caper was running in the same lines. His eyes, peeping over the rim of his third pot, caught me making a disgusted grimace.

'I ought to shove your face into the gas fire,' he said, dropping his voice back to normal.

'I wouldn't do that.'

'Why shouldn't I do it?' He leaned forward and surveyed me solemnly, as if his whole future was now bound up with this question of shoving my face into the gas fire.

'Because,' I said, 'if you did that, you would get yourself mixed up with Wilson in an argument about moral sense which has already been posted as missing.'

And funnily the prospect of arguing with Wilson about the moral sense seemed to scare Oscar a bit and his temper simmered down right away. He started to beam at me as happily as could be, as if I were wearing a lining of haloes and he were the element who had given me these haloes as a gift out of his own large stock. He called for the same amount of beer again. Half-way through the second load I helped him hoist his legs on to that low mantelshelf above the gas fire on which the Macnaffy girl had rested hers a few nights before.

'Oh Christ, Lewis,' he said, blowing the words out suddenly like coughs, 'she's lovely. Boy, she's a pippin.'

'Who? The Macnaffy girl?' I was thinking of her and I assumed Oscar's mind might be on the same target.

'Hell, no. That woman we saw today.'

'Oh, Hannah. She's all right, Hannah.'

'I'd give a lot to have her, Lewis. I've learned a lot about women, Lewis. I'd take that sad look off her face.' He dropped his feet to the carpeted floor with a bang and his hot, bulging face bent close to mine. 'I'd give a lot to have her, and by the time I'd had her a bit, Jesus, I'd make her glad I'd frightened the guts out of her old man and made him drop down dead.' He paused to gulp powerfully at his pot. He was running to a high tide. Breathless, he started to talk again.

'If I had known there was a woman like that living in those bloody Terraces, one of my houses, too, I'd have shot that husband of hers a long time ago. Fancy a dirty, penniless little bastard like that keeping a woman like her from a man like me.' He looked honestly shocked and disgusted that Danny could have done any such thing. 'But he can't keep her from me now, can he, Lewis? He's dead now, isn't he, Lewis? It was my gun that did it, wasn't it, Lewis? Did you see him jump? Did you see him jump and roll and then lie still, Lewis? Oh Jesus, that was something worth watching. Did you see him, Lewis?'

He was laughing now, but the merriment of it was lost somewhere in the vast, swollen redness of his face. He only stopped laughing to take another pot and half drain it.

'I saw him, Oscar,' I said. 'And if I was you, I'd stop bawling about it at the top of my voice or somebody might hear.'

He started fidgeting on his seat and crinkling his eyes as if he were in pain. The fear came up in spouts from that man whenever he became afraid.

'But I want her. I got to have that woman, Lew. How the hell'm I going to get her? That's what I want to know. How am I going to get her?'

'I'll get her for you, Oscar.'

'You'll get her? You're joking with me. That's what you're doing. Don't joke with me or I'll do what I said I'd do with your face and the gas fire.'

'No need for you to get nasty with me, Oscar. Mine isn't the only face that could do with some pushing, and you're not the only one with jobs to offer either. Not these days. Things are picking up. Of course I can get her for you. She'd be keen as hell to get a man like you. There isn't a woman in the Terraces who wouldn't pawn her husband to get a man like you. They're so bloody poor they got no option. Take this Hannah. You own the house she lives in. You own all the tip her old man passed out on. And now he's passed all she'll get is the pension which is sweet Billy Adams to live on if you don't want to live on acorns. You'd be like God to her, just like God. You leave it to me, Oscar. I'll get her for you.'

'Honest?' He was very pleased and a little doubting.

'You see. I'll get her for you. Bring her to you on a lead. Eat out of your hand. She got to eat. May as well be out of your hand as anybody else's.' I stood up, glad to get my face from off the same level as his.

'Where are you going,' he asked.

'You don't want me, do you?'

'I'll be here till stop.'

'I'll go then. You don't need me to help you swallow. So long.'

So I left Oscar to his drinking and made my way, full of thought, towards the top terrace where Hannah lived.

I took my time over the steep road that led to Hannah's house. I stared at the many voters who were moving about on the pavements, making their way to cinema shows, chapels and courting. It was interesting trying to guess which of these characters were going to which activities. And it was often hard to get this guessing right, because life in the Terraces is a large, black item that has been kicked clean out of shape by years of being a lot poorer than even life has a right to be.

So you had very often to be a seer, a prophet or, perhaps, a Means Test investigator to get anything like a correct bead on any particular element you happened to be observing. I would pass, perhaps, some voter with a bowler and a black suit who looked as if he were going to be the central figure in some chapel gathering, but the odds were that this voter would have for his programme for the evening nothing holier than a few hours of rolling about on the grass of the mountainside with a maiden, also in black, in mourning for whatever it was she was going to lose as a result of all this rolling.

Then some other voter with his shirt hanging open at the neck and with a generally pagan look about him, might well be on his way to give a rousing sermon to one of the many sects that thrive in the Terraces. Most of the front doors I passed were wide open. From these open doors came either bits of gentle singing or bits of talk that were clear enough to listen to, and this talk was often of such a sudden, savage and impatient character that one could understand why the front doors were kept open. It was to allow any of the talkers who got a sudden wallop to roll right into the road without danger of being bruised by any immovable woodwork that might be in the way.

When I got to Hannah's, three men and a woman were coming out of the front door. These people had the same short, dark, worried look as Danny, and I thought they were his relatives, although this look I have mentioned was very widespread in the Terraces. I was glad these relatives were going and not coming. The worry was much too thick upon their faces for them to be bright company. They all tilted their hats at me for no reason I could see. It might have been my tie or they probably thought it would mean some fresh trouble if they did not.

With Hannah in the kitchen was an old man, an uncle of hers, an aged element who was called Hopkin the Rasp, because in the days when his fingers had been less stiff he had been able to make some very pretty things from bits of wood with the help of no more than a rasp or two. He had a very high, sleepy voice and no teeth, and it was difficult to listen for more than about five minutes without getting the feeling that life was heading for a great lull.

He was talking away at Hannah as if she were a concert and he a reciter. Hannah looked steadily into the fire with just the same expression as she had worn at the vestry. I sat down and she did not turn to say hullo or smile at me. I thought it was a good idea to have this Hopkin the Rasp to talk to people who were feeling grief. The sound of him was like the drip of dope on the face. After a spell with him, one could feel nothing very much.

Hopkin turned his head my way when he found I had my

eyes fixed on his interestedly, trying to listen. I supposed he would be talking about Danny and I would not have minded listening to that. I remembered then that although I had known Danny ever since I could walk, there was still not much I knew about him.

'You remember Iolo,' said Hopkin to me.

'Iolo who?'

'Iolo the sheepdog.'

'What are you talking about sheepdogs for, Hopkin? This is no time to be talking about sheepdogs.'

'Because I had one once. They're smarter than men. This one I had died before I could give him a trial. Died, just like Danny.'

'I'm sorry to hear that,' I said, very kindly, but thinking all the same that voters who go around putting dogs on a par with men ought to be treated like bones and fed to a couple of dogs.

'That was a long time ago,' said Hopkin. 'It never grew to be more than a pup. But Waldo Williamson the Fruit, who knows dogs – he's got his failings, mind, Waldo, but he knows dogs – he said that Iolo would have been a winner. That was years ago.'

I gave no answer for a minute. I thought that a conversation between Hopkin the Rasp and that Waldo Williamson, who could hardly think with drink and waterproofs, must have been very interesting. I looked around for some way of getting this Hopkin out of the house short of setting him alight or hitting him over the head. He would have sat there for a month by the look of him, wanting to talk of nothing else but Iolo the sheepdog. There did not seem to be any subject closer to the heart of Hopkin. I did not suppose that there had ever been in all his life any event or person as great as that Iolo. But I had no interest in sheepdogs. Nor in elements whose minds wept over their passing. Nor was I fond of the way in which this Hopkin the Rasp sang instead of talked.

'There was a woman looking for you, Hopkin,' I said.

'What woman?'

'Didn't catch her name. Sort of plump woman. Nice-looking woman.' His head jerked up as I said that, and it struck me that I had been wrong in putting him down as having no other interest than sheepdogs. 'She said she was very keen to see you.'

'That would be Agnes, no doubt,' said Hopkin, proudly, as if this Agnes was no more than one of a whole parade of women who went about the place inquiring after him. 'I'll go and see her.'

'She'll be glad of that, Hopkin. She was very keen.'

'I suppose she was, boy, I suppose she was.' And he left the house saying in a very high key that he would be back.

'Hope he breaks his neck,' said Hannah, without shifting her eyes from the fireplace. The dark skin of her face was glazed with the fire's heat and that made her seem prettier to look at.

'He's old and daft,' I said. 'He can't help being like that.'

'He's old and daft. He walks around. People can talk to him. But Danny, he's up there.' She swung her head up towards the bedroom where Danny was.

'Sorry about Danny. Nice fellow, Danny. We'll miss him.'

'You won't. Not as much as me.'

'No. Not as much as you, Hannah. He was a nice fellow. Used to go for walks with him. Over the mountain, when I was a kid. But he was different then. He changed a lot.'

She looked straight at me, surprised, as if I had given her some bit of news. Her face changed slowly, like the sky will change when the sun gives over to rain and you see the black cloud ridges moving without sound into place. She swivelled around on her chair and she brought her face down on to the edge of the table. She slipped and landed kneeling on to the canvas mat. I put my arms beneath her shoulders and lifted her back on the chair. Her face was ugly and flattened out with weeping, and fast as the tears came from her eyes the words came from her mouth.

'He never did any harm at all. He just got harm like he always said. He was so patient, so patient and kind it withered him away being so patient and getting nothing out of it. All his strength went out of him, see, Lewis? For years I could see the strength going out of him. He wouldn't even give me love in the nights, because he said he wasn't fit to love any woman. He said when things were better it would be different. God, how we used to pray that things would be different. I wanted him to love me like he did at the beginning, so much, for so long. But always he said not till things are better. We waited too long, Lewis. We waited too long, Lewis. We waited too long and this is all we got. He goes up on a tip and they bring him down like that. It isn't right, is it, Lewis? A thing like that isn't right, is it? Why should anybody be treated like me and Danny been treated? Oh Christ,

I'm sick, Lewis. I'm sick of being alive like this. I'd rather be like Danny is than sick like this . . . '

'Don't talk like that, Hannah. You're just hurting yourself. Be quiet now, Hannah.' I pressed my fingers into her armpits. I thought she was going to scream, but she quietened and wiped her eyes.

'I'll be quiet,' she said. 'I was tired, listening to that Hopkin. The bloody rasp. I'll be all right. You're kind, boy. Thank you, Lewis.'

'Where do you keep the teapot and the tea?'

She showed me. I made the tea strong and she smiled a little as she drank it. I drank nothing, said nothing and smiled not at all. There were a lot of fists inside me beating to a hard, bitter tune.

'We put up with a lot,' I said after a while.

'Too much,' said Hannah.

'We are stepped on.'

'They stepped on Danny good and proper.'

'He never harmed anybody.'

'They harmed him like hell.'

The pale agony crawled back into her cheeks, into the stiffening red of her lips.

'Seen him, Lewis? Seen him since he's dead?'

'I found him, Hannah. Don't forget that. I found him. I helped to bring him down. Jesus, he was quiet.'

'That was his seat there, where you are sitting. Always he sat there. And in the nights when he came in, he'd sit there and talk. I liked to hear him talking . . . . He was . . . '

I could see she was on the point of starting off on that crying again. I could not have stood that.

'For a change,' I said, 'it's time we stepped on somebody.'

'We ought to do that. We ought to get something out of all the trouble we put into getting nothing.'

'Danny never had the chance to get his own back.'

'No. No chance.'

'We ought to step on that bloody Oscar.'

'Who could get up high enough to step on him.'

'You ought to. Listen, Hannah. Oscar killed Danny.'

'Don't be daft, Lewis. Things are bad enough. Don't make them worse by talking daft.'

'I was there. I was on the tip when he shot his gun at Danny. It frightened Danny when the bullet came right close to him and he fell.'

The silence then seemed to come right out from the walls, to form a thick column around the spot where Hannah and I were sitting. The little alarm clock on the mantelshelf ticked with a hard, unwilling, underpaid tick and I rubbed my wetted fingers up and down my thumb, cleaning it. A beetle moved around on a ball of brown paper that had been tossed into a corner.

'You stood up in that vestry,' said Hannah. 'You told them there how you saw Danny dying. But you didn't say anything about Oscar. You didn't say anything about a gun. What kept your mouth shut, Lewis?'

'Oscar'd have said I was lying. They'd have believed Oscar. Why should I have told anybody else, anyway? Danny's gone. Talking won't bring him back this way again. This is your business and mine, Hannah. That Oscar's not fit to be alive. It isn't only that he stands on that mountain and calls it his and boots the people off it. It isn't only that he gets a crowd of poor bastards to pick coal for him off that tip and makes a pile of dough out of it. It isn't only that he fired his bloody gun at Danny and made him fall. Hell, Hannah, he's dirty, that Oscar. He's dirtier than anything. He's got no pity for anybody, and if he sees anybody who's kind and clean like Danny was, he hates them worse than poison. That morning, the day Danny died, he was lying on his bed talking to me. Said he was feeling a bit stale, wanted something new to amuse him. Said he ought to be allowed to kill a few people, people who were poor, of no account, like Danny, who wouldn't be missed. Said that would give him a new feeling. That's why he shot his gun at Danny. He thinks he's a bloody god sitting up there on a mountain his old man stole, getting policemen to boot the backsides of people who set their feet on it.'

'He said those things?'

'All those things.'

'He said he'd like to kill somebody, somebody like Danny.'

'Like Danny. That's it.'

'Somebody poor, of no account, who wouldn't be missed.'

'That's right.'

'Who wouldn't be missed, by Christ. He said that, did he? When I finish nobody'll miss him.'

'What are you going to do, Hannah?'

'I'm going to kill that bastard of an Oscar. Don't know how, but I'm going to do that.'

'You got a right to do it, Hannah. Somebody should have done it a long time ago. But nobody ever had as much right to do it as you. You . . . you got to do it.'

'And I won't do it to get any new feeling. I'll do it just to get clean again. All the things I went through with Danny, the cold and the hunger we put up with as we waited and the way it finished, those things made me feel dirty. Doing something to that Oscar will make me feel clean again. That'll be good, to be clean again.'

'How will you do it, Hannah?'

'Get him near me. That's all. Just get him near me.'

'I can do that. He comes when I whistle.'

'The last thing Danny ever gave me was a hammer. Funny thing, a hammer. He said he wanted to give me something. So he stole a hammer from a woodwork class he was going to down in the Settlement, you know, the Social Settlement. He stole it because he wanted to give me something. But he was sorry he did it as soon as he brought it home. That's how Danny was. He hid it away, never used it at all, in case somebody would see it. It's in a drawer over there. It's new and big.'

'Danny was good to get that for you.' I did not fancy the notion of Hannah working on Oscar with a hammer, but I gave no thought to difficulties of that sort and took things as they came. There is a rhythm about things when you are angry and I could feel the rhythm strong about me. 'I'll get him here for you, Hannah.'

'When?'

'Tomorrow night.'

'That's soon.'

'Oscar didn't ask Danny if he'd like to wait a while. Oh, you're just talking. You don't mean what you say. I can see by your look that you're just talking. Nobody'll ever touch that Oscar.'

'No, I'm not just talking. I could do it now even as I'm standing here. Bring him here tomorrow night. Bring him when you please. Tomorrow night. The day after that is the funeral. So Danny'll know he's quits with Oscar before he leaves here. Danny'll like to know that.'

'That'll cheer him up. He needs some cheering up, God knows. Get that sofa from behind the table. You and Oscar sit there when he comes. He'll like it sitting next to you. He's fancied you, Hannah. You're pretty. And if you can make an eye at him he'll roll all over you. He's like that, is Oscar.'

'I'll give him roll. I'll have the hammer on the sofa, behind a cushion.'

'Keep it close to you, Hannah. Keep it close.'

'. . . And then I'll stop him rolling.'

'That'll be a new feeling for him.' I was happy, excited, almost shouting. 'That'll be a new feeling for you, Oscar, you sod.'

Hannah rubbed her hands together, hard. I looked down at her. She was biting her lips as if she were sorry for some of the things she had said. I could almost see the old white fears seeping back into her brain. A lot of the temper seemed to have drained out of her and once more she began to look as she had looked before I had said anything about Oscar, a sad woman, short of food and hope.

'You'll be afraid,' I said. 'You'll never be able to do that to Oscar.'

'I'll do it. Honest, Lewis.' Her voice was trailing off into dumbness with every other word. 'The way I feel . . . I could do anything.'

'I'll get you something to drink. Something to warm your blood, see? I'll buy you whisky. You drink that. Then you'll feel nobody's too big or too small any more. You'll just see yourself and that dirty nuisance who took Danny away from you and you'll know what to do.'

'Get some for me.'

'Tomorrow. And here's some money for you. It's a half of what Oscar gave me.'

'It's a lot.'

'It's not much. Looks a lot to you and me. But it's not much. And when Oscar comes in here you better keep the doors locked. You don't want people walking in. But it'll be late when he comes so there won't be many people about to bother you.'

'God, it's quiet in this house.'

'It is, too.'

'What's that noise in the corner?'

'That's a beetle. Only a beetle. What are you so pale for, Hannah?'

'It was so quiet then. Step on that beetle, Lewis.'

I did that. I could see Hannah was afraid, just as afraid as that beetle had probably been when it first felt the graze of my boot on its back. Hannah's fingers opened and shut on the money I had given her. There was no more for me to say or do.

'See you tomorrow evening, early. So long, Hannah.'

I left the house and made my way up the mountain path to Oscar's house. I had to get the horse to get him home. The evening was cool. The air was nice around my head and made me thoughtful. One of my thoughts brought my legs to a halt.

'Jesus,' I told myself, 'I've got Hannah to say she'll kill Oscar. To kill him with some bloody hammer. That's a hell of a thing.' And as I looked at it the idea seemed daft, mad. Then I thought of Hannah's face as she slipped by the table, ugly and flattened out with tears. I thought of the mess her life was in, poorer than she had ever been and not even Danny now to give the business an occasional streak of light, and I knew that these things would not be if it were not for hogs of Oscar's stripe making the world their sty. Then I thought it was good and fair and just that Hannah should take a hand in pushing Oscar from the world which he had helped to make a little dirtier than it needed to be. And if men there were who would blame her or punish her for so doing, then, I told the mountains, God help men. Hannah could not be in a worse mess, anyway. If she could, then God help Hannah, and I could not help thinking that that kind of phrase did not help much.

'In any case,' I muttered, 'I don't give a damn. Mountains, tips, Oscar, Danny, Hannah, work and pain, living and dying, it all looks terribly odd to me.'

Next day I asked Oscar for an afternoon off. He gave it me, because he was pleased when I told him I had seen Hannah and got her to agree to seeing him late that night. I told him the session should be easy and joyful, because Hannah had brightened up no end when I told her that a man like Oscar was interested in her.

'You can always depend on me, Oscar.'

'You're a good boy, Lewis. What did she say when you told her?'

'No much. That sort never say much. But I could see she was pleased. Her old man couldn't have been much use to her anyway. Too weak and they're always cold in those Terraces. This is a kind of promotion for her.'

'Where's he now, the husband?'

'Oh, he's still there, in the house.'

'In the house?'

I could see that Oscar was not much taken with this idea of being in the same house as a dead man.

'But you don't need to mind that, Oscar. You had something to do with him being dead so it won't be so bad. You'll soon forget about him.'

'That's right, boy. Who the hell was he, anyway?'

'Nobody. He's better out of the way.'

'Absolutely.' And he wagged his huge, red face from side to side, solemnly, as if he were having a talk about the hymns at last Sunday's service.

'I'll call for you at the "Harp",' I said.

I went down into the valley. I was nervous, even though I walked fast to keep myself from thinking. Now and then I went cold from head to foot. I buttoned up all the buttons of my leather jacket to see if that would put a stop to these cold spells, but they kept on just the same. I suppose people who have lived in places like those Terraces and who have been kicked around for the sole benefit of others, have been afraid of things for so many years and for such good cause that they get into the habit of being afraid even when their brains are screaming at them that there is no sense in their fear. I thought of what Danny had told me on that subject. There was a man whose brains had done a lot of screaming. But the fear had still kept a jump ahead of him. I felt I wanted to be doing something that would take my mind off Oscar.

I called at the 'Harp' for the whisky I wanted Hannah to drink. Clarisse was there, having a slack time and ready to talk bits off my ears if I had let her.

'This bottle's for my mother,' I said. 'She's got the chills and a birthday today so I'm taking her this. I've got to go now, but I'll be back later. Can I see you tonight, Clarisse?'

'I'll be looking forward. Gee, you're so dark, Lewis.'

'What the hell's so great about being dark?'

'I don't know. I just like looking at you because you're so dark.'

'I can't understand that.'

I slipped the bottle into my jacket and walked, without hurry, to Hannah's. There were some more relatives in the kitchen when I got there. One of them, a young woman, was detached from the rest of the group and was crying away in the corner where I had stepped on the beetle. She was crying strongly as if she were celebrating some kind of plague. She would have drowned that beetle even if I had not stepped on it.

Hannah had drawn the sofa from behind the table and it stood now in front of the fireplace. It was a red, wooden contraption, old, but still firm enough. There were two cushions on it. I could not take my eyes off that sofa. There were two voters sitting on it, two men, sitting up very stiffly, holding their bowlers in their hands, saying nothing and just waiting by the look of them for the woman in the corner to get dry enough to start moving. They must have thought I was staring at them and not at the sofa. They started fumbling at their bowlers and coughing in the direction of the weeping woman. She calmed down when she saw there was a stranger present. She came and shook hands with me and her fingers were wet with tears she had wiped from her face.

'It passeth all understanding,' she said.

I wanted to ask what passeth, but all I said was: 'There's no doubt about that. It doth.' I remembered that word 'doth' from the chapel and I thought it sounded all right. I passed my hand over one of the arms of the sofa.

'Nice bit of wood,' I said to the nearest of the two voters who sat on it.

'Nothing like it to be had today,' he said.

'There's no doubt about that.'

When they saw that I was just going around agreeing with everybody, they prepared to go. I was glad of that. The whisky bottle was hard and heavy beneath my jacket, on my chest. They shouted 'So long' to Hannah, who was in some other part of the house.

When they had left, Hannah came in. She was paler than I had seen her before.

'I couldn't stand to talk to them,' she said. 'I kept out of the way. They drive anybody crazy. Twice today I felt like taking that money you gave me and getting away, right away from these Terraces and never come back.'

'Danny wouldn't like you to do that.'

'Oh, what the hell does it matter what Danny . . . '

But she was sorry right away for that thought and her mouth closed up on the rest of the sentence. But she was right all the same. What the hell did it matter what Danny might think. He was dead. Still pretty near, but dead.

I took out the bottle and put it on one of the pantry shelves. The shelf had oilcloth of a pretty pattern on it. I could have stood there for a spell looking at that pattern, because I did not know what to say when I went back into the kitchen. When I went back in Hannah was sitting on the sofa, a handful of her red apron upraised to her mouth nibbling at it, and looking as if the last thing she wanted was to hear anything from me.

'It's in there,' I said. 'In the pantry. Just take sips of it. Slow sips, till you get to the right pitch, the pitch where the only thing you feel is your anger and that boiling all the time. You listening, Hannah?'

'All right, Lewis. I'll do that. So long.'

'About nine to half past. I'll bring Oscar.'

'All right. Bring him.'

That evening I sat with Clarisse in the kitchen of the 'Harp'. She had built a big fire. Life was easy, full and warm, sitting there with Clarisse. As I lay back in the deep fireside-chair with her sprawled above me, I would dearly have liked to cut every thread that bound me to any other man or woman outside that room.

I had my mouth pressed into the small of her back. I was doing that on orders. Clarisse said she liked it, and, in any case, I had not much choice, because the way she sprawled covered my mouth with the small of her back. I was as near bliss, as I saw it, as I would ever come. But the threads that led outwards could not be cut; they were thicker than I was. From down the corridor came the bawling voice of Oscar, singing.

'What's the time, Clarisse?'

'About nine. No hurry. Plenty time yet.'

'Got to go.' I stirred.

'Stay there, for God's sake. You're a fidget. Lewis. You always got to go. It's early. Stay there.' She slapped at my leg like a mother arguing with a kid. 'It's nice here.'

I lifted her from above me and stood up.

'I know it's nice in here, Clarisse. Nicer than I've known anything before. I'd like to stay in here with you for always, because it's a very queer place outside. Queer men. Queer women. All putting up with queer kinds of trouble.' I talked like that because I was content for a brief spell and so tired I ached. 'But I got business to do and I got to do it.'

'What business?'

'Got to get Oscar and go.'

'There'll be other evenings.'

'Plenty more. I'm very warm for you, Clarisse.'

'I knew you'd be like that one day, Lewis.'

'Time I had some warmth. Never had much. Got to go now.'

It took me five minutes to get Oscar from the room where he was doing his singing. The Macnaffy element was in the same room. He was concentrating on her. He was singing right at her. She was swinging her thin strong arms in front of his face, conducting the bawl of singing that splurched out of his mouth. She looked merry and glad to have Oscar ramming his tonsils on to her face. She seemed to have forgotten the night when she was so savage about him and called him a bloody weight. Elements like that Macnaffy cannot afford to remember things for very long. I grabbed Oscar by the arm and kicked him in the leg, always a good way of attracting attention, especially if that somebody is a hog who has just drunk about eighteen pints and is too far gone to pay much heed to whispered messages.

'Come on, Oscar,' I said. 'You know where we are going. Hannah. You remember. The Terraces.'

Oscar let his mouth drop and stood there swaying. As he stood there I thought by the look of him that, given about twenty years, he might have remembered his name and that would be all. The Macnaffy element took one of his arms and began dragging him towards her. I caught hold of his coat-tail and the thin Macnaffy, while strong in her lean, Brimstone-Terrace sort of way, was no match for me. I got Oscar out of the room in a rush.

We got into the yard outside.

'Start up towards the Terraces,' I said. 'I'll tell Wilson we're leaving the mare.'

'The mare. The mare,' muttered Oscar. 'I want to stroke that bloody mare.'

'I'll stroke you in a minute, Oscar. Start walking and try to keep upright.'

He steered his way by instinct towards the Terraces. I caught up with him quickly and armed him to keep him steady. It was a long hard walk I had with him. The weight of his body against mine wearied me and its warmth sickened.

I pushed him up the steps that fronted Hannah's. He chuckled a little as he glimpsed at the drawn blinds of the house. The blinds were too short and left gaps. We walked softly up the cemented gully that flanked the house. A yard from the end of the gully I gave him a last push.

'She'll be there, waiting. Go on, Oscar.'

I stayed where I was, not moving at all. I heard him shuffle across the paving. I heard him knock upon the door. The door opened. I heard Hannah's voice. It was high, lively, piercing, not low as I had heard it before. The door closed. I waited and did not move. It began to grow dark quickly, as if the dark were racing down that night from the height of the hills to celebrate something.

I moved to the top of the gully and on to the paving. The gas had been lit in Hannah's kitchen. Through the window, which had no curtain, the inside of the kitchen could clearly be seen. With the lower part of my eyes I could see the forms of Hannah and Oscar on the sofa. Most of my vision was taken up with a picture on the wall opposite, a big picture showing Moses bringing a sackful of frogs down on the head of some Egyptian. It was a whole minute before I could bring my eyes downward from Moses and those frogs to the two on the sofa.

Hannah was lying back on the sofa, further away. Her eyes were closed and strange white thrills seemed to be surging through her face causing her eyelids and her chin to twitch from moment to moment. Oscar was bent above her. His body was motionless save for a heaving of the shoulders that kept time with the twitching of Hannah's eyelids and chin. Hannah's arm was outstretched behind Oscar and rested on the fringe of the cushion.

She is reaching for the hammer, I said to myself. The hammer is behind the cushion and she is reaching for it. And soon the hammer would be put upon Oscar, just like a hog being auctioned. Oscar in all his heat and dirt and then Oscar, cold and getting colder and cut off from all the things that make men dirty, would be clean, too. In my eagerness I pressed my body against the window-sill and felt the lime with which the stonework had been washed crush and flake against my clothes.

Hannah's hand dropped out of sight. But not behind the cushion. It dropped to somewhere my eye could not follow, not even my aching, open eyes in a head slanted excitedly on a stretching neck. Hannah's head dropped back. I could see the muscles around her eyes contract as she closed her eyes tighter, as if to lose the sight of herself and the conscience of her from sight. Her mouth hung open. And then, with the unhurried silence of falling snow, she gave herself to Oscar. There was nothing I could not see now. She gave herself, and Oscar, with his huge body flattened in skilled and solemn ecstasy, took her with a rapture and a joy that could almost be seen rising from him like a mist.

I had to stand there, watching them. It was long and the pain of watching them sucked the strength from me as if the pain were a forceps. My sight became clouded. I had been pressing my eyes hard against the window-pane and that had made my eyes water. Sickness passed like a light-flash through my stomach. It had gone before I could think much about it, leaving only my stomach, wonderingly hungry, in me, wonderingly alone. I walked softly backwards and sat on the low wall that divided the house of Danny from my mother's house. I was full of wailing songs that passed through zones of light and dark inside me, and went from very high to very low in their sad, sickening passage.

I sat on that wall for two or three minutes. Then I walked back to the window, calmer, inwardly silent now. Hannah was helping Oscar to his feet now. He looked vacant, dumb and sweaty. When she had got him off the sofa she turned sharply on her side and sunk her head on the cushion that had been beneath her shoulder. I made my way back into the gully. A bat had been caught between the narrow walls and the sound of its flight was the only sound in all the night.

The kitchen door opened. I heard Oscar take two or three steps along the paving. Then he stopped. That would be the night air poking into his brain. He started off again, unsteadier, I thought, than when I had brought him up to the Terraces an hour before. He had gone past the stage of knowing who I was when I came out of the dark gully to take his arm.

I took him along the pavement of the Terraces. Then up right through a stony alley on to the mountain and towards the path that would lead us to his house.

'Where's the horse?' he mumbled, his head nearly down on his chest with fatigue. 'Where's the horse, Lewis?'

'At the "Harp".' I pushed his head up sharply or he would have fallen alseep on top of me. 'A walk will be a nice change for you, Oscar. You did very well tonight. You ought to give thanks by giving the horse a rest.'

We mounted. The old wind met us as we passed the breast. The old wind that made its ancient sobbing home on that mountain with Oscar, and, Christ, it had reason to sob, living on that mountain. It awakened Oscar, and, as ever, he became merrier, started to chuckle and blabber.

'Hell, Lewis. She's lovely, that Hannah. Don't want anybody but her. Said she'd come with me and live in my house. That's what she said, Lewis, boy. Said she was sick as hell where she is and she wants to be with me. Oh, hell, Lewis, she's lovely. Never known anybody like her, Lewis.'

'That's right. Oscar. There's not much you want you can't have. It's a big thing, having a mountain. When you get a mountain there's nothing you can't have.'

The moon, which had shone briefly, now vanished. I did not blame it for vanishing. It had not much to look at. Only me and Oscar pushing his face into mine, breathing into my eyes, scalding them with the heat of his breath.

We came to the point where the path forked. I led Oscar along the path that would lead him away from his house. We entered the ravine that skirted his tip. We ascended the path that led us on to the broad plateau, on the lip of which I used to sit in the sun and stare down into the narrow valley where Clarisse lived. I had no thought for Clarisse.

Oscar slipped on the loose stones of the path. When I yanked him to his feet I noticed that I did so without effort. I was at full strength, because I had never felt as fully wise as I felt then. I had never before known when all the old stupidities, all the old doubts, have been laid to rest. And I knew, too, that thousands of people who slept in their cramped, terraced houses on the sides of the mountain would nod their brave, tired, friendly faces in agreement with what I wanted to do.

Along the path across the plateau, we walked without haste.

'It's long,' said Oscar. 'Where we going, Lewis?'

'Home, Oscar. There's the lights of the house. Can't you see them?' I pointed my fingers into a great distance. Far away, tiny lights of lighthouses came and went. Oscar must have glimpsed them, because he started to chuckle again.

'And we'll get rid of Meg,' he said. 'We don't want Meg any more.'

'I'll tell Meg that.'

'Where's Meg, Lewis?'

'In the house. Where d'you think?'

'You tell her, boy.'

'All right, Oscar. I'll tell her.'

Then he started to sing as he always did when he came near the edge of that deep quarry which lay on the southern side of the mountain. His voice seemed to be louder than it had ever been, drenching the world with it. I made a buzzing sound in my head to make the noise of his singing less. Now and then he would wave his right arm in my face and shout:

'She's lovely, Lewis. Honest to Christ, she's lovely. That Hannah.'

'Yes,' I would say. Hannah was lovely. I knew that.

We came to the fence that had been put up to keep people away from the quarry, the fence that various voters had made it their business to kick down. I told Oscar to lift his legs to keep them free of the tangled tracks of wood and wire which were all that was left of the fence. He did that. He lifted his legs up a lot higher than was necessary and he screamed that the movement made him feel like a bloody woman.

'That's right, Oscar,' I said. 'Like a woman. Go on, boy.'

And on he went, right over the quarry. As his body landed on the jagged shelves and boulders beneath I thought the earth shook, but it was I who shook. The earth was quite still. I stepped back and sat down on a dew-wet knoll and my mind was full again of those strange, blank minutes I had spent sitting alongside Danny at the base of the tip.

From the quarry no sound came. I stood up and the air that circled on the mountain, all the air in the world, maybe, seemed fresher, cleaner, blowing to better purpose. I ran my knuckles up from my temples until they met in the middle of my forehead and I ground them together with the puckered flesh between. It was a waste. All the blood and bone and sight and sense that had been Oscar. A waste that it had been the way it had been. That notion coming from God knows where cooled me with its odd note of pity and I felt less giddy.

I turned and ran along the path I had come by. Passing Oscar's house, I thought I would go in and tell Meg she need not bother about waiting up for Oscar, that she could go to bed in peace for once. But I did not fancy talking to her. There was something in her face that thickened the layers of silence in me. And anyway, I thought Meg had gone past the stage where peace meant anything more. I ran faster towards the house where Hannah was.

The kitchen door of Hannah's house was on the latch when I got there. I walked right in. Hannah was still on the sofa, lying on her side, her head stuck into the cushion as I had seen her last. I touched her softly on the shoulder. Her sleep was hard and she did not awaken. I touched her hard, pressing the flesh of her shoulder with my fingers. She stirred, turned her head and saw me. Her eyes were dull, misty. Then the mist blew up into a storm. She flung her arms around my legs and cried like mad.

'I was going to do it, honest,' she said.

'You're a bright, bloody beauty, Hannah.'

'I was going to do it.' She flung aside one of the cushions and behind it was the hammer. 'I didn't know exactly who he was. That's what it was. I didn't know . . . exactly. When he came and sat there I thought he was Danny and all I wanted was for him to do what I always wanted Danny to do, but Danny never did. I thought he was Danny and I didn't know anything except I wanted him to do what he was doing. I been so cold, Lewis, so cold, so long. And I wanted to be warm again or I'd have died being cold. Oh Jesus, Jesus, Jesus.

Her crying went up like a bird that has had its wings torn off and flies for a few more moments through sheer pain. I kicked my legs from the embrace of her arms. She did the rest of her crying into the mat on the floor. I had never heard such sounds. It was as if the whole world was crying and she was just a part of it.

'You'll wake the dead, Hannah.' I walked into the pantry and filled a cup from the whisky bottle. I took it to her.

'Drink that, Hannah. Or you'll go mad. And me, too.'

She drank it and she did not seem to notice it was not water. Her crying was no more than soft, hiccuped echoes in her throat now. She sat on the sofa. Her head rested back on the wooden support. Her face smiled and her arms came out on to my shoulders, and the look she gave me would have been burning bright had the room been dark. She was lovely, just like that Oscar had said. She was lovely, that Hannah. I shook her arms away and pushed her head to rest.

'In a minute,' I said, 'you'd be thinking I was Danny. For Christ's sake.'

I wanted to move and keep moving. I found myself pushing open the door that led to the stairway. I walked up the stairs. On the small landing, my hands groped for the door of the front bedroom where I knew Danny was. I opened it. The room was lit dimly by a lamp-post across the street. Danny lay on the bed, boxed, unpuzzled.

'You're lucky, boy.' I yelled hard to keep myself from crying, crying in the pained and wingless bird style I had heard from Hannah. 'You're lucky, Danny. There's a very peculiar bunch of sods performing around here.'

Then I jumped back down the stairs, crossed through the kitchen without a glance at Hannah and made my way into my mother's house. I bit deeply, savagely at my thumbnail and I wanted to talk. I wanted to talk in the dark with that quiet, distant woman who was my mother, and who was no doubt wise about why there was so little peace in the strange, tormented area that separated me from Oscar and Danny, the shrinking ditch between the stirring and the resting.

THE DARK PHILOSOPHERS

If, instead of taking the left-hand road that led you up to the Terraces, you took the right-hand road, two things would happen. First, nobody would blame you for taking that left-hand road because the Terraces were not much to look at even in spring when birds appeared on the older and more stagnant houses. Second, along that right-hand road, following a fairly steep slope, you would reach the house of the Rev. Emmanuel Prees. This was a large house with a lot of pretty silver birch trees around it in which birds sang when the seasons suited them, the birds having more sense than to go wasting their song on that forlorn opposite side of the valley where the Terraces crawled.

The Rev. Emmanuel Prees was a notable preacher. He was so notable he was known as the Rev. Emmanuel or simply Emmanuel by those in the valley who had not yet reached the stage of not bothering to know anyone at all. The congregation at Emmanuel's chapel was the largest in our area, and the collections for several years, greater than the total takings of the coal industry in our section of the valley.

Also, Emmanuel had a mop of snowy hair and a pure, remote look. These features helped him a lot in his work. Whatever you say, it is bound to sound fuller and wiser if it is said beneath a layer of white hair. And with a pure look in a world running so much to dirt and antics whose trade mark is a blush, you can often make a whole career without ever bothering to open your mouth except to eat.

Emmanuel lived alone in that house among the trees and he had more room in which to develop this ascetic, meditative expression and gentle, cooing manner of speech than most of the people who lived with us in the Terraces. Among us the standard of living had for long been so low that people tripped over it and took their time about getting up again.

In some houses you would have so many people living in one room they drew lots to decide which ones would have to go and stand on the window-sill when the others stretched out to sleep. In two houses that we knew, when you opened the door of the sub-let parlour, you had to give the people inside formal notice of your intention. That gave the multitude a chance to shift back out of harm's way; otherwise, the person nearest the fireplace moved at least a foot up the chimney, struggling and complaining all the way, and making mocking replies to the women in the room who warned him to keep clear of the saucepans when he dropped. These conditions, dark, noisy and confusing, never bred that serenity of thought and bearing which drew people towards Emmanuel as music draws those who have long been sick of solitude.

In our young days, we had never been keen followers of Emmanuel. At that time we had never been without a fancy blue-serge suit in which to turn out on Sundays and in addition to having suits we also enjoyed what was said during the sermons. Morning and evenings we would march down through the Terraces to his chapel and listen carefully to all he had to say. In those days our standing with the pious was high. Emmanuel was a lot more interesting to us than the average preacher. His hair was still jet black at that period and his voice had in it a passion that rang out like a chime whenever his words struck fire from his heart.

Emmanuel's parents had been poor people from the Terraces. When they died, the schoolmaster had pointed out to Mr Dalbie, the managing director of the colliery in which we worked, what a fine bright-eyed promising look there was about Emmanuel. Mr Dalbie was a hard man. He had three wooden sheds built at the back of his large house. One was for his coal, the second for his wood and the third for his pity.

He was not usually interested in anyone unless that person happened to be looking bright-eyed and promising over the task of digging coal for Mr Dalbie. But he must have wanted a change or a rest when Emmanuel was pointed out to him. He may have left the door of that third shed off the latch one griping night in winter, and glimpsed the slow procession of our more faltering comrades making their way from the pit to their hillside homes. Or, more believable, even the hardest skull might find it difficult to prevent the thought of a young orphan driving a straight hole through to its soft core.

Old orphans did badly in the Terraces, but young ones still had a fighting chance especially if, as in the case of Emmanuel, there was a schoolmaster doing propaganda on his behalf. Mr Dalbie paid the boy's way through school and college, and provided him on graduation with one of the valley's most commodious pulpits.

Then Mr Dalbie had a shock. He had had so little active experience of being benevolent that he created around his services to Emmanuel a private legend of pure gold. He expected, if not a daily salaam, at least a song of complaisant gratitude from the boy who, had it not been for this incalculable spasm of fondness, would have gone into the pit and received a full blast of shot from one of the two barrels of the gun that Mr Dalbie handled in his double function of pit manager and Justice of the little Peace we knew in our valley.

Instead, Emmanuel treated his patron with fierce scorn. Time and again, he dragged into his sermons bitter references to the overlong hours, brutalizing toil and poor housing which were converting such places as the Terraces into catchment areas for oafs and cretins. It was this approach that attracted us and drove us to take the step of buying serge suits and listening attentively twice each Sunday to his warm addresses.

We even persuaded our friends Ben and Arthur, normally great enemies of the organized emotion that is worked up in chapels, to wear ties and collars and come with us to hear him. They put on these garments which hung from their necks in a way that made them look trussed and horrible. They agreed that Emmanuel rang the bell in his surveys of social conditions, but would not relent in their opinion that hymns, as used by the Celts, run death neck and neck as a full stop for mental motion.

We might have nodded a little during the theological passages because our thoughts are simple and inflexible, and do not lend themselves to the rubbery idiom in which these matters are couched. We clung to a notion of truth as the point at which the waving lines of reading, experience and the state of one's stomach intersect.

Mr Dalbie protested to Emmanuel. He pointed out how much harm it would do to society to have this public assault upon the fitness of those social arrangements in the valley for which Mr Dalbie took full responsibility. We took the arrangements and he took the responsibility, and we could have changed over any day. He pointed out also that these passionate sermons were attracting a very undesirable type of riff-raff in the guise of worshippers to the chapel.

He had, no doubt, been taking stock of my friends Walter, Arthur, Ben and myself, the loosely hung and even sinister cut of our clothes, and the habit my friend Ben had of gripping the woodwork of the seat in front of him with his huge hands as if he were going to tear it up and take it home. This led Mr Dalbie to say that even if Emmanuel was not prepared to look after his pastoral duties he, at least, was going to place scouts at various points along the gallery to look after the woodwork.

This did not unsettle Emmanuel, though his crusade to make the valley a place unfit for Mr Dalbie to live in was sucking the energy from him and making him ill. On the day after receiving a most solemn warning from Mr Dalbie to come back into the camps of the mighty or be damned, he went into the pulpit and gave a sermon that moved whole into our minds like a pillar of burning sand, savage, gritty. He called upon us, the half-dressed, the shambling and the outcast, to be his comrades. He wept. We nearly wept. Mr Dalbie would have done something, too, but before he could commit himself, Emmanuel reached a climax, had a collapse and went crashing to the floor of the pulpit. As people bore him home, it was said he was dead. We had seen many dead men in our time and had an instinct in these matters. We knew he was not dead; nor, of course, was he.

Mr Dalbie nursed Emmanuel back to life. There is no doubt that the man loved Emmanuel like his own son, in a way that warmed the whole pond of darkness that had formed in his being around the impersonal harshness of his relations with us. The seizure whitened Emmanuel's hair and thinned the great bugle of his voice to a reed. The fires had gone down.

Mr Dalbie kept him secluded for many months and talked to him for long periods and with great earnestness, as you can do when you have a bedroom with a door, a man in the bed and a key for the door. Mr Dalbie showed him how foolish it was to hurt one who had treated him with such charity, how foolish to pour forth the very substance of his life and well-being on wretches as lacking in gratitude as cleanliness, wisdom and beauty. These arguments Mr Dalbie topped off with a kidney-punch which stated that if Emmanuel was tempted to ignore the lesson of this seizure and to direct further jets of bitter oratory at himself and his colleagues, Emmanuel would find his pulpit pulled from beneath him with little hopes of finding another.

Emmanuel could not resist these arguments for long. He agreed not to see any more motes in the eyes of the strong or any shadow of cretinous squalor over the Terraces. We did not know whether he was concerned mainly with his chapel or his strength when he made this retreat. We have seen so many men turn tail and run away from what they used to say was the truth, that we have given up wondering why they should feel this urge to pay life the gross compliment of burning, to appease it, that very dignity without which life is as mean a dish as can ever be contrived.

That was why we thought it just as well that his hair went white. When he emerged into his pulpit again he was a soft-spoken, smiling, negative echo of Mr Dalbie. There was nothing left in him for his hair to be black about any more. It might well be that it is a man's conscience that helps to keep his hair black. When he has tossed that conscience to the dogs, what could this hair do but turn snowy?

Emmanuel kept his word. From that point on, he developed the gentle, fatherly manner of pulpit talking, which led people to believe he was conversing with them rather than preaching to them. Nor had he any reason to preach, for preaching is passion and with what passion can a man stand up and advance a thousand reasons why the golden rule of life should be devotion to the wealthy and obedience to an order that may be condemning his closest neighbours to a lifetime's diet of worried wondering.

It was he who said, when soldiers were sent into our valley to bring the great strikes to an end, that we should give warm welcome to the soldiers and return forthwith to work, inspired with a dutiful terror. He described as cannibals such people as my friend Ben, who saw no point in these soldiers, and claimed that they could be keeping the peace and passing on the time more profitably elsewhere. Emmanuel argued that the soldier was simply our well-beloved brother, for was he not doing the duty that was imposed upon him by the whole family, which was the State.

Whenever there was upheaval in some foreign land, there would be a procession of refugees from that land filing through Emmanuel's pulpit, with quivers full of piety, singing ballads of a sad and lowering sort like 'Russia, Holy Russia, I will die to set you free', and telling a sackful of stories about their narrow escape from the grip of the half-dozen or so godless persecutors who were at the bottom of all this trouble.

My friend Walter was convinced that these refugees were all people from the next valley, trained in the part by Emmanuel and Mr Dalbie, fitted with shawls, an overborne look and accents that only a police dog could follow, and released in clutches of suitable size as revolt succeeded revolt.

During the first world war, Emmanuel called for the lynching of so many Germans we wrote to ask him where he thought he was going to get all the time and rope needed for such a heavy programme. Then, during the age of unemployment that came upon us at the war's end, it was Emmanuel, clairvoyant and bland almost to the point of magic, who saw most clearly that golden days were just around the corner, that all we had to do now was trust in the skill and kindliness of our betters, grow stocks of patience as we used to grow potatoes and have faith in faith.

Another item in this recipe of how to go though ten kinds of social hell and still not feel that anything is amiss, was that we should keep our self-respect fresh and sound during this period of trial, as if self-respect were something you could store away under the bed during such times as you were not using it for ordinary living purposes.

Thus it was that Emmanuel, a keen and worthy man as we had known him to be at one time, stricken with the fear of destitution, which is a horrible fear in those who have lived close to destitution and escaped from it, sold his soul to his enemy. He would do nothing of which Mr Dalbie did not approve. What Mr Dalbie told Emmanuel, Emmanuel told the people and the people, drowsy and top-heavy with all the soft consoling axioms that came from him in a broad flow, sank.

We were told that even when Emmanuel, responding to a furtive return of virility to his veins, fell very much in love with some girl in the valley who gowked her adoration of him from the front row of the gallery, Mr Dalbie refused him permission to marry on grounds of health, saying, possibly through the keyhole of a locked door, that absolute rest in week-nights was a primary need for such a nervous and apostolic type as Emmanuel.

Emmanuel laid the girl aside as promptly as last week's shirt. That must have been surprising to the girl, for even we could imagine that she might have been far gone on so refined, meditative, white-haired and well-off a man as Emmanuel. For these services Mr Dalbie paid well. We were pleased to know that he paid somebody well, for while that was done, there was always the chance that the impulse would branch out if he ever decided to take the same high view of digging as preaching.

During all this period when Emmanuel was doing so much better out of the coal trade than we had ever done we mostly stood still and cultivated our discontents. We had them trained and disciplined to a degree that amazed visitors. They answered to their first names, begged, did cartwheels and jumped through dialectical hoops at a word of command. The only contact we had with Emmanuel was when he referred to us, on and off, as enemies of the faith, dangers to the state and enemies of mankind.

We objected to that last charge, for in the line of harm and malice we always got a lot more than we would ever give. We never listened to his sermons. Those fancy blue-serge suits had long since been handed over to neighbours as patching material or, green with age and decline, hung on trees to help on a spring that never arrived. Long before the slump our interest in the metaphysical stretches of theology had gone up the chimney and there it had stayed, because we could not even afford to get such useful articles as soot from the chimney.

During those years when our brains had all the room they needed to move about in the stillness that came to our valley with the closing of the pits, we became bitterly opposed to Emmanuel on topics like the right to work, the right not to work, the October Revolution, the State as a Family, Patience as a Virtue. The only time we ever felt inclined to use patience was as a shoe lift when the urge to kick somebody caught us in our stockinged feet.

Indeed, in moments when distress weighed upon us more heavily than usual, which was at the beginning of every fresh week, and despair shook us like the clapper of a funeral bell, we sometimes looked upon Emmanuel as being in every way, despite his hair and his expression which was so pure, a poor human. We thought it a pity that among the improvements that Mr Dalbie had lavished on Emmanuel's pastorate, room could not have been found for a simple, inexpensive fitment of seasonable honesty.

Mr Dalbie died some time between the first and second big coal strikes. The manner of Emmanuel changed. It crossed our mind that Mr Dalbie might have laid a charm on Emmanuel and, with his departure, it was likely that Emmanuel would rise from the grave of his defection and return among us, his face bright with the old convictions. He seemed to lose himself, to become listless, jumpy. But he continued to utter the same nerveless, servile precepts of acceptance which, taken in and learned by heart, brought such a glassy look to the features of the people who listened regularly to him, their Adam's apple assuming the shape of a window catch.

Mr Dalbie left him well provided for. He inherited the roomy mansion on the hillside opposite the Terraces, and we heard about him only when we argued fiercely in the Library and Institute with those of his flock who made regular transmissions to us of Emmanuel's wisdom, and who regarded our infidel passions as being high up on the list of reasons they advanced to explain the presence in our midst of such a bewildering scale of plagues like rickets, leaking roofs and hearts that lay in perpetual shadow. We did not think our path and that of Emmanuel would ever cross again. But the paths did cross and this is the odd way in which it came about.

*

As you know, the slump in our part of the world eased somewhat in recent years. When people started making guns and such things in preparation for new wars, a muffled echo of this interesting process was heard even in the Terraces. Various of our neighbours, who had seen no work or wages save in cinemas or sleep for ten or fifteen years, drifted back on to jobs, in the different stages of stiffness and inefficiency you might expect from people who have had to put up with such long stretches of exile from useful labour. The miracle was that they had anything left to be stiff and inefficient with.

We thought it a pity, of course, that this increase of jobs and prosperity should be due to the making of guns, for we were no fonder of war than we were of unemployment, but the attitude of most of us was that anything that brought life a heightened sense of meaning and direction, and a more flippant attitude towards Social Insurance was our notion of a sound religion. It was a notion we hated but we fell in behind it as behind a hearse. You would denounce it as pagan if you had none of our experiences, but you would not if you knew anything much about the Terraces.

Nothing would seem very strange to you if you knew anything about the Terraces. Even my friends and I, who were considered desperate, unmanageable and useless characters by the Ministry of Labour, were found things to do that we got paid for. We looked as astonished as the clerks who gave us a hearty send-off on these new experiences.

My friend, Walter, who was a handy penman and wrote in a clear way which even voters who could not read could understand, was made a storesman at one of the Council's supply yards, keeping a check on such articles as picks and shovels. He also watched that the people who worked for the Council did not leave the yard wearing more than two sets of the Council's oilskins at once.

The Council, knowing my friend Walter for a discontented and rebellious man, had made him promise to keep off politics before giving him this job. Walter had given this promise and kept it for about half an hour. There was an oppressed look about the boys who went walking in and out of that yard oilskinned up to the eyes, and sunk in a soaked gloom that drove Walter to take the matter up with life in the bold, keen way he had. For eleven years he had lived on a diet of politics and dry toast, and he had lost all sense of responsibility in such things as promises and words of honour. However, his penmanship was so good and he knew so much more about the stores than the previous storemen, who had scarcely known where they were themselves, that Walter kept his job.

My friend, Ben, went back to his old trade of bricklaying, and was so out of practice that the first wall he helped to build was so crooked and covered him so well that it served as a good shelter from the rain, even if it was not so bright as a piece of wall.

My friend Arthur made a bad start by getting a job with the Water Board as a shoveller of frogs from the filters of the reservoir. This made his weak stomach much weaker; so weak that he had to protest to the foreman that if he developed any less affection for this work, the frogs would be noting his helpless and beaten look and shovelling him off the filters. Then he got a job as a warehouseman at a large Co-operative Store where conditions were good, and Arthur grew to look quite well again. The only trouble with this job, as we saw it, was that it involved a lot of counting, and even after he had left his work Arthur could not help counting things that did not need counting at all, simple things like the legs of tables, just to show us how skilled he had become in this line.

I was taken on as a decorator with the County Council, and I entered on this job with a lot of joy, because I had noticed during my years on earth a lot of places which badly needed decorating; minds, bodies and even whole lives that had been loose on the hinge, or had taken to rust since humanity had first gone humid. But the County Council kept me to such small jobs as painting the outsides of places like schools, workhouses and other large establishments which are set up by County Councils for the very young, the very poor and the very sick.

I was not much of a painter. A foreman whose manner and ideas I disliked, but whose opinion in these matters I trusted like a book, told me that my brushwork was the worst that had been seen since the invention of paint, which was a long time ago. That was not a fateful fault. One thing about schools and workhouses, which are now called Institutions, is that the way in which their outsides are painted does not seem to be of any great importance. As long as the ratepayers see some sign of the paint their money buys, no one grumbles, except those elements who object to County Council establishments on principle, with or without paint, and want a return to the days when only about ten people could read, and all the sick people were kept stuck away in the attic or burnt as witches if they chanced to gibber.

The ratepayers certainly saw enough signs of their paint on me, for my method with the brush was never steady. My friend Walter told me that if I painted myself with any deeper thickness of County Council paint, the Council would start enlarging me for use as a school or a Union just to cut their losses.

Naturally, with this increase in prosperity, our lives became a lot freer than they had been. We could now afford to abandon the brick wall at the bottom of our yard, where we had talked our way through innumerable evenings. That was one thing that made us glad. Our clothes had been thin, the bricks cold and we would, no doubt, have contracted various complaints if we had been doomed to sit permanently upon that wall, to do all our talking upon that spot until our tongues, the bricks, or time itself caved in.

Our new meeting place in the evenings was the refreshment and confectionery shop of Idomeneo Faracci, an Italian, whose shop was on the third Terrace, not far from the Library and Institute, where we had now taken out fresh membership cards for the sake of attending lectures and borrowing books. This Institute was a useful place for all voters whose minds liked to dwell on those serious topics with which the Terraces slopped over, and there was room there, too, for those whose maximum in the way of mental action was billiards, ludo or just coming in out of the cold.

The Institute had several rooms set aside for the playing of simple games, and these rooms were much used by backward types whose speciality was horseplay or sitting in a sort of trance at the portals of puberty with their ears to the keyhole, and learning the facts of life at second-hand and fainting every so often from pure surprise.

During the years when we had no work we had discontinued our membership at the Institute. We would have found it hard to pay the subscriptions and to wear the keen, sociable look one is expected to put on in places where large numbers of voters gather for quiet enjoyment. We had that lost, haunted look which would have caused a sense of wonder to form, soft and sad as moss, around the brains of those gallivanting, groping lads in the horse-play department. We had greatly missed the Institute.

But for the purpose of a quiet talk among ourselves, when we felt a strange craving for that loneliness we had known so often on that brick wall during the cold years, we preferred the back room at Idomeneo's. This room was cosy and cheerful, having sawdust on the floor and a large stove in the middle, which had a complicated system of airshafts that made the layout of an ordinary man or woman look simple. Idomeneo had never properly mastered the ways of this stove, and every now and then thick clouds of smoke would come from it and blot out the person to whom you were talking.

When that happened Idomeneo came rushing in from the shop in front and started poking about with a long bamboo rod in this direction or that, doing nothing, it seemed to us, except increase the amount of smoke and occasionally wound with a thrust of the rod some voter whom Idomeneo could not see on account of the smoke-screen.

My friend claimed that this stove must at one time have been a pipe organ to explain the presence in it of so many pipes, and he often urged Idomeneo to give the inside of it a good scraping out to see if it contained a keyboard. If it were found we could arrange to have Ben crawl in and give us some such number as 'Lead Kindly Light' on this keyboard every time we lost sight of each other in the smoke. But once you got used to the antics of this stove it was a comfortable room in which to sit and talk with your friends.

Besides the stove there were also some tables of various sizes on which the customers could drink hot cordials and eat the sandwiches that Idomeneo served, and we always praised the hot cordials of Idomeneo for being prepared with deep skill and great heat. Our own drink was tea and we drank a lot of it. We had taken a vow to get our stomachs as dark as our philosophy before we finished, and every time we ordered a fresh round of cups Idomeneo always put an extra pinch in the pot as a tribute to the fine brooding quality of our spirits.

The hot water for this tea Idomeneo obtained from a big shining cistern which stood on the counter of the shop. This cistern, when the taps were opened, went off with a sharp hiss that always made my friend Arthur say he had no time for snakes. To me this hissing of the cistern sounded as if Idomeneo had decided to deal a final blow at the stove in the back room by getting the Fire Brigade to bring up their strongest bit of hose, so I always ducked when the hissing started.

The cistern had been made in Italy, and just above the name of the manufacturer, which was stamped on a chrome plate, there was engraved a bundle of rods and an axe. My friend Arthur pointed out to Idomeneo that these rods and so on were the trade mark and symbol of the Italian Blackshirts, and no very healthy sign to be showing in a place like the Terraces, where the voters had never failed to show a great respect for democracy and a will to strive for equal justice.

Idomeneo, who was a short, cheerful man with black hair, said he knew all about this symbol and that he liked it no better than we did. He added that even then he had two brothers in Italian jails because they had happened to be in Italy when they said they did not like this symbol either. As far as politics went, said Idomeneo in a whisper, he was with us to the end. The way in which he did this whispering and especially the way in which he said those words 'the end' made us feel that he thought that the end was going to be on the rough side, and we were sorry that Idomeneo should take this dark view of the future, for we had spent much time and energy agitating for a better life all round. But it might not have been a dark view at all, it might only have been Idomeneo's Italian method of exaggerating his tone in order to get his point across. We saw very well what he meant. He meant that he was all for the common people, as we were, being of them.

From the moment of that explanation onwards we were good friends with Idomeneo, particularly after he had told us of those two brothers who were in jail. We looked on him after that as being a splendid character by our standards, and a valuable link between ourselves and all those humble brethren on the continent of Europe whose aim, as ours, was to cut down on the number of nuisances who flourish on this earth, and to reach the grave without paying too many and too heavy toll charges on the way.

But my friend Walter told Idomeneo one evening that if his sympathies lay with the poor, as he said, why did he not take some steps to get those rods and axes removed from the belly of the cistern, where they did nothing but cause a lot of suspicion and grief in the minds of all his clients who did any thinking at all.

In reply, Idomeneo bent low over the table at which we were sitting, and as he did this bending, he wore a cunning and confidential look. Many times, he said, had the thought of removing the emblem come to him, of filing it right away, but two things had always made him pause. First, he was no great hand with tools of any description, and any attempt on his part to file away the emblem would probably have ended in his filing clean through the metal, which would have been bad for the tea- and coffee-making side of his business. Also, the man who had loaned him the money to open up this business, an Italian living in London, was very partial to Italy and to the party behind the rods, so partial that the only reason he had for living so far away from them was that he did very well out of being in London, and in a position to lend money to poor Italians like Idomeneo who wanted to open shops and refreshment bars. If this man was to discover that Idomeneo was showing his contempt for the doctrines of force by filing away the Blackshirt emblem from a nice shiny cistern that was still no more than half paid for, he might call in the loan and cause Idomeneo to close down.

We all told Idomeneo how sorry we were to see him in the grip of such a type of moneylender as this Italian. Moneylenders as a body we condemned, but for moneylenders who used their loans as a reason for sticking up unpopular emblems in the shops of those traders to whom they lent money, we had less than no use. We told Idomeneo that the next time this man called around to inspect his investment, he should tip us the wink, bring the water in the cistern to the boil and then we would dip in the moneylender and hold him there for a long period. Then, on top of all our other interesting experiences, we would know what it was like to drink tea flavoured with black reaction.

Another pleasing feature of the back room at Idomeneo's was the regular presence there of a youth named Willie. This Willie was, from any viewpoint, a very admirable person. He did a lot of thinking along serious channels, could talk like a mill stream, and wore clothes that looked as if someone had thrown them at him on the same principle as you throw rings at a ringboard. If they catch on a hook, they stay on: if they do not catch, they fall to the floor.

This Willie had such a smiling, confident attitude towards all things that I do not think he would have minded much if all the clothes had landed at his feet and he stood naked. He had hair as black as Idomeneo's and his face was broad, strong and had a wondering kind of look on it most times. This Willie had a great love for music and a promising tenor voice, which he would flash out to express any mood as if it were part of his brain. It was this fondness for singing that had brought Willie to be such a regular patron of Idomeneo's.

Idomeneo had an old cabinet gramophone in the back room, and a large bundle of records containing such items as very sweet arias from operas, also duets, trios and choirs, and to these Willie and ourselves would sit and listen by the hour, with Willie bursting out with his own version sometimes if there was a tenor on, and Idomeneo giving him strong support in a baritone voice that seemed to us very deep and rich for so small a man. And when the music had ended and Idomeneo was bringing us our last cup of tea of the night, Willie would sit looking very sadly at the stove, his eyebrows high up on his forehead and his lips moving as if he wanted to cry. One night sitting like that, he said:

'We feel warm and happy now and that is good. The music reaches us and we are willing to hear all the things it has to tell. But, hell, man, what about the people around us, most of the people in these Terraces for a start, whose lives are sad and ugly because they never understand what all this music means.'

'True enough, Willie,' said my friend Walter. 'You have a tender conscience, which is always a very nice thing to watch. You see the moment of your own happiness, full of those sweet melodies that Idomeneo allows us to hear, to appreciate the troubles of other voters whose way of life makes it impossible for them to share that happiness. That shows true humanity, Willie, and augurs well for your future as a voter. But see here. The need for beauty comes a long way after the need for food and warmth, and while people are still worried black and blue from the guts upward by that second need, they will see no need for beauty except perhaps that sort they get in thimblefuls from such articles as prayers, picture postcards and young passion kindling among the mountain ferns. The education of the people will only truly have begun when the desire to express the need for beauty will be a common feature of one and all. As things are now, we would not see a fat lot of difference if I or one of you were to wake up one of these mornings and find that we were sharing the world with such creatures as rats, beavers, wolves or skunks. Not much difference, not with regard to this business of beauty, anyway.'

'I am looking forward,' said Willie earnestly, 'to my future as a voter.'

Then we all fell silent and the only sound in the shop was the roaring of angry, complicated draughts through the twisted air shafts of the stove, the beat of Idomeneo's tired fingers on the counter (he opened the shop at six in the morning), rain outside beating down upon the Terraces. We thought of the music we had heard and of what Willie and Walter had been saying.

We cursed within our own minds the sterile cold and loneliness we had lived in for many years when misery and anger had killed the memory of all such loveliness as that music within us, and we thought sorrowfully of all those many voters lying around about us in the Terraces who had been made numb and stupid by poverty, dead even to the divine beauty created by man.

Many of Idomeneo's records were worn and very often all the music you heard from some of the older ones was a scratch that went up and down to a certain beat, like a hoarse ghost following the music about, quarrelling with it. Idomeneo said he was sorry he could not buy new ones because, while he was paying his loan back to that man in London, he was so short of money he could not even afford to buy a new tie, and would probably have to be wearing brown paper underpants before the winter was out.

We all thought it strange that a man keeping a shop like Idomeneo should be in such a predicament as this. We were especially moved by the reference to brown paper underpants, a notion that set even our teeth on edge, since such a garment as that would surely be horrible to the shanks of any voter, quite apart from the risk you would take of having somebody sticking strings and stamps on you in mistake for a parcel as you were getting into bed dressed in this fashion. It made us feel that with shopkeepers like Idomeneo going short of comforts, there must be a lot more misery in the world than even we had imagined, and sometimes we had thought that our imaginations were going mad because they imagined so much.

Willie suggested that we should all club in sixpence a week to buy new records, and since we were now earning as much as three or four shillings over and above what we needed for such items as rent, food, clothes and tobacco, we agreed to this plan. The money mounted up quickly, and soon we were marching down into the valley with Willie, one Friday evening, to buy a new record.

We had decided beforehand that the only records we would buy were trios and quartets from the operas, because if there was one thing we enjoyed more than a good singer it was several good singers singing in harmony; also, trios and quartets would allow Willie and Idomeneo to join in the singing to their hearts' content without blotting anyone out, which was what sometimes did happen when they were competing with just one solo singer.

In choosing our records we were helped greatly by the manager of the music shop, a man of very sound democratic outlook, who was pleased to see a band of voters from the Terraces, particularly young voters like Willie, listening to music and examining his stock with so much enthusiasm. We would listen to dozens of records before choosing the one we wanted, so on those Friday evenings when we had clubbed in money enough to go down to the gramophone shop, we always had a very good concert in addition to the pride of actually being able to buy something that did not have to be eaten or worn. We would make our way back to the Terraces and Idomeneo's back room in a very happy state of mind, with our skins full of melodies and trailing as fast as we could behind the swift Willie, who always carried the record.

When the new music was played for the first time, Idomeneo would suspend any activity that might be going forward in his shop, such as serving sweets or changing silver into copper for some voter's gas meter, and he would come and stand with us in the back room, his dark face tilted thoughtfully down towards the lapel of his brown shop coat and gently tapping the sawdust on the floor with his dull, unpolished shoes, nodding joyfully once in a while at Willie, who nodded joyfully all the time.

The only trouble we had during these sessions was when my friend Ben tried to steal a bit of Idomeneo's thunder by cutting in with snatches of the baritone part. We had to argue with Ben on this point and we got him to stop it because my friend Ben, while being a man who bears an unblemished record of political activity in defence of the common people, and being very strong in point of muscle and very keen and quick to use that muscle in pursuit of narks, scabs and other nuisances, is no singer. He is perhaps the worst singer ever produced in the Terraces.

When the music was finished Willie would ask Idomeneo many questions about the operas from which these trios and quartets were taken, and he would listen thirstily as Idomeneo, who had seen a lot of these operas on the stage in Italy, told stories about them, their plots, the kind of scenery you would see and the kind of singers you would hear.

'It's not right,' Willie would say when Idomeneo had told him all these things. 'Why haven't we had the chance of hearing such things as these operas here in the Terraces?'

'Because,' said my friend Walter, 'there's no profit to be made from beauty of any sort, opera included. That is why there is so much profit and so little beauty to be observed in such a community as this one. Unless you are a man who can see beauty in profit, you get a thin time. These Terraces were put up so that people could eat and breed in between shifts and working in the pits. They were not put up with any notion of giving the voters a full and happy life. What room is there in these Terraces for such things as operas? Every spare inch is taken up with houses and people. Even if it was only an extra urinal you wanted to build, you would have to build it on somebody's roof.'

We became very fond of all these trios and quartets, and Idomeneo said one night he thought it would be a good idea if there were some girl who could come along and give a hand with the soprano part. He said a woman's voice among men's was like yeast in bread. Willie considered this idea to be useful, and told us he was friendly with a very nice girl who would be such a bit of yeast as Idomeneo was suggesting. We all agreed that any friend of Willie's, yeast or no, would always be most welcome among us.

But our evenings in Idomeneo's were not all given over to music. Willie was a lad whose curiosity was wide awake, whose mind went rapping at the door of many serious questions affecting the world we lived in. We thought this a good sign for the generation that was coming up behind us, because we have always believed that those who do not rap hard upon the doors of problems will soon find the problems rapping upon them. So we were pleased to see this keen interest in Willie, though he tried to tell us that personally he found most of the lads of his own age very dense in all matters except love.

We were eager to put at the disposal of Willie any knowledge we had picked up in the course of our pilgrimage. True, we were not men who knew much about the whole globe. We had never seen Bombay, Moscow, New York, Alaska. We had lived our lives in the Terraces, and had had great difficulty in keeping ourselves alive in that tiny part of the world's surface without traipsing around the rest of it. But for all this lack of travel, we did claim to have arrived at certain deep ideas regarding the present and future of the human race, ideas that had arisen from all the things we had seen and felt in the Terraces. We also claimed, having read as many pamphlets as men can read without going blind, and having attended as many meetings as men can attend without going deaf, that we had a pretty wide selection of ideas about the state of the world at large.

'Knowledge,' said my friend Arthur to Willie one night, 'is not what you've seen but what you've felt. The man in the Terraces, who works too much and eats too little, knows a lot more about the man in Bombay who works too much and eats too little, than the man who works too little and eats too much, but who gets the chance to stare at the man in Bombay for years on end if the fancy takes him. The scenery of this world, the mountains, the rivers, the plains and the seas, the things people write books about, mean nothing to us who have lived from birth onward locked up in these Terraces. But the people of the world, the people who are like us, who live in places like the Terraces or worse, whose lives are a freezing day and their hopes the water that freezes, they are as real and as near to us as the fingers on my hand.'

But Willie was not a youth who took in all we said like a sponge. Indeed, in many of the discussions we had concerning such topics as World Peace, Labour and Unemployment, What is Faith or the Red Dawn, Willie would often become very fierce in telling us that we were men who were stumbling about on the wrong track.

One night he stood up in the middle of a talk we were having on the subject of slavery past and present, and reproved us in a loud voice for being narrow and intolerant. We were men, he said, who had become lost in our own bitterness, whose intolerance was a deadly weed, a poison that would end by drying up the very spring of human brotherhood, that we were judging the whole world by reference to the grey wretchedness of the Terraces, and that that was a very wrong thing for such nice fellows as we were to be doing.

My friend Ben took offence at these remarks from Willie, and was on the point of pressing Willie back on to his chair or even to some point lower than the chair, such as the floor, but my friend Walter called them to order. We all wondered where Willie could have gathered up such a stock of strange ideas, for they sounded very strange indeed to our ears especially coming from a youth for whose brightness we had such respect. We thought at first that Willie's father might be one of those products whose brains had died at some date prior to the Labour Representation Committee, and who had passed these horse-hair notions on to Willie as a kind of family curse. We considered that if that were so it showed a very mean streak in Willie's parent, for the children of the Terraces have quite enough curses passed on for their attention whether the parents wish it or not.

But Willie soon explained to us where he got his stocks of philosophy. He was a follower, he said, of the Rev. Emmanuel the white-haired pastor and spinner of soothing axioms, who lived in the lonely and tree-surrounded house on the opposite side of the valley. He was more than a follower, said Willie. One could say he was a lover, a disciple of the Rev. Emmanuel. Emmanuel was the saintliest character that had ever breathed (the whiteness of his hair, unsupported even by the whiteness of his linen would prove that, said Willie). And his doctrine of universal peace, brotherhood, meekness and charity was the very last word in wisdom as far as Willie went.

We all thought it odd that so wide awake and curious a youth as Willie should have taken and swallowed such a mindful of doctrine from so shifty an influence as the Rev. Emmanuel, whom we deeply distrusted as a man who had abandoned his love for the common people and gone straight over to the forces of the earth's mighty in the person of that deacon-coalowner.

But we treated Willie with the patience and understanding which we always wore as proudly as a crown when we were dealing with any good, sincere comrade who failed to see eye to eye with us on this point or that. (My friend Ben, it is true, had a weakness for beginning and ending most arguments by letting his hands fly, but even Ben, when reasoned with by us, would become most temperate and accommodating in his method of conversation. The man who took the class in biology at the Library and Institute that Ben attended one winter, had told him that this impatience of his was due most likely to his glands, and Ben was always telling us that even so you could not blame his glands altogether for that because they had probably been put up to it by the dark forces.)

We understood Willie's position even better when he explained to us the full story of his devotion to the Rev Emmanuel. At twelve, Willie had left the Council School to become a scholarship pupil at the County School. He had taken this step with the full assurance of his teachers that with his brain, a bit more book learning, and the ability to use his knife and fork with less savage motions, he would become a great power in the land.

At this time, Willie had been an attender at the chapel and Sunday School of the Rev. Emmanuel. But he was one who took only a drowsy and enforced interest in such events as sermons. The broader syllabus and the more adult atmosphere of the County School had jerked up Willie's wits no end, and the subject of biology in particular had set him thinking in a very critical way about such topics as the beginning of the world, topics which had always attracted a lot of notice in the Sunday School, because the bulk of the elements who became pupils at this Sunday School were the sons of voters who were so poor and got so little in the way of a reward for all the labour they performed, that their sons were very fond of asking why the world should ever have taken the trouble to begin.

It was Willie's conviction very early on that if we were to consider as creatures with an equal right to live such types as men, newts, apes, fleas and stars, then the world must just have wandered into the midst of so much nonsense and not just begun as a concert or a disease would begin. The world, to Willie, from himself to his old man, and from those two points outward and upward as far as the eye could reach seemed full of things that did not quite fit. Willie, in a halting but very sincere way, placed these ideas of his before his Sunday School teacher, a stern man, a wood merchant and such a firm believer that he thought the stars were angels' hearts.

He had never heard of newts and thought Willie was making them up out of his own head just to annoy him. He believed so firmly in a deliberate and organized creation that he had the date of the world's creation, in years, months and days engraved on his watch chain, this chain being very strong and securely fastened to the wood merchant, making the date handy to get at and not likely ever to get lost. This voter, like most voters who are firm believers and go around covered with watch chains and have never heard of newts, was a difficult man to argue with on such a theme as equal rights to live, which was Willie's strong point. And as he was the employer of Willie's father, he had even more cards up his sleeve than any biologist when it came to taking up the offensive in an argument. Such a card, for example, as threatening to sack Willie's father from his timber works if Willie did not immediately foot it back to the Kentucky Hills in the matter of religious thinking.

Willie's father, an ailing man on account of the tons of sawdust he had swallowed in the wood merchant's yard and a social contract he had never quite managed to swallow, threatened at once to plane at least two inches from the top of Willie's skull if Willie continued to annoy the wood merchant by trying to make him out to be no better than an ape, when everyone knew he had next to no hair on his chest, such a tail as only his best friends would quibble about, fifteen thousand in the bank, a contract with the County Council and two sons at college, one learning to exploit his father as thoroughly as his father exploited Willie's father, and the other learning to be a vicar.

But Willie refused to mend his ways. He continued to anger the wood merchant by bringing along each Sunday to the Sunday School a large bundle of facts that proved instances of great disorder and discontent in the living arrangements of man and beast. Finally, the wood merchant told Willie's father that the boy was getting nothing but harm from the rubbish he was learning in that County School. In any case, quite apart from the matter of Willie trying to make him out to be an ape, the wood merchant thought that there would be enough education in the world to get along with when his two sons had finished their course without having lowly types like Willie cluttering up the market with unnecessary thoughts and learning. Moreover, Willie was of an age to work, and he would be far better employed earning a few extra loaves for his father and mother, especially since Willie's old man was never sure about when he might not be ailing himself out of a job.

Willie's father took the hint, and after some protest from Willie's headmaster who saw a promising, revolutionary shape about Willie's skull, the lad was withdrawn.

The wood merchant had promised Willie a job in his yard as a kind of compensation, but when Willie turned up at the yard for this job the merchant did no more than laugh, look wise and send Willie away empty-handed, except for the advice that Willie could now meditate in peace for a year or two on the disadvantages of impiety in a world where the strings of all power rest in the hands of the pious.

Even Willie's father thought that this conduct was open to question, and got so worked up by rage that he threw a beam of wood at the wood merchant and fell ill as a result of this activity. The family of Willie had a very thing time during the father's illness and Willie, wandering about the roads in search of work which was never there, felt that if this search went on for very much longer he would be able to write at first hand regarding the attitude to life of such small neglected creatures as newts, he feeling twice as small and three times as neglected.

Things got better when Willie's father started work again with the wood merchant, for the wood merchant always believed in creating a good impression on the local voters by forgiving somebody once in ten years and, on top of that, Willie's father, flabby as many of his ideas might have been, was a very useful hand in all things connected with wood.

Willie, at sixteen, having heard his father quote a wise axiom from a sermon of the Rev. Emmanuel about it being easier to go around a thing than through it, and being impressed by the consoling sound of this thought, softened his bitter attitude to religion and drifted back to the chapel. He confessed to the wood merchant, into whose Sunday School class he had been once more admitted, that the only date that would mean anything to him from now was the date on the wood merchant's watch chain.

The merchant was very pleased by this and took Willie along to see the Rev. Emmanuel, introducing him as a youth of promise who would bear watching. The Rev. Emmanuel treated Willie with great kindness, took him to his house for tea, explained to him that the upsets we meet in this life are really no more than upsets within ourselves, which are in turn no more than growing pains of the soul struggling towards ripeness and full courage.

Willie joined the Young People's Club, which had been formed as a subsidiary of Emmanuel's chapel, an organization that had such events as plays about missionaries, puzzle games and jumble sales well up on the agenda. Willie threw himself with great zeal into the work of this club, making a name for himself as a young actor who could play to perfection the part of any missionary in the plays that were performed: but of all the things that Willie valued about this club, outstanding were the talks he had with the Rev. Emmanuel, soft, simple, persuasive talks of patience, brotherhood and charity that lay like swan's down on the listener's ear. Then Willie, having in the course of many evenings got a record load of this swan's down on his ear, was taken along one day by the Rev. Emmanuel to the chain works which is situated just outside the valley, and Willie, as a result of this visit, had become an apprentice welder, a trade in which he had continued and which he considered very healthy and satisfying.

'So you see,' said Willie, 'if I had kept on being intolerant, where would I have been? But I saw my error, I discovered the lesson of patience, brotherhood and charity. I owe it all to the Rev. Emmanuel who made these things clear. Don't you think that was a wonderful thing he said about our upsets being no more than the growing pains of the soul.'

We thought of the cold, dismal years we had known after the closing down of the pits in which we had worked.

'We had so many growing pains, Willie,' said my friend Arthur, 'our souls died.'

'We won't argue with you, Willie,' said Walter. 'You are young and things have turned out fairly well for you. We are not so young, and we can say quite honestly that things turned out hellishly for us.'

'You should forget all that. Banish hatred,' said Willie zealously.

'You cannot forget things that have been your entire life for many years. The insult of a moment, Willie, is hard enough to forget but when men have to endure the insult of being idle, degraded and useless for years on end, not only is it impossible to forget that, it becomes an act of faith to cherish the memory of it every moment one lives, because one's duty as a human being from that time on is to fight against the possibility of that insult being levelled against oneself or against others again. You're young, Willie. You only caught a glimpse of the knife that went right through our bodies.'

'You should have had patience,' said Willie with great obstinacy.

'Patience,' said my friend Ben. 'Oh holy God. He tells us we should have had patience. There wasn't any before we started it.'

'Had we lacked patience, Willie,' said Walter, 'we would have listened long ago to the reasoning that told us we would be saving the State and ourselves a lot of time and bother by hanging ourselves from a beam.'

'You hate too much,' said Willie, weakening a little now, we thought. 'You have lost the sense of brotherhood.'

'Willie, during all these years, the strongest fibre in us has been a sense of pity and comradeship. It has often been betrayed by others who have left us for a life of more ease and less struggle. It has often been strained by one temptation after another within ourselves, but it has never broken.'

'You missed the hand of charity.'

'If we had seen it, Willie, we would have bitten it, hard. There is no greater dispenser of poison than charity. Only slaves need charity. The only things that men need to be at their best are freedom and intelligence. Simple things, no doubt, but only a tiny fringe of mankind has them at the present.'

'Oh, you tie me up, Walter,' said Willie with a laugh. 'You're so old and hard and far away sometimes, like an image. But I still think that what's wrong with all you brethren, you and Ben and Arthur and John, is that you locked yourselves away in these stinking Terraces to go grey, dirty, like them, to close your ears against all the fine messages that might have come to you from the outside. You should have been followers of the Rev. Emmanuel. If you had heard him you would have loved him as I do. There is no man, however he might sin against you, who cannot be forgiven and persuaded by your forgiveness to act decently towards you.'

'You would forgive even such a type as that wood merchant?'

'I did forgive him and look how kindly he acted to me when he saw I had made my peace with him.'

'But don't you think you were right about the newts and the stars and so on, about the disorder and discontent?'

'One lives to be happy,' said Willie, 'not right.'

'A very queer attitude, Willie, and one which, if adopted at the time of the so-called Flood, would have converted all men into mackerels.'

'Happiness is what I want and happiness is what I'll have.'

'Good luck to you in that venture, Willie. But look. You've told us yourself that many things about the way people live in these Terraces make you sick inside. The bulk of our neighbours live lives of little comfort and less beauty. Do you imagine that people will continue to live in that odd fashion for ever more, without regarding such wholesale misery as an unnecessary fetter that might be broken. And how do you imagine that that fetter will be broken if not by one or two bouts of uneasiness and intolerance on the part of the people? You work in a foundry. You've seen enough fetters to know that not even a community most skilled in weeping would ever melt it with their tears.'

'I know that,' said Willie, 'and that is where you friends are at such a loss through not hearing the Rev. Emmanuel. He's got a theory that explains all that. He says there was once an Ice Age.'

'It finished,' said Ben solemnly, 'when I got back into the building trade.'

'Not that Ice Age. I mean the big one, the real one, with mountains of ice over everything.'

'I've heard about that,' said Ben, eager now to show Willie that he had not spent all his time cultivating muscle and slapping backward voters, but had gathered some learning from such things as those classes in the Library and Institute.

'Well, that Ice Age,' said Willie, 'gave way to an age that was not so cold. The ice melted and the earth was fuller of life and movement and sound than it had ever been before.'

'All these changes must have been very confusing to the voters,' said Ben.

'It was a slow change, Ben. People didn't notice it, it was so slow. Well, according to the Rev. Emmanuel, this is a new Ice Age now, but this time the ice is in men's minds and hearts and takes the form of violence and hatred. But this ice is melting, too, as the fires of charity and peace grow stronger. One day the thaw will be complete and man from cradle to grave will be full of hymns of love for all other men, and such love will make war and misery impossible.'

'Sounds like one of those miracle stories to me,' said Ben, looking at Willie with a lot of wonder on his face.

'I've seen more than one voter in my time on earth,' said Arthur, 'in whom the ice seemed to be getting harder. I am thinking in particular of such types as landlords and certain clerks connected with the giving out of the dole, who seem to thrive on giving a lot of harsh and needless lip to the boys in the queue. Don't tell me that such elements as those are on the thaw, Willie, or I will tell you that this new Ice Age you talk of has left you with a frost-bitten brain.'

'As for me,' said Ben, 'it seems as if this Rev. Emmanuel has been spilling pints of eywash over Willie. Emmanuel is one voter who is doing very well out of the Ice Age. He gets a good living from just telling people that there's a lot of ice around the place, and that seems to me to be a very pleasant way of keeping off the Insurance. Emmanuel has been, as I see it, one of the leading cold snaps responsible for this Ice Age, so he's doing the right thing in telling young Willie here to sit back and expect a long thaw. But here's my viewpoint, as one of the coldest ice men breathing. Many people have treated me in my lifetime in a manner that can only be called rough. They have got great pleasure from chivvying and bullying me, especially when they've seen that my wife has just persuaded me not to tear their ears off and go to jail for it. I've hated those people, and if I live out the rest of my life as happy as Santa Claus is painted up to be, I would have no other feeling for them, because I think that people who can grow to enjoy being mean and brutal towards those weaker than themselves are an ugly mess on the face of life, and to melt any hatred I might feel towards those people, you and the Rev. Emmanuel would have to go down to the chain works, forge a red-hot pellet of charity and proceed to jerk it up me.'

'You'll never understand,' said Willie. 'You should listen to the Rev. Emmanuel. I'll never make you understand.'

'We did listen to him,' said my friend Walter.

'When?'

'Before you were born, I should say.'

'Didn't you like him?'

'We liked him all right.'

'Then why didn't you follow him and his teachings?'

'Because what he said then, Willie, was a lot different from what he's been saying since. He didn't talk about Ice Ages then. If someone had talked to him about them he would have laughed, as we felt like laughing when you explained the notion to us. He was interested in just one age, the age he lived in, and he clearly saw the lives of the people in it. He saw then that you cannot harness the strong and the weak together in a golden chariot to paradise. He supported any struggle among the common people for a better and more sensible life here and now. The miseries and upsets of the people he saw around him he described as the results of a greed and stupidity which could be righted by curbing the greedy and instructing the stupid. He was a very fine, brave man in those days, Willie, and we heard him with respect. Also, his hair at that time was black and he did not look so much like a saint.'

'He had a collapse,' said Ben, 'and sold out to a coalowner who was helping to finance his chapel.'

'The coalowner,' said Arthur, giving Willie no rest, 'was a man with a great number of nasty ideas regarding the common people. The voters would have disliked these ideas coming from him, and would no doubt have gone to the length of dropping him down a shaft to cure him of these ideas. But the voters lapped them up when spoken by the soft voice of the Rev. Emmanuel. The Rev. Emmanuel sold his mind and heart over to that man. Even when he stretched out his hand to get that kind of happiness you think so highly of, the coalowner said he wouldn't like it if the Rev. Emmanuel got married, so he stayed single. The coalowner said that Emmanuel's heart was weak after that collapse, and such a thing as steady love might do him harm. But what kind of a man was Emmanuel to give up a woman he thought much of, a chance of happiness, just because someone else told him to.'

'He gave her up?' said Willie, looking very moved, struck

more strongly by this fact than by any of the others he had heard.

'That's it.'

'How happy would be woman be who was loved by the Rev. Emmanuel.'

'How sick would the woman be who was given up by the Rev. Emmanuel. Think of that, Willie.'

'Perhaps she was a bad woman. There must have been a good reason.'

'Couldn't say. Never knew. Why should Emmanuel fall in love with a bad woman in the first place. A very pure character, Emmanuel.'

'So you see,' said Ben, in triumph. 'This Rev. Emmanuel of yours has his weaknesses, Willie.'

'Perhaps so,' said Willie. 'Perhaps so. . . . Unless you're lying to me.'

'We never lie,' said Ben, 'except to foremen and officials.'

Idomeneo, from behind the counter, said it was getting late, and that we had better be going or the police would be thinking we were running a seance or organizing a riot and break in on us. Always willing to help Idomeneo avoid getting in any worse trouble than he was having already with that element in London, who loaned money and dictated opinions to poor Italians, we made ready to go.

Willie, looking a bit shaken and hesitant, managed to work up a smile as he got his coat on and said there was nothing like a good argument to improve the mind. Before he left us, he told us not to forget to be at Idomeneo's the next night because he was going to bring along his friend, the girl who was going to sing the top part in those trios and quartets we played on Idomeneo's gramophone. Thoughts of this girl must have made Willie sentimental because as he walked through the door, he said:

'I'll never believe what you said about the Rev. Emmanuel giving up the girl he loved. He's too full of love. He loves all men, all women. He would have made her his no matter what stood between them.'

Ben said that sounded so much like one of those mottoes you get in the Christmas crackers he would stay behind to help Idomeneo scrape out the stove to get the taste of it out of his mouth.

*

The next day, my work as a rough work painter with the County Council took me to a large Union Home, or workhouse, which stood at the top of the valley. This Union Home had grown to look so dowdy through the lack of such articles as paint that it was beginning to depress the master and the matron, and to annoy the inmates whose state was such that they would have laughed heartily at being so lucky as to be no more than depressed.

I spent a lot more time feeling sorrow at the sight of these inmates than I spent on my brushwork, and I hoped that the foreman, who had an opinion of my brushwork as low as the opinion I had of communities that shove their elderly paupers into Union Homes, would regard this as a mark in my favour.

I recognized one of these inmates, and during a lull when we were sitting on the grass waiting for one of our colleagues who had forgotten, lost or broken one of the ladders, I engaged in talk with this inmate, eager to bring him a breath of human solidarity from the outside world. His name was Abner. This Abner had exhausted himself over a period of many years with activities like drink and women.

Not long before, his family had given him the choice of staying sober or being thrown out. As Abner had now reached a stage where he did not care much about anything, not even his family or drink or women, he answered this by getting drunk and going straight to the Union Home, and this move, no doubt, saved a lot of wrangling from one quarter and another. Abner seemed very glad to see me and asked how my son Wilfred was getting on. I had no son Wilfred, but, rather than give Abner the idea that his wits were beginning to wander, I said that my son Wilfred had never been better.

'How do you like it here, Abner?' I asked.

'Very peaceful. Just as I like it,' said Abner, patting himself, for all the world like a man who has just completed his fortieth year as a very law-abiding monk.

I remembered that Abner, during his civil life, had combined a great taste for gossip with his other fancies.

'Abner,' I said. 'Do you remember the Reverend Emmanuel?'

'Remember him? Know him like a brother. A very notable man, that. I think I could have done something in that line myself if I had given my mind to such things.' And Abner put on a look that said he was not sorry he had been firm in his stand against ambition, and had been content to stay a simple monk.

'Do you remember the time he fell in love with that girl in the valley?'

'Remember it? Remember it like my birthday.'

'Why didn't he marry her, Abner?'

'There was a certain party who did not agree with another party getting married.'

'The coalowner?'

'That was him. A notable man, but hard.'

'What happened to the girl?'

'Married somebody else like girls do. Girls got to. Can't wait about for ever. No prospect for single girls.'

'Where are they living?'

'The chap died. Name of Radnor, as I remember. Decent chap but never strong. Left a daughter. Last time I heard anything about it, the widow and child were living somewhere in the Terraces.'

'The Terraces? Never heard of her.'

'Quiet people, widows.'

'Why didn't Emmanuel seek her out and marry her when her husband died and the coalowner man wasn't there to stop him? It couldn't have made him very happy to see her a widow with a kid to bring up.'

'Forgot about her, most likely. These very godly chaps are great at forgetting. In any case, Emmanuel is a very pure man, and he must have been in love with this girl when she was pure. But you can't expect a pure man to keep on loving a girl when she's belonged to somebody else, because that make her stop being pure.'

I was grateful to Abner for explaining these things so clearly to me, but for the life of me I could not understand why such a character as Abner, who had lived the love life of a very red-blooded goat, should single out purity in men and women for such special praise. I could only guess that life in the Union Home, with the paintwork so rusty and the master and matron so depressed, had the effect of putting the brains of the inmates in reverse. I thanked Abner for all he had told me and, seeing the foreman approach, I climed up a tall ladder to show willing, without knowing where exactly the ladder would lead me.

That evening we waited in the back room at Idomeneo's with some curiosity to see what sort of female friend Willie was going to bring along. Idomeneo's stove was in very special form as we sat around it, and had entered into a new stage of life which consisted of bright clusters of ashes being shot up through the top of it. This was in addition to the old caper of smoking which continued as before.

My friend Ben told Idomeneo that this new shooting-ash caper was very pretty to watch, since it reminded him of volcanoes and other such wonders which he had heard of in the Y.M.C.A. lectures at the Library and Institute, but which were never to be seen in their natural state in the Terraces, where men and women did all the erupting that was necessary. But all the same, said Ben, these ashes were a nuisance when they landed on a customer's clothes, being liable to set him alight.

Idomeneo explained that he had placed a lot of packing paper at the bottom of this stove and there was, no doubt, some chemical on the paper that was causing these little explosions. We helped to clear out some of this paper because spouts of ashes might take our minds off the music that was to come and, in any case, there was so much smoke rising from the stove, a lot of it caused by this tricky paper wrapping of which Idomeneo seemed to have thrust about two ton into his stove, there was a danger that by the time Willie's friend arrived, we would not be able to see her, and we considered that it was already pity enough that there should be so many comrades on the other side of the world that we could not see, without having people in the same room added to the list on account of Idomeneo's stove.

None of us could explain why we were so curious to know what this friend of Willie's looked like because, for our own part, we were men who had lived strange, disordered lonely sorts of lives that had contained little of such things as love. But we liked Willie and while we would have regretted seeing him fritter away too much of his time and conscience on a thing like passion, which does not bring in very great returns, mentally, we were glad to see that he had friends.

There was a lot of noise from the shop in front. It was raining hard outside. It nearly always rained in the Terraces, and this very heavy and frequent rain accounted for many of the marriages that kept on taking place in the Terraces, even though most of the voters had reached a point in the knowledge of misfortune where they thought children were silly things to have. But marriage was the only thing that could be relied on to bring young couples out of the wet and into the dry when the rainy season was on, which was all the year round.

If the Terraces had not been built on a sharp slope that let the rain drain away, all this rain water, collected up, would have risen to the voters' hips, and we would no doubt have had a lot of such troubles as drowning and rheumatism to put up with as well as the better known troubles connected with coal and poverty of which we had already had a bodyful. There were not many voters who were clothed and shod in a way to cope with all this rain. In our time in the Terraces, there were never more than about twenty men equipped in such a way that the rain bounced off them. Nineteen of these were men connected with activities like road mending and investigating cases for the Assistance Board, activities which sort of overlapped because by the time you came to have dealings with the Assistance Board, which relieves voters who are in great distress, you were usually so thin you kept on slipping through cracks in the road from which the road-menders fished you out and handed you back to the Board with nobody's compliments.

The twentieth of these men we remembered as being able to laugh at the rain was some element who went around dressed in oilskins like a fisherman to advertise some article like cod oil which was very good, said this fisherman, for all sickly voters and kids. There was no one in the Terraces, as far as we knew, who either did not need or could afford this cod oil. We knew some voters who were so weak and sickly in all departments of the body as to need soaking in some such substance, but all the same we were glad to see this fisherman because he was a cheerful man and all his layers of oilskin reminded us that one day we might all be protected from the rain if the fish of this world could be persuaded to support the Government and produce enough fish oil for us all to go around advertising it.

When the rain came on very sharply, the voters who were in the street would have to seek shelter, because the rain would soak quickly into their boots, the rain being of much better quality than the boots. This made the boots heavy, so heavy that it became very difficult for the voters, with all this great weight dragging at their feet, to tackle the steep climb up through the Terraces. Also, the rain was so fierce it would carve deep ruts in the roads of the Terraces, so it was no new thing to see some voter making his way upward and weighed down with too much water, vanishing into one of these ruts and being stuck there, struggling to move forward but not moving an inch, just deepening the rut with all his struggles, which was as unpleasant for the voter as for the Council which had to go about filling in these ruts, sometimes, if the hole was deep enough, with the voter still inside.

Therefore, such places as Idomeneo's shop which never seemed to close, were very popular shelters with the voters and on this particular night, as we were sitting in the back room waiting for Willie, a large number of these elements, drenched, had crowded into Idomeneo's shop out of the rain. They would have bulged over into the back room if Idomeneo had not told them that he had his sick mother in there. This brought a sharp reply from one of the voters, who could see the smoke from the back room stove curling over the partition, that it was no way to treat a sick mother to smoke her to death.

Some of the people, to thank Idomeneo for letting them in out of the rain, bought small bags of sweets such as pennyworths of hard mints or twopennyworths of toffees in paper, which were considered very classy things to eat in the Terraces. But most of the voters just stood there dripping wet and making a great noise.

My friend Ben did not like this because he had been working that day on a house that had managed to grow twenty feet without his having had much to do with it, and he was still feeling giddy from all that height. He said it might do good if he marched out into the front part of the shop, hauled one of the noisy voters into the back room and held him with his rear about an inch from the top of Idomeneo's stove, which was now getting very hot. That, said Ben, would teach all these elements to behave in a better fashion.

But Idomeneo said his parents had always told him it was wise policy to be friendly with all, whether they bought articles or not because it was a very poor voter who went through life without ever buying anything.

At eight o'clock came Willie, wearing a big raincoat which had a large system of small capes at the back, as complicated to look at as the air pipes of Idomeneo's stove. All these capes must have given the drenched voters standing outside the idea that a large number of voters were marching in to see Idomeneo's mother. With Willie was a girl, a very handsome girl as our tastes went, dark, thin and tidily turned out. Beneath her raincoat she had a dark blue costume which fitted her tightly. It was not new but looked as if someone had been trying to keep it looking new for a long time.

We knew a lot about guessing the age of clothes with our eyes, because many of the voters in the Terraces wore clothes that went right back into history, and we had passed on a lot of time pleasantly during the idle years trying to name the century in which some of these garments had been stitched into being. We always kept our own clothes a very long time, but we never managed to keep them looking new. Even clothes bought the week before seemed to give up the ghost and the gloss at the sight of us. But this friend of Willie's looked very neat and tidy and bright of brow and eye. We were glad of this because Willie could just have easily have brought along one of the division's looser bags, cheerful and willing maidens, no doubt, but liable to be very dumb in company unless they were being busily worked upon physically.

'This is Margaret,' said Willie, and we all stood up and scraped our chairs about as we shook hands with Margaret in a very civilized way.

Willie started playing the records and we settled down in our chairs with the deliberate idea of being fully entertained. Willie, Idomeneo and Ben sang to these records with great force, Ben with a lot too much force, and we had cautioned him twice to be silent before he became interested in a fresh spout of ash from the stove and gave most of his attention to that.

Willie, with his hand, encouraged Margaret to sing with them but she remained silent, sitting still and huddled on her chair, enjoying the music. After each record there would be a little clapping from the wet voters on the other side of the partition, and this clapping pleased Willie because it meant the music was giving pleasure to more people than just us.

Ben maintained that this clapping was not meant for the music at all, but was part of a general policy on the part of these voters who, when wet or otherwise without comfort, made a noise regardless of any purpose. But Willie would not touch this interpretation of Ben's, said it was unkind, said Ben was being made very bitter by all the bricks he had to fool around with during the day.

Later on, Margaret grew less shy and whenever a record came along with music she knew, she would sing. She did not sing loudly but in a sweet voice that brought a tender look to the faces of my friends Walter and Arthur, and this tender, smiling look sat oddly on their faces for, as a rule, the expression they wore was a fixed, sad one, the result of great brooding upon our many problems, such problems as would have caused the merriest of apes to go grey in every hair.

We all felt a pleasant, gentle happiness in the presence of Margaret, a feeling that made us conscious of all those kinds of soft delight that fill man's poetry, that must make life pass very quickly for those that have them but which we, in the main, had lost touch with and nearly forgotten; and this sense of loss, biting at our minds as sharply as the smoking stove bit at our nostrils, made us drift into a mood of calm sorrowing around which the music was set like a deep, golden frame.

At nine Margaret rose to go.

'So soon?' said our eyes, for our lips were not accustomed to working off such smooth phrases as that at a moment's notice.

'My mother is ill,' she said. 'She misses me if I am out too late.' And she went, promising to come again many times in the future, and we mumbled that we would all be looking forward to her coming again, and so we were, for we had enjoyed the mood of peaceful, rageless regret we had felt in her company.

'I'll take Margaret home,' said Willie, 'and then I'll be back.'

While waiting for Willie to return, we sipped at our cups of Idomeneo's tea and began to discuss with Idomeneo the difference between British people and Italian people. We could find no difference that mattered and that discussion dropped. Then we set to talking of a lecture we had heard at the Library and Institute a week before, in which an oldish man, wearing a thick suit, had told us of the troubles that people had had trying to climb Everest.

My friend Walter maintained that this had been an interesting lecture, especially the part that dealt with the climbers getting short of breath when they got too high. Ben decided to oppose this point of view. What Ben really objected to was the idea of any voter standing on a stage and showing off in a thick suit, but he did not say so.

'Climbing such places as Everest,' he said, 'can't be much worse than climbing up these Terraces when the ruts are bad after the rain. Why all this mountain climbing anyway? What's going to go on on those mountains when they've been climbed?'

'They climb mountains because it's instructive, Ben.'

Ben would not have that. He claimed that all this business of looking for high mountains and getting such elements as the voter in the thick suit to monkey about on them, was all part of a new plan to get in some more blows at the unemployed. When there was so much to be done on the lower levels, how else could you explain people wasting their time on the higher levels? No, it was part of a plan. When we had a lot of unemployed again, what nicer than to bundle the whole issue of them on to a couple of high mountains, so high nobody'd ever be able to get at them from below, and the only contact with life the passing over of a weekly balloon from which the Ministry of Labour would drop the dole and odd bottles of lung mixture.

In the old days the one thing the unemployed had plenty of was breath. Under this new order, said Ben, the unemployed, placed at these great heights would be short even of that, and thus they could be persuaded without difficulty to give up the ghost if that had not been taken away from them already as part of a scheme to send them up the mountain travelling as light as possible.

When Willie came back he asked us straight away what we thought of Margaret. He looked as if he were very eager to have our opinion on this issue, as if our opinion on this issue was one that he would be willing to trust to the death even though our opinion on such an issue as the Rev. Emmanuel was one he thought to be all wrong. We told him in our various ways, that we thought she was a lovely girl and did him much credit.

'Tell us about her, Willie,' said Walter, who collected the life stories of the people around him as other people collected stamps or stones or money.

Willie looked around as if he were going to let us into a great secret.

'She's very poor,' said Willie, and he looked at all our faces as if wondering how we would take this news.

'Hell, Willie,' said Arthur, staring at Willie. 'What's so odd about that, boy? Don't you know what system this is? Who's rich in the Terraces?'

Then Willie told us the story of Margaret. He told it in a clear, straightforward way with all the right details thrown in at the right places, which showed that he was one who had looked at life from many various angles and was a bright youth, for all his attachment to the Rev. Emmanuel.

Margaret's mother, said Willie, was a widow. Her father had died while Margaret was still young, and the mother had supplemented her pension by doing such things as sewing and laundering, which, if done too often, have a knack of shortening breath if not life. She was determined that her being a widow would not cause Margaret to lose chances she might otherwise have had. She kept Margaret in a Secondary School for three years. From there Margaret went into a Commercial College. After four or five months there, her mother became very ill, and, doctors and nourishing foods being the price they are, Margaret had to leave this Commercial College and look for a job.

She found one that left her with five shillings a week after paying her bus fare, with her mind full of worry about her mother the whole time she was working. She had job after job, giving up each one as her mother took turns for the worse and needed her at home, or being sacked because sometimes she'd go half mad with thinking about her mother alone in the house and, failing in that state of mind, to give as much attention to the work in hand as the employer would like. Finally, Margaret had given up any attempt at holding a job and was now staying at home for good to give her mother, who now never left her bed, all the care and comfort she could.

'On a widow's pension,' said Walter, 'a rent allowance, and six bob a week for Margaret. Not much ground to manoeuvre in there.'

'That's it,' said Willie, looking rather shocked as if he had never thought of the matter in such bald terms as that. 'Margaret doesn't get out much. Now and then a neighbour will come in for an hour or so to chat with her mother, and then Margaret's able to slip out for a bit like she did tonight. But her mother is very touchy and proud about neighbours, so that doesn't happen very often.'

'It's a hell of a life for a girl,' said Walter.

'It's a hell of a life for the mother,' said Arthur.

'It's a hell of a life all round,' said Ben, and I sided with Ben.

'It seems to me,' said Walter, 'that poor widows are a class of voter who would do a lot better for themselves if they were chucked outright into a thick jungle and allowed to chum with the leopards. They couldn't do much worse for themselves. Think on that woman for a moment, brothers. She lived on the wind for God knows how many years, eating probably as much good food in a year as the rich would eat in an evening. For what? To give her kid a flying start in life, a start that would make her fly, too. And look how she flies. She's on her back and the only life she's got in her, as like as not, is the love she gets from her kid. God, it's no wonder some men think in music when words are used to tell of things like these. For such people as Margaret's mother, Willie, and the exceedingly rough lives they are asked to lead, I suggest that the Rev. Emmanuel should rush up a full set of heaters to deal with the ice.'

'He has a great pity for such people,' said Willie, on his guard again.

'Pity's like buns, boy. It fills without feeding. All blast, no body.'

'He would have helped Margaret and her mother if he had known them. They never went to him so what could he do?'

'Don't they go to chapel?'

'No. So they never came into touch with the Rev. Emmanuel. He would have helped Margaret as he helped me, but her mother never wanted her to go.'

'Is she an agnostic?'

'A what?'

'An agnostic. Doesn't she believe in God?'

'Suppose she does. Never talked with her about things like that. Suppose she does. Most people do. Must have been somebody at the beginning. I suppose she didn't want Margaret to go to chapel because she's been so ill and wanted Margaret to stay at home with her.'

'Where do they live?'

'The Terrace above this one. They live in rooms. They've got two rooms in a house. The rent is cheaper like that.'

As I listened, I thought of Abner, the old voter at the Union. 'What did you say her name was?'

'Radnor. Her name is Radnor. There's nothing funny about that name, is there? What are you looking so surprised for?'

'Nothing, Willie,' I said, feeling sorry for myself because I must have been looking at him in a stupid, mouth-open sort of manner when he mentioned that name. 'That's a very uncommon name in the Terraces.

'Margaret's father was a stranger here. He came here from the North.'

We fell silent for a few minutes, thinking of the pattern of things that causes some to live on the wind, to desire to fly like the wind, others to come South from the North and to have the fruits of the journey kicked aside by dying, and we all thought the pattern was as vague and shapeless as the clouds in the sky.

Then Willie, becoming restless at the touch of all these deep thoughts going on around and hanging over our faces like dark, transparent gauze, said we should have some music and we had some. It was the duet from *Tosca*, said Willie, and it jerked our brains up like your stomach jerks in a ride on the switchback. Soon after, Willie said he would have to go because tomorrow would be a long shift for him at the forge. We helped him into his many-caped raincoat which was as tricky to get into as a safe. We bade him good night.

'Now that,' I said after Willie had left us, 'is a very funny thing.'

'Which of the many things that are funny is this thing?' asked my friend Walter, shaking the dust from a butt before lighting it.

'That girl. Do you know who I think she is?'

'Tell us.'

'She is the daughter of that very woman the Rev. Emmanuel was so much in love with and gave up on account of the coalowner, who was a deacon.'

'Stop making up plots,' said Arthur.

'Honest now. I'll tell you why I think that.'

I asked them if they remembered old Abner, the ancient voter I had met in the Union Home.

'The only people,' said Ben, 'the only people in this division who do not remember Abner very well are his own family. I suppose they had such a gutful of Abner and his capers when he was cutting loose they took a special course in how to forget their old man.'

'Well, Abner told me the name of the man who had married that woman of Emmanuel's and the name was Radnor. Abner said this Radnor died and left the woman living in the Terraces with one kid. Doesn't that fit?'

They all said it did fit, without a doubt.

'Now isn't that the funniest thing you ever heard, the funniest thing except for fairy-tales and speeches by the wealthy about the workless. There's Willie fonder of this Rev. Emmanuel than ever a kid was fond of his parents, so fond of his little tin god he accuses us elements of perjury when we tell him that Emmanuel gave up the woman he was passionate about, just because a bloke told him not to get married, and now we find that Willie is courting the daughter of that very woman.'

'No wonder,' said Ben, 'that she is not keen on such things as chapels.'

'If I know anything about the Rev. Emmanuel,' said Walter, 'he most likely forgot right about her a few days after he found that his emotions were not meeting with the approval of the coal-owner. It's so easy to forget someone who's dumped down in the middle of these Terraces when you happen to be living in a large house on the other side of the valley.'

'I don't know,' said I. 'I don't think he could have forgotten like that. I've never forgotten anybody who ever had anything to do with me.'

'You never had anything to gain by forgetting.'

'That's so. Think we ought to tell Willie of this?'

'Let him find out if he wants to. Since we cheated the dead past of the chance of burying us, we ought to leave it to bury its own dead, anyway. We won't tell Willie. But it would be very interesting, all the same, to know what the thoughts of the Rev. Emmanuel have been about this woman, if ever he had any thoughts.'

We saw Margaret often after that. One evening a week she would come along to Idomeneo's back room, fill herself with music, fill our ears with the reflection of it from her own throat. She grew to like us, for life had taught us sympathy of many shades and sizes, and she sensed this in us even when we did no more than sit dumbly around the stove trying not to cough with the smoke.

Sometimes we would talk about things in general with an idea of getting Margaret to express her views. She talked swiftly in a low voice, and she talked much sense with a kind of lilt which would have made it all right to listen to even if she had been talking the flattest nonsense. She told us the whole story of herself and her mother, and it was a tale of struggle just as Willie had told us.

A nice feature of Margaret was that all this struggle and scraping had not driven her to take up the women's magazine notion that these sad events should be looked on as a brief and accidental interlude, to be ignored or lied about until some prince or polo-playing empire-builder would come along and restore reality by opening up the gates of paradise, in which event the bedroom pot would be pure pearl. No rubbish like that from Margaret. She had used her eyes, read some Upton Sinclair and pamphlets, had seen that her own difficulties could be matched in nine out of ten of the houses around her.

And she had a serene conviction that sprang from her even when her lips were still that such difficulties and disappointments as these should be lessened or removed promptly in case they started making people mad or rotten right and left. In these matters she had a clearer outlook than Willie, whose brightness had undoubtedly been a bit cotton-woolled by the Rev. Emmanuel with his myths of ice and meekness and so on. Margaret never made any mention of the Rev. Emmanuel, so we thought her mother must have kept this business very dark.

One evening, when Margaret was there, Willie said it was a great pity that Margaret's mother should be leading such a silent and cheerless life pinned to that bed of hers from day to day and week to week. We said that was absolutely so, a great pity. Then Willie said it would be a big help if, one night, my friends Ben and Walter and Arthur and myself would come along and try to cheer Mrs Radnor up.

We protested at this idea. We said we were a very rough collection of voters, too heavy about the voice and feet and brain to be led into the presence of anybody sick. True, we said, we sometimes showed the wisdom that springs up in the heart of any man who has seen a lot of hunger and hates it, and has met a lot of oppressive nuisances and despises them. But the sort of pleasant smile and manner that the sick require, no, we had pretty well lost that at birth.

'Oh, no,' said Margaret. 'I never want to meet any nicer men than you are. You've been so nice to me, and Willie thinks the world of you.'

Now we all thought that was a great tribute for men to receive after spending eleven years or so having all our limbs pinched in the grip of an economic crisis which had pitched us on to a lower social level than the ancient serfs, and we were glad to hear Margaret say these things.

'My mother would like to hear you talking. She would like to hear you talking of the things that have been going on in the Terraces. She always worked too hard trying to keep me clothed and in school ever to play any part in these things, but I'm sure she'd like to hear about them.'

'We have met many voters,' said my friend Walter, 'who have been given nothing but earache by the things we talk about. So it will be very encouraging for us to find your mother taking a sisterly interest in the political history of this division.'

'It's music she should have,' said Arthur. 'She'll know enough about the hard side of life. She's been through that, and nothing any voter will tell her will teach her more about it. Music is the sweet side, the side of us that not even the combined princes, priests and profiteers can ever make a thorough mess of or properly destroy. Let's give her that. Here's the gramophone and the records. There you are.'

Willie said that sounded very promising, but it was Idomeneo's gramophone and he might not like the idea of it being carted around the Terraces. We told him that he had only a very poor knowledge of Idomeneo to go thinking things like that. When we put the facts before Idomeneo he said straightaway we could consider the gramophone as our own, and that there was nothing he would not do to ease the loneliness of anyone in the Terraces, for he, far away from the place he had been born and up to his temples in work and debt, was very often lonely himself.

We thanked Idomeneo for this and told him, in our gratitude, that on the day Europe would cease to be an armed camp of fighting cocks, and would entrust its peace and happiness to the common people whose knowledge of discomfort was long and deep enough to have taught them all there was to know about what discomforts it was best to avoid, Idomeneo would be made something worthy, like a mayor or a tribune of the plebs. Nor did we forget to mention that Idomeneo's brothers, who were in jail, would also have their share in these awards.

So, on the next Sunday evening, Ben carried Idomeneo's gramophone and Willie carried the records to the house of Mrs Radnor. A thin procession of religious voters passed us on their way to worship, and they gave us many a dark and intolerant glance as if to say we were up to our usual depraved capers, and that these far-seeing voters had always known that one day we would reach the stage of carrying musical instruments about the streets on a Sunday evening to seal the pact we had no doubt made with the pagans.

We found Mrs Radnor's house to be one of a group of small houses in the top but one Terrace. The woodwork of the house looked as if the landlord thought paint was a deadly poison to be obtained only after getting a note from the doctor, and not even then if the tenants lacked the means to burn down the woodwork and move off to some quarter that had a fresher look.

While waiting for the door to open, Willie, whispering in a very important way, told us that the two rooms of this house, that were not occupied by Margaret and her mother, were lived in by a voter called Hector. We knew this Hector by the back. A backward element who looked like an ape and acted like some animal that has not been found yet and has not been named for that reason; unless you want to take a short cut and call it Hector.

We knew him well. He was the sort of man who would run away from a thought or an argument as if it were the smallpox. He had very big shoulders and black hair falling over his brow in such thick locks it was hard to know where his skull finished and his face began. He could work for so long without resting, and could shift such quantities of stuff like earth or coal or timber in such a short time and was so dense on topics as trade unions and wage-rates that Hector was a hand-picked gift from the gods to the employing class, and there was always a long procession of people waiting to employ him.

It is likely that this Hector never even heard of the depression. He was a single man with a great love for pleasure, and in pursuits like drink and women he had jumped into the throne left vacant by that very loose living old voter, Abner, who was now in the Union Home, talking about purity and taking a rest after about forty years of goating about. As we stood before Margaret's door waiting for an answer, we thought it a pity that a nice couple like Margaret and her mother should have to be sharing a house with a dirty and thoughtless element like Hector.

Margaret took us upstairs. Mrs Radnor, in the bed, greeted us in a very soft voice. Margaret had her mother's face and voice exactly, but we could see that the face of this Mrs Radnor had been much changed by illness. She seemed to be very small but we could not say anything very certain about that, she being in bed.

At first she seemed surprised and shy at seeing this parade of solemn-looking voters in her bedroom. It was a small bedroom and we must have looked very big to her. The room was badly lit. There was a candle on either side of the bed. I though the smell of candles in the nose of a sick person must be very unpleasant, but one look at Mrs Radnor told me that the smell of candles at the side of her bed was not the worst thing she had put up with.

We cleared a place for the gramophone on a washstand which had a white marble top, and which might at one time have been a very elegant bit of furnishing but was not any more. The washstand swayed on its legs every time you touched it, and we hooshed a lot at one another in case one of us would cause the thing to sway too much and bring the marble top and Idomeneo's gramophone crashing to the floor. We did not want to be the cause of any more trouble than we could help.

We got seated, two on the side of the bed, the rest on chairs. As we sat, we kept hearing a grunting, thumping noise, and we thought it might be Ben, not knowing exactly what to do with his hands, being nervous, playing about with the washstand and making it rock. But Willie went 'Sh' and jerked his finger towards the next bedroom and said 'Hector', meaning, we took it, that this thumping and grunting noise was being made by Hector, but how or why Hector should be making such a loud and regular noise in his bedroom at that time of the evening was more than we could imagine.

My friend Walter started off the talking with a remark about the great rainfall in the Terraces, and assured Mrs Radnor that complaints like rheumatic were on the increase as a result of voters never being dry. That put us all in a proper state of mind for conversation, and Mrs Radnor asked us if we recalled the bad floods of fifteen years back when four voters had been trapped in a flooded bakehouse while trying to rescue their bread. We all agreed that that had been a notable flood even without those voters who had gone wading in after their baking. We found Mrs Radnor knew a lot of people we knew, and between her knowing a lot about people's families and our knowing as often as not how long these same families had been in or out of work, we were able to fit together some very interesting life stories.

We could see that Mrs Radnor was as ill as a woman could be, and sometimes her head would slip down on the pillow and she would let us do all the talking, but even then she would continue to smile as if she found a roomful of voices as pleasant as a dark sky full of lights. She said she was always glad to hear talk of the valley because the valley had turned out some very nice characters, and we asked her, thinking of such novelties as black lists and Industrial Transference Schemes, whether she used the words 'turned out' to mean produced or ejected. She gave a wise little laugh when we said that, and she answered that she probably meant a bit of both.

Willie chipped in here to say that the Rev. Emmanuel was a great supporter of these Industrial Transference Schemes which meant transporting the young from broken down areas like ours and giving them a fresh start elsewhere. At the mention of the Rev. Emmanuel we saw Mrs Radnor's eyes grow very thoughtful and her lips purse. We gathered from that that she did not think so much of Emmanuel, and we could understand that. We told Willie we agreed so much with him on this point that we thought it was a pity that the Rev. Emmanuel was not young any more so that he could be transported, too.

Then we had some music. After the first two or three records, there was a great thumping on the wall of the next bedroom as if someone were beating on the wall with a chair or a boot. Margaret looked upset and embarrassed, and Willie whispered again, 'Hector'. Mrs Radnor shrugged her shoulders as if to say that her thoughts on Hector had gone far beyond the stage of speech.

Ben motioned to me with his head. We walked out on to the dark landing which had the heavy, oniony smell which goes along with damp walls in the Terraces. By running our fingers along the walls we found the door of Hector's bedroom. We pushed it open without knocking. It was not worth knocking on that door because a voter like Hector is at no point familiar with such things as courtesy, and if you knocked at his door before entering, he would only think you were training to be a drummer and that would make him wilder.

We found Hector standing near the wall with his fist upraised for a fresh barrage, and by the wild defiant look on his dark face this fresh barrage was going to be a big improvement on those that had gone before, and would have landed him and his fist well on the inside of Mrs Radnor's bedroom. Hector dropped his fist as he saw us. He took a few steps towards the door and bawled to us that if we did not stop that music there would be trouble.

We looked around the room. On Hector's bed there was a woman, half covered, looking dirty, tousled, impatient and full of experience, a woman, we should have said, below the stage even of reading women's magazines, which is very low.

Ben stepped up very close to Hector and told him that if there were any more disturbance from him he would toss Hector and his bed right through the window. As he said that, Ben stood still, his big hands resting quietly at his sides, looking as rough and ready for violence as ever I had seen him, in no mood to be annoyed by anyone, least of all by backward elements like Hector, who acted like an ape and had not even heard of the depression.

Hector looked hard at Ben, and I began to wonder about the state a man is put into by being tossed through a window. But Hector must have been feeling very weakened because he said 'All right' very gently, and fell back into silence and on to the bed, where the tousled woman, looking drowsier than ever, started groping with him as if Hector were a slice of darkness that had just come her way. We left them to whatever they wanted to be left to, which was not a discussion on What is Faith.

When the time came to go, Mrs Radnor made us promise that we would come again. We said we would. We told her, too, that with a nice daughter like Margaret she would soon be well again. When we said that her head lifted slightly from the pillow and there was a glad, hopeful brightness on her face and then, as if a strong mouth had bent low and breathed on it, the brightness left her face and she said she did not think she would ever be much good again. As we went down the stairs, the darkness seemed much darker than it really was because we all felt that Mrs Radnor was most likely quite right about herself. She would never be much use again.

'As for that Hector,' said Ben to Margaret as we got out on the pavement, 'if he ever gets on your nerves and you feel you would like to see him bruised all over in various shades, just let me know and I will come along and deal with him. A good spell on his back with different shades from blue to black on his body would bring nothing but benefit to a backward voter like Hector.'

One evening the following week Willie came along to Idomeneo's back room in great excitement. We thought that to see any subject in the Terraces looking as excited as that meant that we had just set up something big and valuable like a World Commonwealth or a Means Test for those rich and clever voters who first thought up the Means Test.

But all that Willie was excited about was a slender book wrapped in brown paper to provide a second cover which he held tightly between his hands. This slender book, said Willie, was a new play especially written by the Rev. Emmanuel himself. It was a missionary play dealing with an incident in the life of Livingstone, and it was going to be put on at a missionary festival that was due to take place at the Young People's Club, which was run by the Rev. Emmanuel.

We could see by the very neat way in which Willie had bound the book that he thought highly of this play, and would not stand for any criticism about the book being so slender or about missionaries. He told us that he was going to take the part of Livingstone. We told Willie that except for his looking very young, and not answering in any part to the pictures of missionaries we had formed in our minds, and being Welsh, not Scotch, he would do very well as a Scotch missionary.

'Would you like me to read this play out to you?' asked Willie. 'The part of Livingstone was especially written for me, and the Rev. Emmanuel says I should do very well in it.'

'No doubt,' said my friend Walter. 'The Rev. Emmanuel, it seems to me, has a plan about you, Willie. He'll get you to act as so many missionaries, you'll feel a lot more at home as a missionary than as a foundryman, and you'll start getting delirious for the sight of a few Negroes to try your hand on. That'll be Emmanuel's cue to bundle you off to Africa, convert a fresh tribe to the Gospel, and create a fresh vacancy at the foundry to cheer up some young voter whose patience with this social order has come to the end of its tether.'

'No Africa for me,' said Willie, smiling. 'I won't say I wouldn't try arguing the darkness out of any savage tribe that happened to land on my doorstep, but I like the Terraces too much to leave here and look for them.'

'All right,' said Walter. 'Read this play.'

Willie started to read, lowering his voice so as not to disturb a man and woman who were cuddling away in one of the corners in a way that Idomeneo would surely have called to a halt if he had not been Italian and very sympathetic with these methods of open cuddling. And we, of course, being followers of the Love-is-warmth and Coal-is-dear school of belief, felt no urge to disturb these two voters providing they drew the line at some point where they were still partly clothed, and we could hear Willie reading his sketch.

The sketch was short and dull, not as short and twice as dull as that large placard they plastered the valley with some years ago which said: 'Thousands now living will never die', which slogan we took to be a very great threat indeed, for life seemed rough and dark and dirty to whole legions of us at that period.

This play that Willie read was made up mostly of speeches by Livingstone, who could certainly speak, if this play was any guide, and who was curing a native chief of a broken leg. These speeches were about Livingstone serving under three banners, God, medicine and geography, showing that there was more work going the rounds in Livingstone's day than in ours, and if he really talked as much in life as he did in this play, the chief would have got up on his broken leg before the curtain dropped and started to treat Livingstone for lock-jaw.

It was a very dull play. But the chief was an interesting character. All he did was grunt now and then and say, whenever Livingstone took a minute off to get a fresh splint or take a deep breath for his next speech, 'T'ank, bwana. Oh, bwana. Pain, bwana.' This was the Rev. Emmanuel's notion of African talk, and we thought it was a great libel on the oppressed coloured peoples. But the chief learned a lot during the half spent by Livingstone in almost solid talking, because, after all those grunts and scraps of talk that would not have done credit to a budgerigar, 'Oh, bwana, pain, bwana,' and so on, he opens out at the end of the play with a speech as good as Livingstone's, explaining in a very fine sprint of oratory that such a method of fixing broken legs as he has just seen, is a very fine method, and one that could only have been revealed to a race that was a chosen race.

As the play stood, if it had ever got up, its only moral seemed to be that the only hope you had of talking religion into a black man was first of all to get him on his back either by kicking his legs from under him or throwing him over a cliff, then getting out the first-aid box to do its work, supported by a stream of talk that you could no doubt get from any one of the thicker missionary leaflets, and make the black man listen whether his leg was broken or not. After thirty minutes of this talk we thought that any sensible black man would be willing to break his own leg to keep his mind off the conversation, which is bound to be very one sided when you are practically dumb and the other man is a missionary.

My friend Arthur dropped to sleep during the reading. He was very open in his dislike of missionaries, and had often said that the Missionary League would have done far more useful work if, instead of going around tropical areas persuading the natives to wash their sins away with British-made soap flakes, they had imported a few of these natives into such areas of Britain as the Terraces, with the aim of teaching the voters how to get along with fewer clothes, clothes being very hard to buy and, for some, a hindrance to the fuller life when bought. On top of that, Arthur was tired, having had a busy day at that warehouse where he worked, having carried practically everything except the Board of Management from one place to another.

My friend Walter kept awake the whole time and paid close attention, because this play was a very simple thing for him to listen to. Walter was a man who had read through the Regulations of the Assistance Board three times in one day: it was the longest day of the year when Walter did this particular bit of reading, and he said it seemed like the longest night as well, on account of the large masses of very dark reasoning that had been worked into this document. Also, it was often Walter's fancy to read items like reports of political congresses and tracts on Supplementary Pensions at mealtimes to help along the slow business of chewing.

So, after years of training on the sort of hard literature mentioned above, Walter took this little play in his stride, and would no doubt have enjoyed it even if Livingstone had made a speech a year long and with twice as many bends and mud-flats as the Congo. As for myself, I kept awake while the play was being read because the smell of County Council paint that kept hanging about me made me feel so much like an Indian warrior on the eve of a great battle, it put sleep out of the question lest I should doze off and find that I could not put my hand on my quiver when I awoke.

Ben looked quite interested, too, especially when the native chief said anything. His eyes lit up also at any bit of talk coming from a third character in this sketch, a native boy who marched backwards and forwards, looking out of the window now and then and saying that the tribe outside was getting restive, and muttering that white man practise bad medicine on great chief.

When Willie finished, he asked us what we thought of it. We told him politely, weeding out all coarse oaths before they reached the tip of the tongue, that the important thing was that the Rev. Emmanuel liked it or he would not have asked a reliable performer like Willie to take the chief part in it. Willie gathered from this statement that we ourselves were not too stuck on the piece and looked disappointed. He said you did not get the full flavour of the thing unless you had read it through at least twice, and he added that he had read it through three times himself in bed, and we thought that that was a terrible waste of bed, but we could see from Willie's face that he was chock-full of the flavour that you were supposed to get from this piece after reading it twice or more times.

'We got a tremendous lot of the flavour the last time, Willie,' said my friend Walter defensively. 'I don't think we need to hear it again.'

'Just once more,' said Willie. 'And this time it will be a lot more interesting because I want Ben to read the parts of Tongo and Batali.'

'Who the hell are they?' asked Ben, looking insulted.

'Tongo is the native boy who keeps on saying that the tribe is getting restive.'

'No bloody wonder,' said Ben.

'And Batali's the chief.'

'Not much of a chief to my way of thinking, Willie. Listening to all that propaganda with no more than a few grunts to answer it with, then selling out at the end in gratitude for a few splints, and him surrounded by a whole jungle full of trees the whole time.'

Walter and I thought we could stand it a second time with such an interesting feature thrown in as Ben playing the parts of Tongo and Batali. Ben made a very good job of the grunting and the way he said 'Bwana' made a big windy sound that caused Idomeneo to lean over the counter and say, 'That stove,' and caused the cuddling element in the corner to release his woman and bark out that what he did was his own bloody business. He thought Ben had been reproving him with that windy roar for the public character of his performances.

Ben's interpretation of the boy Tongo was also very interesting. For this part he pitched his voice on a high fluty note to emphasize how young this Tongo was and also, no doubt, to show us that in this line of quick change acting he ran second only to such very skilled voters as Boris Karloff. But this fluty note that Ben had brought into his voice made him sound so much like a nance it brought a big broad sneer to the lips of the element in the corner, who was now thoroughly roused against Ben and probably wanted to show that although he might be a little indiscreet when stuck away in corners, he at least liked his pleasure normal.

'Yes, it certainly sounded better the second time,' said Walter, when they had finished. 'Ben making that range of noises made it very lifelike, though he baffled me once or twice. Sometimes I could not make out whether he was supposed to be Tongo, Batali or the tribe outside getting restive.'

'It will be even better when you see it on the stage,' said Willie. 'You will come and see it, won't you?'

Without saying so in so many words we notified Willie that we would much rather be found dead in a ditch than alive at any missionary gala in the Rev. Emmanuel's Young People's Club. Willie was hurt by this attitude, and he said he had been looking forward to giving us great pleasure with his performance.

'We are out of touch with such things, Willie,' said Walter, in the tone of a man whose viewpoint is fixed and not to be shaken. 'We are well known in the Terraces as voters with very red, advanced principles, and if we were to be seen patronizing such an event as this missionary gala, many of the reactionary elements in the Terraces would be only too glad to hail this as another split in the ranks of the common people.'

'But I had planned for Margaret to go along with you,' said Willie. 'She said she wouldn't want to go on her own, and I told her you'd be going because you were so fond of all sorts of culture like plays.'

This made us weaken. Then Ben said he would not mind going because he was interested to see what kind of a job would be done by the two voters selected to play Batali and Tongo. All this acting and grunting and falsetto work had no doubt gone to Ben's head, because his general rule was to be fierce against Emmanuel and projects like missionary plays. So we said we would go.

'When is it?'

'Three weeks Thursday.'

'All right. As a favour to you, Willie, we will be there.'

We got Arthur to wake up and he said drowsily that he had just been dreaming of a gale. We said that that was no gale but Ben-Batali blowing into his face and Arthur, not quite understanding what we were talking about, was starting to ask Ben what the hell he meant with all this blowing into the face of a voter dead beat and sleepy after all the carrying he had done. We explained and then we had some more tea, and talked with Idomeneo about priests of whom he knew a few, and Ben said he had come across a lot of them in the building trade. He looked annoyed when we asked what he meant by that.

*

On the night of the missionary play we met Margaret outside Idomeneo's. It was raining and she wore a nice dark mackintosh, which she explained was a special line in an outfitter's shop that ran a clothing club in her Terrace. She said she would have to hurry back because her mother had been feeling worse that day.

Walter said it was a pity that some trader in the Terraces could not organize a club from which simple happiness could be obtained as easily as raincoats. We noticed that Ben was looking very buoyant and happy, and we thought he might have come across just such a club as Walter had suggested, but he explained that he was wearing for the first time a black crocheted tie his wife had made for him which, said Ben, was impressive. He was wearing a muffler so we could not see this tie. Having learned all these things, we started to march down the hill towards the Young People's Club.

The club had been built in one of the few clear spaces at the bed of the valley. It was about sixty feet long and had a low stage covered over with a red curtain at one end. The inside was kept looking very bright and clean by the followers of the Rev. Emmanuel who were, no doubt, all as zealous as Willie in the service of this club. Some earnest-looking young voter, who was an usher, put us into the back row, which was as near the front as we wished to be.

When Ben took off his muffler we had already surveyed the inside of the club to our heart's content and we were ready to settle down and study this tie of which Ben had told us. It was broader and blacker than any tie we had seen before. As he pulled back his waistcoat to show us the real width of the thing, we saw that it practically covered his whole chest. Ben explained that his wife, while strong on such items as meat pies, was not very good as a tie-maker, but the rest of us thought that Ben's wife, while knitting this tie, must have let her eyes stray on to a pullover pattern. However, it gave Ben a very respectable look to have all that mass of black around his neck, and it made us feel more at ease to have Ben there in our midst looking as sober and respectable as an old deacon.

There was some clapping as the Rev. Emmanuel came in. We stood on our feet, not to cheer, but to have a good look at him. It was years since we had seen him last and we were interested to know how much he had changed. He had grown very thin, especially around the face, and his hair was so white he looked like one of those before and after advertisements you get with soap powders, or like an actor playing the part of somebody very old on the stage who has just broken the flour bag over his head. There was a vacant, musing look on his face and he smiled a little as the people clapped, but we had the feeling all the time that his mind was many miles away, in other times, in other places.

At that time, Emmanuel would have been about fifty and he appeared no older, no younger than that. With Emmanuel was the chairman for the evening, the manager of one of a local chain store who had managed to crawl along the chain on to the Council: a very keen, neat-looking man, a man who had no doubt arranged his life very tidily in rows like a well-kept garden. Every inch of him was taken up by himself and there was no room in that thin, tight, tidy column of successful effort into which any doubts could crawl and breed. Even as he cast his first glance around the hall, you could imagine that he knew right off which of the voters present bought from him and voted for him.

He must have guessed that we never bought from him or voted for him, for he gave us a very dry, stiff look, or, of course, it might only have been Ben's tie that got this tidy man's goat. Alongside the keen, glaring efficiency of this element, Emmanuel, in his loose black suit and floppy bow-tie, seemed lost and ghostly.

'Isn't he lovely?' said Margaret.

'Who?' asked Ben, trying to get his hand around the knot of his tie. 'The chain-store bloke, you mean.'

'No. Not him. The Rev. Emmanuel.'

'Too white about the head for me. Looks too much as if he's just come into the Allotment Holder's cheap lime scheme. What's so lovely about him?'

'Can't say exactly, not straight. Something I feel. He's so lonely-looking, so pale, just like a saint.'

We thought these opinions were very strange and unhealthy coming from Margaret. We did not like this idea of singling out Emmanuel as a prize-winner on account of his pale and lonely look. We believed that our Terrace produced paler and lonelier-looking voters than any other area in the land, and if they managed to work up a pure look in the process they made nothing out of it.

We noticed that Margaret kept staring at Emmanuel, and we were coming around to the notion that this might be some part of her mother's old weakness for Emmanuel cropping up in her. Ben was shaking his head from side to side in a mournful way, so mournful that to study this head shaking in conjunction with his black tie was to get the impression that either he or we had just died. Ben was mumbling some fact about heredity that he had picked up in that class on biology.

'It comes out,' he was saying in a sad voice. 'You can't help it. It'll hide for a while but it'll come out.'

Ben fell silent when the chairman stood up and announced that the Young People's Glee Club was now going to favour us with a few carefully selected items. The Glee Club turned out to be four boys and four girls bunched up near a piano, and faced by a conductor, a big man who kept his hands so busy he blotted out the biggest part of the Glee Club.

Their items might have been selected, as the chairman said, with care, but they sounded rough and backward to our ears. Items like 'We'll build the maypole high, tee hee, We'll build it to the sky, ho ho, And then we'll dance so spry, tra la' and many other similar verses that made such things as social change seem very far away indeed. Half-way through this item the Glee Club formed a circle on the stage with a tall, glum glee boy stuck in the middle, with the object, no doubt, of looking like a maypole around which the others could cock their legs and go tra la. Indeed, this tall glee singer looked the part, very tall and wooden like the pole of a dead barber. This tall singer never seemed to have been so prominent or important in his life as he was at that moment, because every once in a while he would grin in a broad, sickening fashion that made it look as if the maypole were warping.

After a time this glee turn came to an end. The song they sang came to no definite end, because that kind of song is so silly that there is no definite point at which you can say its job is done, as you can with the baritone song they call 'The Desert' in which the baritone is eaten by vultures and can do no more singing for that reason. And even when the glee singers were climbing down from the stage one or two of them would sing tee hee or tra la, their minds, no doubt, fixed in this rut.

'It is a strange thing,' said my friend Walter, 'that when a country has done a lot of stupid and ugly things, and does not wish the voters to start thinking and acting about these things, the elements who run the country will strain every nerve to keep the mind of the country as childish as possible. When the history of this land's latter day childishness comes to be told, I hope that the history books will have a page or two given over to these Glee Club voters we have just heard who sing tee hee and tra la, and work off a lot of bloody nonsense about maypoles centuries after the last maypole has been chopped down and used to burn the body of some honest rebel or heretic.'

'Down with all glee clubs and tra las,' said Ben.

Then followed a flood of solo singers. Half the audience must have got up to sing a solo or a duet. At first we thought the concert was being run on the principle of a drag-net sweeping from the front row to the back until the hall had been wrung dry of talent. We decided that if we were to be called on, we would go up on the stage, stand in a small circle around my friend Walter and allow him to make a full statement of our views on glee singers while we swore and hummed a bit in harmony. But we were not called on and no one heard the statement.

The flood of solo singers kept flowing at a very steady rate. Many of these songs had a religious bent and the very sick look of most of these singers must have been due to their carrying such songs as these about inside them for many years. One woman came on the stage with a copy of the song she was to sing and also an exercise book. She explained that in the exercise book she had written down six additional verses of her own, making to stretch out the original three in the song. When we heard the three original verses we felt that the woman had done quite rightly to freshen them up with some stuff of her own. It would have been a miracle to invent any verses worse than the original three of that song. But that woman pulled it off, having, no doubt, thrown herself into the job with might and main.

Apart from this woman there was only one other outstanding item in this part of the concert. That was a duet for tenor and baritone called 'Watchman' which Ben told us in advance had some very nice melodies attached to it, and to hear this in full we bent forward in our seats. It was sung by a short tenor with a wig, an element called Abrahams, who had sung himself hairless doing a lot of open air singing during one of the long strikes, and a tall baritone with very large lungs and an impatient look that seemed to say he had very little place for Abrahams or for any tenor with a wig.

A woman sitting in front of us turned around to tell us that these two singers were really the best of friends, and that impatient look was only a dodge of the baritone's to get a laugh. Since we felt no urge to laugh at this look, we thought it would be better if Abrahams were chosen as the comic element in this duo and asked to do tricks with his wig, or stand still with uncovered head while the baritone tapped out the rhythm of the duet on Abrahams' skull with his teeth.

The duet started off with a fine flourish of notes from the tenor, and whenever it was the baritone's turn to come in, he would bend low over the tenor's head and blow the note out with tremendous force as if he were trying to drive Abrahams into the floor like a nail. The tenor's wig could be seen moving about under all this blast, and the various ways in which Abrahams tried to manoeuvre himself into a position where he would not be driven into the floor or his wig blown through the fanlight were very comic, comic enough to have provided that woman with the exercise book with nine additional verses, if she could bring herself to forsake the religious bent that was uppermost with her at present with serious results for poetry and the exercise book.

Then there was an interval before the play. Many remarks regarding the items that had taken place were in our minds ready to be made, but we sat silent because our ears were aching from all that singing. We sat quite silent, except for Ben, who asked just once, 'Where do you think we might lay hands on the ignorant chap who sold that woman the exercise book?'

The chairman got up and read out a speech that was not so good that it needed to be read. Not that we blamed the chain-store manager for reading a bad speech. Many of the best speeches we heard that came from the heart in the valley and were not read, landed the orators in court or jail, and this chairman was good enough a salesman to know that there are not many things you can sell in court or jail when you happen to be on trial or locked up in such places. So we did not blame him for reading a bad speech. The most he said was that these activities we were witnessing were very healthy.

We agreed there. These activities meant a lot of breathing, and where there is breath there is hope and, often, lungs too. The Rev. Emmanuel seconded the chairman. He spoke in a voice like a cello, which, even to calloused and bitter and unbelieving voters like ourselves, was as soothing and relaxing as syrup of figs. Emmanuel celloed thanks in all directions. He even thanked the people in the back, though, outside of Ben with the widest tie we had ever seen, we did not know what we had done during the evening that deserved thanks.

Emmanuel was seconded by a black-moustached man. This man's moustache was so heavy he sometimes toppled over on to his face when he was not wearing big boots with thick soles. This moustached element was connected with giving out Public Assistance, which is that form of relief handed to those voters who do not even qualify for the Insurance, a very depressed class. This man was called Simon by many of the voters who had to go to him to be assisted by the public, because he had a very harsh and barking way with his applicants, and everybody thought for that reason that he took his issue from the old Legree stock, a well-known family in all parts of the world. But now, as he spoke, he was almost soft and cooing and thanked as many people as the Rev. Emmanuel.

And this change in manner was explained to us by Ben, who said that this man had a reserve set of glands hanging up in the bathroom to be fitted on just before he had his tea, just as you would fit on an electric belt or corsets, so that he would never be tempted to treat any of his relatives or friends to the same kind of subhuman chatter he poured daily over the paupers. We thanked Ben for this interesting explanation of the dark-moustached voter's double personality, and Walter added the rider that it was a great waste of glands that this element had even one set without counting the fresh set he had hanging up in the bathroom.

The play started. Knowing what it was all about, and disagreeing from first to last with its plot and theory of life, we concentrated on the acting and the costume. They had fished out a very ancient sporting suit for Willie, and he was covered with grey pleats all over, all of them bulging as if Willie was emphasizing the medical side of his mission by carrying a full first-aid kit in each pleat. We also liked his trousers, which were a kind of baggy plus-fours with a puffed and drooping seat that gave Willie a deformed appearance, and gave us the impression that he had taken up this open air missionary work because he had never been able to find a chair low enough for him to become an office worker or a simple lounger.

On his face there were tufts of hair that had been put on very carelessly, without any effort to match up one side of his face with the other. We could see the point of all these tufts. They were to give Willie a look of age, but we did not see why he should have aged so much more quickly on his left side than his right. From one side you could see thick tufts two or three inches long which stuck right out and made Willie look like a gorilla and, from the other side, weak, scattered tufts that made us think Willie might have been shaved that morning by the very gorilla he looked so much like on the other side.

The chief Batali was very well dressed for a native. He had black tights over his legs, and covering his top part he was wearing what looked to us like a railwayman's waistcoat. He was also covered with big beads that jangled like a xylophone every time he turned. What made this matter worse was that for the first ten minutes Batali kept wriggling about on the floor as if he were sleeping on a snake, no doubt to suggest pain, and this made the jingling of the beads very loud, so loud Willie had to hold him down firmly to have enough quiet to make his speeches without bawling in a fashion that made the audience think he was talking to the tribe outside as well as to Batali.

Tongo, the young window-peeper and announcer, was a slim lad, also wearing many beads but nowhere nearly as heavy a load as Batali, who had most likely ransacked every chest of drawers in his street, and boiled down the china on his wife's dresser to get his collection.

We doubted whether Tongo could possibly have worn as many beads as Batali, for with his physique, so slim it was only his fuzzy wig that made him look any different from his spear, he would have had to walk about with his head touching the floor beneath the total weight of Batali's beads. Tongo did not know his part too well. We knew it better, having heard the play only twice before. During the first half of the sketch he simply marched back and fore the stage, keeping an eye on Livingstone and trying at the same time to keep the front part of himself turned away from the audience, because he was ashamed of having so little on. This gave him a twisted and suffering look that made it seem as if he, too, should have been stretched out on the floor alongside Batali, receiving his dose of treatment and persuasion.

We could hear a lot of prompting from one side and the other, and this prompting was being done loudly and by many voices, causing us to think once in a while that the tribe outside knew the play a lot better than the elements on the stage, especially the Tongo character who seemed to have very little idea indeed of what was going on, and what purpose was being served by his standing there half naked in front of us. We heard one of the voices from the side of the stage instructing Tongo to stop idling about on his beat and start reporting on the mood of the tribesmen.

Tongo wandered back-stage to the window and talked in English with some voter behind this window, and then started to announce so often that the tribe was getting restive that between his interruptions and Batali's grunts Willie was thrown out of joint, lost his place in his speeches and must have felt more than once like thrusting his tufts down the throats of his companions.

When it finished the woman in front of us turned round and said:

'Now it'll start.'

'What will start?'

'The fishing sketch.'

'What are you talking about?'

'The fishing sketch. That thing you saw was just working up to it. Didn't you see the man's drawers and whiskers. That's what they always wear for fishing sketches.'

'Florence Nightingale, I presume,' said my friend Walter, very calmly, to this woman.

'Less of that bloody lip from you,' said this woman, but she was not bad-tempered because she sat down again and settled herself on the bench in readiness for the fishing sketch which she would, no doubt, have enjoyed greatly if there had been one. When she saw the people moving towards the door, she said:

'Well, I'm damned. It's over. What do you think of that now?

Never mind. The sketch will be next time, they sometimes do it like a serial. Oh yes, I've seen it done like that often. And this particular one will be good, too, when it comes on. I like the cut of that man's drawers. And that hair they got plastered over his face is good, too. Puts you into the right mood for the jokes right off.'

We were making ready to go when Willie came running up the aisle. He had not changed his clothes or got rid of his whiskers, and at close quarters he looked more like a distressed area than ever. The woman whose mind ran to fishing sketches as other people's run to food, rocked on her heels and blew a lot of appreciative laughter into Willie's face as he passed her. She pulled him by the arm and threw her own arm up and down in the fashion of a fisher casting the fly from a rod, and doubled her laughter in the thought that Willie would take this fly-casting caper as a tribute, but Willie only looked at this woman as if she were crazy, which could not have been far off the mark.

'Wait a minute,' said Willie to us. 'Don't go yet. The Rev. Emmanuel would like a word with you.'

'If he's offended by our being here,' said Walter, 'he can take that up with you. We came to please you.'

'Oh no. He wants to meet you. I told him about you all, and he wants to meet you.'

We stood awkwardly in our seats, waiting.

Up the aisle, so slowly we thought he would never reach us without being shoved, came the Rev. Emmanuel. With us standing in that corner and him advancing towards us, his white-haired head bent beneath the bright lights, it was like being caught in a snowstorm. He stood before us and for many seconds he looked at us as if we were ghosts, as if he were a ghost.

And ghosts, indeed, we might have been for we and the Rev. Emmanuel were separated by a long period of time during which we had been at opposite poles, time full of deeds, some bright, others so dark the whole series had seemed like successive acts of living and dying. Then, after looking at us, Emmanuel looked at Margaret. There was on his face a look of brooding longing such as you get on the face of a man who has been a long time sick, or on the face of a wise and thirsty man who is staring at the waters of the sea.

'You remember us?' asked my friend Walter. One of us had to say something. We could not stand there indefinitely like a set of mopes, with him gazing at us as if he were wondering whether he should scrape off the moss to find out the date on the headstone. So we were glad when my friend Walter started off the talk in that very polite way.

'So well. So well,' said Emmanuel. 'Every face that has come into my life or gone from it is always well remembered.'

Margaret bade him good night. She slipped through the door of the hall. He turned his eyes from us and looked hard at the door through which she had passed, and we thought that Emmanuel's brain must be getting very soft for him to be doing all this hard silent staring of which he seemed to do just as much as a man paid to hypnotize the voters on a steady basis.

'A good thing, remembering faces. Many different people here and there. Very useful to know who they are.'

'Excellent, excellent. You were quite young men when I remember having seen you last. Now you look quite different.'

'We nearly died.'

'Were you ill?'

'We were all right. The world was ill.'

'Oh yes, yes. That unhappy slump. But there you are. All passes. Times are better now. More life, more hope. Already, those unhappy years of poverty and bitterness are far away, it would seem.'

'To some people,' said my friend, 'those times were always far away.'

'Yes, perhaps, indeed. But it really does make me most glad to see you here tonight. You have great hearts, you Terrace folk, and I love you all for it. I would dearly like a talk with you. Could you come up to my home on Saturday evening? Then you can tell me of all that has been happening to you. I am sure you all have interesting stories to tell.'

'We'll come,' said Walter, and we all agreed by shaking our heads up and down.

'About six-thirty then. Saturday night.'

We said good night and walked out. Near the entrance we found Margaret waiting for us. She asked us eagerly what the Rev. Emmanuel had said, and we could have seen that she was very interested in the Rev. Emmanuel even if we had been four times as dense as nature made us.

'He said,' murmured Ben with a threatening disgust, 'that he loved the good hearts of the Terrace folk.'

'Oh, that is just what I could imagine him saying. Don't you think that was a wonderful thing for him to say?'

'For God's sake, Margaret,' said Arthur, 'don't get worshipful about a man who looks saintly because he can afford the soap to keep cleanliness up to saint level, and has kept his expression pure because he has been careful to keep himself away from all the impure capers that come by the ton as a natural heritage to such elements as ourselves. He loves our hearts, does he? Won't our hearts skip a beat for joy when that fact sinks in. He loves our good hearts. That interests me. Why are our hearts good? Because they continue to beat after many years of being shoved hard against a wall with life petering to a close in us and around us, with our ribs being quietly stoved in by every wicked misfortune that could be worked up by human stupidity under cover of a slump for our delight. And we are delighted. The Rev. Emmanuel would have shown the kind of love we could have used if he had joined hands with us during the rough years instead of joining in as best dressed pall-bearer at what he hoped might be our funeral. For all that time he forgot the Terraces. He closed his eyes to us, hoping that we would oblige him and society by going into liquidation and saving him the bother of wheeling yet another problem about on the handcart. No, Margaret, we cannot say that the Rev. Emmanuel strikes us as being a very admirable type of voter.'

'You're all too prejudiced,' said Margaret with much vigour, very much as Willie spoke in similar arguments. 'How can you judge any man so lightly? How can you possibly look into the heart and soul of the Rev. Emmanuel. You cannot judge a man without looking right down deep into his heart and soul.'

'Nobody ever looked into ours and we do not see why we should do all this deep burrowing you suggest into Emmanuel. Our hearts and souls have always been around waiting to be looked into and sized up, but no one ever bothered. To the rich we were labour for the using, and while there was profit for them in our labour they used us. To the Government clerks we were cards for rubber stamping, and there were some of those clerks who worked up a lot more dislike for us than they ever could have worked up for ordinary cards. Who's ever thought that we had hearts and souls? If we had had hearts and souls dangling from our backs like hundredweight sacks, no one would have paid them the least attention. And I would not blame anybody for not doing so. Look, Margaret, there are many people hanging around on the crust of this earth. So very many it makes you sick to think how few of them you will ever see and how few of them you'll ever know. The job of all these people is to live as well as they can together without shoving their feet into each other's mouths, or their finger-tips into each other's hearts. Now, the world being as crowded with people as this, you would have a very hard time if you went judging every man you meet only after you had examined his heart and soul as the gas man examines the gas meter. So we have to go on results. Either a man promotes the greatest happiness of his neighbours, or he stands to one side and gives not a damn about his neighbours providing his own skull is whole or he can actively take steps to reduce the happiness of his neighbours. You can tell in which of these three paths a man is treading without crouching beneath his bed at night trying to work out the quality of his soul from the things he might be muttering in his sleep. The Rev. Emmanuel started off in the first road. Then the good old whip of the money-bags was cracked above his head, and for a while he switched over to the third road where he did great harm to the people by putting his signature to every silly little lie that was spread forth by the mighty to divide and stupefy the people. But most of the time he had been in the second path, enjoying a prosperous tranquillity and giving as much help as he would if his pastorate were on the further side of Mars, and you know well that Mars is a very distant place and no part of this division.'

'All the same,' said Margaret, 'I think he must be a great man. He looks so wise. He must have thought so deeply about so many things.'

'That's picture-postcard stuff you are talking, Margaret. I thought you had more sense than to be taken in by a mop of white hair. It was not wisdom that bleached the Rev. Emmanuel. It was a sickness. It might have happened to any one of us, but we were kept so busy being kicked around we weren't ever long enough in the same position to have the bleaching well done.'

'Not only his hair,' she said. 'Look at his eyes.'

'What about his eyes?'

'So deep, so pitying.'

'He's got plenty of pity, no credit to him. And I suppose we'll have to tolerate a mass of hunger and disease in the world just to provide a pitying look for the eyes of secluded thinkers. I can't understand you at all, Margaret. Why should a bright girl like you be wanting to wave flags for the Rev. Emmanuel?'

We all stopped. The rain had finished. The steep climb had shattered our breath. Ben and I got behind Arthur to prop him up if he should weaken and start running backward at some point of the steep road that had still to be climbed. Arthur was getting very unsteady in steep climbs and we could hear him whispering 'Thank Christ' when we stopped for a spell.

'I'm not waving flags for him,' said Margaret. 'But he looks as if he's all on his own, unhappy as anything, wanting somebody to be near him. I'd feel the same about a dog if it looked like that.'

There was a sound of feet running down the hill towards us. A voice shouted, 'Margaret, Margaret.' She called back 'Yes' in a quiet, frightened voice. A woman, wearing a man's raincoat over her head, came running out of the darkness ahead. She was gasping with great swells of her red throat which we could see in the light of a lamp-post, and trying to talk at the same time and the talk from her mouth sounded very strange indeed.

My friend Walter told the woman to go lean against the wall and get her breath, because such gasping as this woman was doing seemed to be very dangerous for her health. The woman did that and leaned with the full weight of her breasts against the wall as if the run had made her ache, and she wanted to press the ache from her body into the stones.

'Your mother, Margaret,' said the woman, without turning her head around to look at us. 'She's been terrible. For half an hour now she's been terrible. Come quick.'

Margaret hurried forward. We followed her. As we reached the house, the doctor was getting into his car. Margaret rushed at him, caught him by the arm and nearly pulled him off his balance on to the pavement. He was a young doctor, new to the Terraces, a friendly, smiling element, nice enough.

'How is she, Doctor?'

'I've made her sleep. She's very ill, very weak. You know that?'

'Yes, I know.'

'She might die. You must expect that.'

'Yes, I know.'

'I'll be around again in the morning.'

Margaret went into the house. She said no word to us. Nor did we want one. Near the house was an iron seat the Council had fixed up for the halt. We settled ourselves on this seat, trying to get as comfortable as we could on the thin iron bands of it, and thinking that the halt would be a lot halter after a short spell on such a contraption as that.

As we sat there, we felt, the four of us, that what we wished to know about the mother of Margaret we should know soon enough. I have said that we have great instincts in these matters. For all who had lived in the Terraces we had a kind of love, a comradeship that has beauty for having no axe to grind, and that love made us quick to sense the coming in or going out of life. To all those who have lived without wealth, importance, purpose or consolation, the simple act of living acquires a meaning that increases to a point when we can never describe the feelings we have before the simple act of dying.

Above us, in that small bedroom, there was ending in a silence that was sweet and intelligent to the ears that listened, a brief story of great effort that had proceeded to failure as naturally as a thirsty animal would proceed to water. You may read the story of poverty, oppression and human failure in learned books and feel your brain burn at the wretched spectacle of the stupid tormenting the weak, but try sitting on an iron bench in a dark night meditating upon the death that is shortly to come, a few yards away, to one of stupidity's victims, who has put more intelligence, strength and valour into trying to win a civilized standard of decency for herself and a child, than ever any of history's revered baboons put into the exploitation of their kingdoms, strip mills or coal mines, and yet dies without any outward evidence of having made anything but a hell of a mess of it, and your brain will do something more than burn. It will have the grey, dusty fragility of coke.

The night grew mild, less dark. Ben pointed to the broad range of hills five miles away, and began to describe a walk there a year ago, looking for blackberries. He went on with this tale, his deep voice a bluer streak in the shadow until we told him that we had been with him on that walk and we had gathered no blackberries, because we had been driven off from a very fine blackberry hedge by a farmer who looked crazy to us, a man with a glaring, twisted look of the sort that often comes to the faces of men who get the idea that things like hedges on broad mountains can belong to anybody. Anyway, we got no blackberries, and we reminded Ben of that, and he said he could quite believe that because that would be just like our bloody luck, and we agreed with him.

An hour later the same neighbour who had run down the hill to meet us came out of the house and said that Mrs Radnor had gone.

'Got to go back up now,' she said. 'Got to comfort that poor little Margaret and see to things. There's a lot of work with death. They were very close. She'll be hit very hard.'

'It's a misty life, sister,' said my friend Walter.

The woman looked around for signs of the mist that Walter was talking about, saw none and went in. We made no move to go. The hills were becoming clearer now all around, and the sight and the shape of them accorded well with the thoughts we had, full of the anger of years and of the angry, wanting years our fathers must have known as well and died upon. My friend Walter sat with his chin low on his chest. My friend Arthur sat sideways on the iron bench, his hand running over his brow as if there was poetry or just some ordinary rash crawling below the skin. Ben fidgeted about on the iron strips.

From down the road came the noise of a man singing. It was Hector, drunk. Hector rolled into the house. We could see the gas being lit in the front room downstairs, which was the room in which he lived. Through the undrawn curtains we could see his dark, thick body sway beneath the gas mantle. We could see the flood of curses that blustered through his lips when the paper taper burned low to his fingers. Then, when the pain of that had passed, he started bawling some song again, in a voice that had layers of damp dirt swept into every corner of it.

He was singing a song called 'Moonlight and Roses', and we knew that song very well because it had been a very popular number with all the boys who had had gazookas to play on during the strikes, and between all these gazooka players half the guts had been blown out of this song 'Moonlight and Roses', but it remained for our ears a pretty tune except when sung by such an element as Hector, who, as we have said, was like a gorilla in hair and brain.

It was hard at times to tell really what tune Hector was supposed to be singing, but we could hear the words 'Moonlight and Roses' being mumbled every once in a while and that gave us a very clear clue to the title. We saw Hector drag a fat parcel of fish and chips from his pocket and lay it on the table. The man, no doubt, was very drunk. He did some more pretty swaying as he stood beneath the light. He took up the package again and tried to read some item of news that had caught his eye on the newspaper wrapping. We thought that the only news that a voter like Hector was ever likely to get from the outside world was what he picked up from the wrapping around his fish and chips. From inside the house we could hear the voice of the friendly neighbour screaming:

'Stop that noise, you pig.'

'Where are you going, Ben?'

'In there. I'm going to give Hector some moonlight. You can bring the roses.'

'Hector is very backward,' said my friend Walter.

I followed Ben into the house. We walked into Hector's room. When he saw us he said something so loud, so sudden and so dirty we could almost see it floating through the air as if it were a dark cloud or an ink-stained cloth. Then he threw the package of fish and chips at us with a very strong throw. The package burst like a shell in Ben's face. The paper of the package was soaked with vinegar and grease. Ben blinked his eyes as the vinegar made them smart. His two hands swept over his chest to dislodge the falling chips that had stuck there.

Then we beat Hector very hard in one way and another. We beat the senses out of him. But that made so little difference to Hector it was hardly a punishment at all. We lifted him up and laid him on the sofa. He breathed loudly but apart from that he was very quiet, very bruised. From above we could hear Margaret wailing. We left the house. Walter and Arthur were waiting for us on the pavement.

'A backward element, that Hector,' said my friend Walter.

*

On the following Saturday evening, we went, as we had promised, to the house of the Rev. Emmanuel. This house was on the hillside opposite the Terraces. It was a large house, and except for Ben, about ten times larger than any of us had ever known. Ben had been to jail for cuffing anti-social voters so he knew much more than we did about large buildings. We all felt a bit strange as we walked along the gravel drive to the big house, feeling that we were being admitted at last to the Refuge for the broken-down.

Emmanuel himself opened the door to us. He had no wife or servant. He showed us into a large, brown-looking room that had a lot of old-looking wood on the walls. On a table in the middle of this room was a light supper to which the Rev. Emmanuel invited us straightaway to sit down. We were given hunger by the sight of that clean, tasty food. Emmanuel might have had the idea that voters of our calibre got so little to eat that we were always marching about on the look-out for a meal. We were not exactly at that point but we were glad of food at all times, and we ate this food of Emmanuel's with very willing appetite.

We did no talking at the meal. We ate and the Rev. Emmanuel watched, and both sides showed very smooth form. We thought that part of his saintly look might have come from watching people eat. It must be very uplifting to watch other people eat if you do not happen to be hungry yourself.

Then we sat around a fire that was well piled up. We smoked peacefully, and we considered that such a room as that would be a nice room in which to spend one's whole life with things like crises howling themselves to a standstill outside if one had the leaning towards that kind of solitude.

The Rev. Emmanuel asked us how long we had been working and what we were working at. We explained that we had found things to do with the Urban and County Councils and the Co-operative Society. Emmanuel said that these organizations should consider themselves fortunate to have obtained the services of such mature and shrewd voters as we were.

To this my friend Walter replied that if such bodies as the Councils and the Co-ops were always going to wait until men were as mature as we were before offering them jobs, then there would either be a very sad state of things or a flood of voters taking steps to become mature long before their time.

Then the Rev. Emmanuel, in his softest voice, which seemed to match the old brown wood, began to open up about the Ice Age of Hate and the Melting Age of Love and he stopped short and fell silent when he saw that we thought little of this theory, and that we had heard it once before. When he spoke again it was jerkily, uneasily, as if he were ill or had something on his mind, a trouble.

'You don't think much of me, do you?' he asked suddenly.

'Not much,' said my friend Walter, who never allowed a gift of food to stand between him and the truth.

'You think that what I say is very largely nonsense.'

'Maybe. It does not square with what we think to be the facts.'

'Quite right, quite right. It doesn't square at all. Nothing I have said for the last twenty years has squared with the facts.'

He smiled at us and settled himself more comfortably on his chair. He watched us as we looked surprised.

'Then why did you say it?' asked Walter.

'Because a man is weak, friend. Either his mind is, which mine isn't, because it has never ceased to believe that the misery of man can only be righted by man, or his body is, which mine is. They tell me I live always very near to dying, and to remain alive I must live in a constant calm. To oppose misery on earth means the end of calm, so I accepted what I should have opposed.'

'How do you feel about it?'

'Oh, rotten.'

'I thought you would.'

Emmanuel bent towards the fire. When he spoke it was as much to himself as to us, as if he were speaking things that he had often spoken into the fire with no one but himself in the room.

'I've been in the warm. You've been out in the cold. That has been going on for a very long time, and I don't suppose anything could happen now to alter the way in which our lives have been formed by those two experiences. Judge me as you please and I will make but little effort to change your judgement, for I have grown very sceptical about the value of judges. But something in me is changing and the feeling of a strange new harvest inside me coming to fruit makes me want to talk. You are interested in change, too, aren't you? So you might be interested in what I have to say. When I was young I had two great desires. One was to help usher in a reign of peace and beauty, free from all the ugliness and pain you will have seen so much of in the Terraces. The other desire was smaller, simpler. I desired a girl whose companionship would have given me great happiness. Both these desires I surrendered because, when faced with the prospect of a struggle I might well have lost, I preferred a life of peace with failure to a life in which I might have had to mix up a lot of misery and the danger of death with the accomplishment of my desires.'

'We had no choice,' said Arthur. 'It's just as well for the reign of peace and beauty that most of the people who struggle for it are never offered the chance of comfort or peace.'

'You'd be surprised,' went on the Rev. Emmanuel, 'how quickly one settles down after the surrender of desires you once considered sacred. Man must be a mean animal. I accepted my own Ice Age with great resignation. I saw the social misery against which I had raised my young voice rise to greater heights, greater deadliness as pits closed down, and the people lost their hope of ever seeing the face of sanity or justice again. I made not a single inquiry about the girl I had wished to marry. I stuck my head and the brain thereof into the adulation of my flock as completely as a sow would stick hers into the slop-trough. In relation to what I had been, to what I had felt, I died as thoroughly as a man can ever die without being boxed up and buried in the process. Simply for the sake of keeping alive. Simply for the sake of avoiding various kinds of penury and discomfort that you and thousands of your comrades have endured for the major part of your adult lives. That is very interesting, isn't it? No, I see by the sombre look on your faces that you do not think it very interesting. You have lived too far away from the cosy little subtleties of the inner heart to have much sympathy with them. But here is the point I wish to make, the point I wished to place before you tonight. I am growing tired of my own calm and resignation. Why? That is difficult to say. I never thought it possible that a refuge, where one had found for many years the most pleasant comfort and rest, could ever become disagreeable. Perhaps it is because I have spent many evenings lately thinking of such men as you, whose comradeship and affection gave me much happiness in the old days. Perhaps sheer solitude is piling up like dry ash in my inside and beginning to choke me. Perhaps I have realized that to live for five minutes with one's desires raised high and blood-red in one's hands is better than a lifetime nursing an immortality of calm and rancid contentment on the grave of those desires. Perhaps my tongue has grown very tired of teaching the faith of total acceptance and submission to people who have now become so witless in the practice of that faith, so dumb with obedience they have lost the ability to refute even those things that are most painfully and evidently evil. Perhaps I have felt the longing that every man must feel for a friend. This mood of mine is a mood of reawakening. It finds me very unsteady, very uncertain of the way I should go. That is why I wanted you to talk to. You are not friends of mine. Your attitude towards me is bitter. Yet I have said things to you I would not have said to any one of the hundreds who throng my chapel and hang upon my words. You are different. You held the post that I abandoned. Your minds are the bridge between myself and the past I wish to return to.'

'You wish to return to the past,' asked Walter, wondering.

'I do,' said Emmanuel, very firmly, like a man being married.

'It's no easier than it used to be, no brighter; you might get worked up and die because there are still lots of items around about that cause a voter to get worked up.'

'That bothers me,' said the Rev. Emmanuel, 'not at all.'

He stood up and looked at us in turn.

'You men,' he said. 'When you have seen in your lives any chance of happiness, I don't suppose you ever thought twice of stretching out your hands and taking it?'

'Never,' said Walter. 'The chances have been few but we've been eager.'

'How wonderful,' said the Rev. Emmanuel, and we made no sense of that utterance.

'Come with us,' said Walter.

'To where?'

'Just come with us. It's a part of the past I'd like you to see. And, anyway, your mood, you said, was a mood of reawakening, and I think this thing is the sort of thing a peculiar man like you should see when he is coming out of a long sleep. It will also teach you how very silly it is ever to exchange the chance of a sweeter span of life for the multitude for the chance of a longer span of life for oneself.'

The Rev. Emmanuel got his coat and hat and wrapped himself

up in a white scarf that was very long and looked something like that crochet tie of Ben's only it was white. He also wore a black slouch very long in the body and smooth to the touch. We disapproved of that hat because it made Emmanuel look like a money-changer, and we did not want the local voters to see us in the company of a man who looked as if he had just been changing money for us, our policy being ever to get rid of or steer clear of such elements.

Together we walked down the hillside and across the valley-bed and up to the Terraces. Ben, Arthur and I walked on ahead. Walter and the Rev. Emmanuel came on behind.

'Men like Emmanuel,' said Ben, 'who live like he's lived, lonely and keeping things all bottled up inside them with regard to politics and women and so on, are bound to go crazy. That's where Emmanuel is going now. Crazy.'

We heard Walter's voice from behind.

'To Margaret's house,' he said.

We turned in that direction, wondering what it was that Walter might be wanting to do there. We had thought that Walter might have been planning nothing more for the Rev. Emmanuel than a tour around the houses where there were to be found voters suffering greatly through the system, from bad lungs or legs, and getting so little compensation one would have thought their lungs and legs had actually improved as a result of being made bad.

When we reached Margaret's house, the door was opened by the friendly neighbour. Margaret, she said, had gone out with Willie, to make some arrangements. She was surprised to see us in the company of a preacher, and she looked very hard at us to make sure that the element in the black slouch and white scarf was really Emmanuel, and not some prominent agitator dressed up to look like a preacher and baffle the faithful as well as the police. When she saw it was, without doubt, Emmanuel, she gave little squeals of astonishment, for she knew us well and had often taken us to task for our independent attitude with regard to all such things as creeds and sects. She was very pleased to see Emmanuel and gushed over him.

We took him upstairs to the room where Mrs Radnor was. We stood at the open door of the bedroom. Emmanuel stared at the dead woman, bewildered.

'There she is,' said Walter. 'Your second desire, now gone very cold indeed. The girl you wanted to marry and didn't. Like us, she had no alternative to struggle and struggle she did, without much success. I can assure you, Reverend, she had a hell of a life.'

Emmanuel started to shake as if he had a palsy. He bolted out on to the dark landing. My friend Arthur and I stood by his side supporting him, because he would have toppled over the stairs in all that dark and with all that trembling. He shook so much we and the landing shook too.

As he was growing steadier, Margaret and Willie came upstairs. As soon as Emmanuel saw her, he went up to her and put his arms around her neck and his head upon her shoulders, crying.

'Oh, you poor child. Oh, you poor child,' he said, and followed that with a lot of other statements of a like kind, which are to be found in great numbers in such things as old-fashioned stories and plays, and Emmanuel seemed to have read nearly all those plays and stories judging by the speed at which these statements came flooding from his lips.

Margaret started crying, too, and she and the Rev. Emmanuel stood on the top of those stairs rocking and crying at each other, showing more ability in this line than ever I had seen before, except in the cinema where voters get paid for doing this. Willie, who was wearing a bowler which looked like something that had grown up slyly in the dark, kept running about on the edge of the group like a terrier, and grinning with great delight at all this emotion that was running out of the Rev. Emmanuel. On balance, I should say that the only people in that house who kept up a fair standard of quiet, proletarian dignity were my friends Walter, Arthur and Ben, myself and Mrs Radnor.

We saw no sign of Willie for a week after that. We were kept busy every evening at the Library and Institute where there was a non-stop discussion going on about the subject of syndicalism among a group of voters, who had been arguing steadily for three winters past on the subject of what was pure politics. Being very interested in such questions as syndicalism and pure politics, we thought we should try to help these voters to reach a conclusion, so that they could spend at least one evening in three at home during future winters.

It was at Idomeneo's the following Saturday that we saw Willie.

He was still wearing his bowler and he kept it on indoors. He spent a lot of time staring at himself in the big mirror that Idomeneo had fixed on the wall, and we thought that Willie must have grown very fond of this bowler, a process whose nature we could not fathom.

He looked most happy and he was not slow in telling us why.

'Didn't I tell you that the Rev. Emmanuel would help Margaret once he had the chance. He's given her a job.'

'What job, Willie?'

'Oh, it's hard to say exactly what she'll be doing. She'll be a sort of housekeeper and secretary. She can do a bit of shorthand, and Margaret thinks that that will be a great help to the Reverend Emmanuel with his sermons and so on. He can talk and she'll write.'

'She'll be living in his house?'

'Where else would she live?'

'That's it. It'll be a nice change from the Terraces.'

'It will, that. It would have been terrible for Margaret to keep on living in the Terraces now that her mother's gone.'

'It'll ease the blow for her to be somewhere pleasant.'

'That's exactly what I told her when she asked me what she ought to do about the Reverend Emmanuel's offer. You know, you ought to take back all you said about the Reverend Emmanuel. He's taken to Margaret like a daughter.'

'That's very good, Willie, and we're glad, boy.'

We asked Willie if he were going to have some music. He said no. He said he had to go down to meet Margaret down in the valley. We said it would be a pity if this job with the Rev. Emmanuel would mean that we would not be seeing Margaret so often.

'You'll be seeing her,' said Willie. 'You are her friends and she thinks well of you all.'

Then he went his way, leaving us to drink our tea and have thoughts about mankind.

'All this is very strange,' said my friend Walter. 'Let's talk about it.'

'All right,' said Arthur. 'What I'd like to know in the first place is why the Rev. Emmanuel got us up to his house that night. I'd also like to know why he told us all that stuff about his soul.'

'A man does that,' said Walter, 'when he's got so tired of whatever he's doing, he's either got to talk about it to gather up enough courage for a change or he gets rid of himself, which is the shorter and fuller way of talking about one's soul.'

'He said he wanted to return to the past.'

'He did enough shaking and crying about it on that landing in Margaret's,' said Ben, 'you'd have said he'd been shot back to the past from a cannon.'

'Do you think he could ever return to the ways of thinking he had before fear and Mr Dalbie nobbled him?' asked Arthur. 'Do you think that after twenty years of denouncing the discontented as cannibals and savages and God knows what, that he could suddenly change his tune and march in line with us? Do you think he could turn around and start kicking the teeth of the people whose backs he's been stroking for pay ever since he found that this is not such a bad life after all? Personally, I don't think so.'

'You can't tell,' said Walter. 'A man's mind bobs about a damned sight more than any grasshopper, and has even less notion very often of where it's supposed to be bobbing. And there's no doubt that the Rev. Emmanuel might have been clamped down by his fear of dying, he being frail and liable to pass over if he ever shouts too loud or foams with passion. As he gets older the fear might be growing less, because the older you get in such a community as this the more point and purpose you see in passing over. Also, there are quite as many things for him to kick up hell about now as there were twenty years ago. The bad things of that time have got a shade riper, that's the only difference between then and now. If the Rev. Emmanuel wants to change his line; if he wants to stop looking like an over-soaped saint and to start pointing out that rents are too high, wages are too low and whole streets of houses too foul to be lived in, not to mention the legions of voters who are too ignorant to be talked to without the talker lying full stretch on the floor to get down to their level, we should be the last to discourage him. He can get as worked up about those things as ever he likes, and if he does drop down dead one day in the middle of an attack on the dark forces, we'll be the first to cheer and the first to point out to the voters what a hell of a world it must be to drive a saint like Emmanuel to drop down dead by just talking about it. Such an event would, no doubt, cause these elements to think, who have never used their brains before for any other purpose than keeping the draughts out of their heads.'

'You can't persuade me there's any goodness at all in that man,' said Ben. 'It wasn't the red part of his past he wanted to return to. He's a yellow belly and you can save up that statement to put on his gravestone. He let himself be muzzled because he had grown frightened of his own voice. He put the lead around his own neck when he saw the coalowner wanted to make a dog out of him. You won't see any change in the Rev. Emmanuel for all his talk about returning to the past. He'll keep up the same old smooth, smarmy line about patience and obedience and Ice Ages. I'll tell you all what was wrong with that man. He wanted a woman. He'd been itching for a woman ever since that coalowner told him to stay single and save his strength for the faith. It's amazing what wanting a woman will land a man into, especially if the element who does the wanting is somebody that the other elements look to for a very high standard of purity, a monk or a preacher, for instance. Look at that Job Jefferies in the top Terrace. Not that anybody looked to Job for anything special in the way of purity, but he's an example of the strange things a man will do when he's got the itch. He was a very strong, lustful fellow, Job. He became a widower and started biting bits off his knuckles for want of a woman. Then it drove him silly, and one day he started marching down through the Terraces without a stitch of clothing upon him and laughing like a hyena. It was a very terrible sounding laugh, and it made me very glad at the time to be clothed and married, because, no doubt, being naked had something to do with the quality of Job's laugh. They had to put Job away, because a few hours of that performance and Job would have had everybody in the Terraces doing it since he seemed very happy about it, a lot happier than most of the elements who took one look at him as he marched down and then bolted into their bedrooms shouting for the law. Then, one day when Job was in the Mental somebody told him that he'd been living next door to a very well-known whore the whole time he'd been chewing his knuckles, and that news made Job sillier still, because it galls a man whose nerves are a bit on edge to find that such useful facts are kept so dark. It was a woman that the Rev. Emmanuel wanted when he gave us that long talk about his soul and the inside of him changing. He dressed it up in fancy language when he talked to us, because he's too deep and well respected a man to go flashing his lust like a gun in the manner of so many voters known to us in these Terraces. Also, he's a lot too frail to take up Job's method of walking about naked, and he's not allowed to raise his voice high enough to sound like a hyena. With a body as slender as his, if he howled anything like Job, the force of it would send him through the air like a football. Look at the way he carried on the night he saw Margaret, the night we took him to see Mrs Radnor. And why, do you think, has he given her this job?'

'It's the rearmament,' said Arthur, who had been reading a pamphlet on that subject before we had called for him that night, and whose mind was very full of that theme. 'Even we've got jobs and we were at the bottom of the hat, so this must be a very great war that is coming along.'

'What the hell,' asked Ben, 'has the Rev. Emmanuel got to do with rearmament? They won't be firing off any of his sermons because they are all about ice, and they can't use his white hair for blowing anything up. He gave Margaret a job for a different reason.'

'You mean he'll try to sleep with her?'

'That'll depend on her.'

'She seemed to think a deal of him. Talked about his soul, remember?'

'That's the first step to bed if I'm any judge of souls.'

'Hell.'

'What do you mean by saying that, Walter?'

'I was thinking. It would be a hell of a blow for Willie if what you say turned out to be right. I don't know though. You might be quite wrong. After all, forget for a minute that the Rev. Emmanuel has done many things that we've disliked. Just think of him as a man who spent many years on his own, who's got very tired of being on his own. You can understand that. This is a very frosty life for all who are without comrades or lovers. During all those years he's most likely thought of this Mrs Radnor and I bet he's got as far as putting on his hat on many cold evenings to go and find out what had become of her. Mrs Radnor might have become in his mind the chief image of all that life had cheated him of. Every man gets some image of that sort in his mind and the simpler it is the better he likes it, because he has to carry it around with him the whole time. Then we take him along one night to see this very Mrs Radnor. He sees her dead and over her body he probably sees a great white pyramid of all those talks he's had with the thought of her, over his own fire, in his own solitude. And he sees her dead after a lifetime made stupid and shapeless by poverty, and ready to be buried by the Public Assistance. Wouldn't that shake him? Wouldn't that nerve him, even after twenty years of being half nark, half monk, to start once again his own struggle against all the daft, horrible things that happened to Mrs Radnor? Having Margaret near him would only make his anger the sharper. As for lust, I don't think there's a scrap of it left in the Rev. Emmanuel. Ben here was prejudiced by his deep knowledge of rampant stallions like Job Jefferies, and put Emmanuel into a wrong light for that reason. There's no lust in Emmanuel. He looks just like I feel. Bleached. And you know me. I wouldn't stir a hair for Venus.'

'We'll see,' said Ben. 'If we get any fiery speeches from the Rev. Emmanuel about the sin of widows having to work themselves to death just to provide a decent schooling for their kids, I'll admit to being wrong. We'll see.'

Then we had some music and we were glad to hear it, because this question of Emmanuel, coming on top of several nights of talk on syndicalism and pure politics, was wearing our brains down to a fine point. So we were glad to sit back and stare at each other, and listen to the outpour of great, high notes from Idomeneo's gramophone.

There was a man in the Library and Institute with whom we played an occasional game of chess. This voter was very sad in all his ways of looking and thinking, and this sadness came from the fact that his wife had run away from him twice, and with the same man on both occasions. He gave us the impression that he would not have minded so much if his wife had chosen a different man for the second run, but choosing the same element had made the thing seem too deliberate and it had driven him to chess.

Besides chess and work and waiting for his wife to turn up after her latest trip, his only other interest was listening to the Rev. Emmanuel. And for many months past we had got from him ever lengthening accounts of the sermons preached by the Rev.

Emmanuel. No doubt, the lonelier he got to feel as a result of being run away from as if he were a fire, the more he turned to such events as sermons to smooth out the pain.

So it was this voter we consulted now to find out if he noticed any change of tone or style in the utterances of Emmanuel. We did this for four or five weeks, and we kept the chess player so busy with our queries he had no time for chess, and he grew to look very sorrowful, the only counter-consolation to this loss being that he thought our being in work again was making us softer in our attitude toward Emmanuel and switching us back to the faith of our fathers.

We had to admit, after listening to his long and reliable reports, that for a man who had said he wanted nothing better than a return to the past, Emmanuel was making a very good job of sticking to the present. It was the same old story he seemed to be telling. His statements, his whole line had not changed a jot. There was the same calm, the same delighted acceptance of things as they were, the same angelic blindness to such pikestaff issues as the silliness of extolling meekness to elements whose employers had the general outlook of leopards.

The chess-playing voter raised our hopes for a moment by mentioning a reference Emmanuel had made to widows, but he went on to say that this was in connection with widows' jars, a well-known Biblical feature, he told us, and we did not see that this led anywhere unless to some future appeal for a distribution of free jars to widows on the occasion of some jubilee or silver wedding. We began to feel very severe towards Emmanuel, for we had marched down the Terraces and climbed half-way up a mountain to his house to hear all those things he had said about his soul, and we had been made to believe, by the tone he had used, that he was shortly going to cast his old skin like a snake, and we knew many voters living near us who could have done with Emmanuel's old skin for winter wear. But the old skin stayed stuck to the old line, Ice Ages and all.

But something else developed then that was of great interest to voters of an inquiring mind like ourselves. As you know, life in the Terraces has never been anything but rough, and the thin times have caused the bulk of the voters to have such bitter thoughts about the world they live in that if you dissolved a few of these thoughts in a glass of water and drank it, the stuff would most likely burn away the lining of your stomach. And if ever you saw smoke coming from the ears of these voters either it meant that they had just been talked to by an official of the Labour Exchange, or that they had swallowed some ot their own thoughts in lieu of vinegar, which gets dearer the more it comes to taste like life.

So, naturally, the bulk of these voters had never had much inclination to listen to or accept the doctrines of the Rev. Emmanuel. These doctrines indicated that any bitter-thinking voter was as much a menace as strikers, drunkards or Russians of the kind who had placed a hand on the neck of those refugee elements who had streamed through Emmanuel's pulpit in the old days, singing that lowering ballad 'Russia, Holy Russia, I will die to set you free'.

It was only those voters who were very slow or very small about the brain who had gathered around the Rev. Emmanuel during the dark years, and had remained faithful to all his teachings. Many of these voters had been peasants in backward countries before coming to the valley, and they still thought that a salaam for the preacher and a cheer for the squire would bring them a slice of pie in the sky with a foot-thick crust and a half-mile filling of the best meat and potato. You could not argue with them. Either you broke your teeth on them or they broke their knuckles on you, for they were very strong, having lived in just the same way as horses for centuries past, and could be very violent in defence of their darkness.

Now, many years of listening to stuff from the Rev. Emmanuel that had confirmed and sanctified their superstitions had not made these voters any brighter. It had the reverse effect. They had grown so sloppy with the faith of acceptance that what little brain they might have had in the beginning had now been washed away by the blood-stream to do some job as bone-building. Indeed, at that time, it would have been hard to find, unless in a slave pen or an open air school, any collection of sillier people than those who hitched their wagon to the star of the Rev. Emmanuel.

Stupid people are easy to manage as long as you can keep on leading them along the line that you have laid down. They will follow that line in their ready, brute-like way so well that they get the idea that they must be very intelligent people to be moving so consistently in the same direction. If the direction is along the bottom of a drain-pipe and their destination nothing more than a main culvert, they will have the same pleased feeling, and that is why you have so many stupid people in the world and such a great sound of marching in the drains.

Present these elements with a change of line, however slight, and they protest with what they consider to be the full weight of their intelligence, because the only thing they know is sure is the line along which they are supposed to keep their feet. So they protest with the full weight of an intelligence which has no weight, and all this business of making protests with the aid of brain that is either dead or stunned causes great confusion everywhere. That is why all who are sensible are advised to walk about this earth with iron skull-caps and heavy insurance, until we have a very drastic law against these stupid voters.

The Rev. Emmanuel had spent many years impressing his followers with his saintliness, his indifference to such capers as fleshly love, and indifference to this last caper was bound to give any man a special flavour in the Terraces where, as my friend Walter has often said, the tenants are so often short of coal and firewood that love is valued more as a means of keeping warm than as a means of being happy. And no doubt these followers had grown to look upon Emmanuel as those early Christians looked upon those leading fanatics who made a point of sleeping night after night alongside naked women, doing nothing but praying, purely just to show that for all they cared the women might have been wrapped from head to foot in bullet-proof steel-plate.

It is likely that this side of Emmanuel's character was more popular with his listeners than any of his theories about the Ice Age of Hate and the Melting Age of Love, which must have sounded more like weather reports than theories to the thin-brained elements who gave their faith to Emmanuel.

Now they learned about Margaret, a pleasing and well fashioned maiden, being taken into Emmanuel's home as housekeeper and secretary. They were shocked, hurt and revolted and talked the hind legs off the topic every time they got together, after the fashion of voters who knew so little about the economic system and the international situation that they are driven to discussing the sexual capers of their neighbours, just to avoid the realization of their own dumbness.

The Rev. Emmanuel had brought them through the world's largest slump on a diet of chaste saintliness, and now here he was introducing maidens into his house. They saw only one meaning in it. These voters saw no reason at all for Emmanuel wanting a housekeeper. His loneliness in that large house on the mountain side had been one of his main charms. As for a secretary, if these voters were told of shorthand, they would have thought you were telling them of a voter with stumpy fingers and they would not be interested.

On top of this, it was soon being heralded from all the roof tops, which were strong enough to be stood on without suddenly letting the heralder down into the cellar, that Margaret was the daughter of that very woman from whom, years past, the Rev. Emmanuel had been saved by that firm authoritarian, the coal-owner deacon. Emmanuel's followers added one to one, made four and held it up like a sword.

Within six weeks of Margaret's admission to his house, Emmanuel was visited by a deputation who said they would sit on his doorstep and starve if he did not at once put Satan, a dark character disliked by these voters, through the back door and Margaret out at the front. The Rev. Emmanuel made no promise, said he would speak on the matter in due time, and the deputation went away to starve at home where it was warmer.

My friend Walter in the Council yard, Arthur in the warehouse, Ben building walls that leaned, and I painting large buildings at so much a mile for the County Council, were most interested in this crisis in the life of Emmanuel, and we pondered the issue with great zeal during those intervals when the various foremen, who kept our noses to it, were busy keeping somebody else's nose to it.

At Idomeneo's, on a Thursday night, we put on the sixth record of the evening. This record was perhaps the nicest piece of music of all the pieces we had bought, and Willie loved it deeply, but it did not cheer him up at all that night. In fact, as he sat there among us and scowling at the stove, it seemed to us that either his own internal pipes were as much mixed up as those of the stove, or that he was not listening at all to the record that was being played.

'It's a duet, Willie,' said Idomeneo. 'The duet from *Tosca*. The one you like, remember?'

'Oh,' and that was as much as we could get from Willie until Ben told him that if he grew to look any more miserable he would push Willie's face right into the stove, which was now blazing and hot and likely to cause pain to the face of any voter pushed against it.

'I've got cause to be miserable,' said Willie loudly. 'Nobody can stop me being miserable if I want to be.'

'No doubt. This is a free country and there is nothing as free as being miserable. It's amazing what provision this world makes for such things as that, Willie. So I suggest you leave it till later to start brooding. For half an hour you've been crouched there like a mute. Talk to us.' At a signal from Walter we all bent forward very attentively to hear what Willie might have to say.

'All right then,' said Willie. 'It's about Margaret, if you want to know. It's about her being in the Rev. Emmanuel's house. People are saying rotten, terrible things about them and these things make me mad to hear, and I'll be killing somebody if they keep on saying them.' And Willie kicked the surround of the stove with a force that sent a brilliant shoot of ashes blossoming from the top of the stove, and brought Idomeneo from the front part of his shop with the old bamboo rod at the ready.

'You're what Emmanuel would call a bad case of Ice Age, Willie,' said Arthur, in a satisfied tone that showed he was glad to see Willie getting worked up and intolerant on the subject of the bigoted and backward voter who had it in for Margaret.

'What things are they saying, Willie?' asked Walter.

'That the Rev. Emmanuel wants somebody to keep him company, somebody to play with, a young girl to play with. It makes me sick just to say it. Why can't people say the truth? Why can't they see that the Rev. Emmanuel never had a dirty thought in his head in all his life. Why can't somebody tell them that it was out of pity for Margaret that he took her into his house, out of the Terraces where she'd have been sad all the time after her mother died. He only did for her what he did for me, what he'd do for anybody who was in distress. But people are saying these things and I've got to listen. Once, today, I even found myself believing these things, and I had to go out of the foundry because it made me feel so bad. Why can't people say the truth?'

'Christ knows,' said Walter. 'We've puzzled a lot over that very point, Willie, but we haven't puzzled it out yet. Have you seen Margaret?'

'Not for a week.'

'Where's she been?'

'Busy, she said. That's what she said. Busy.'

'At what?'

'There you start, too. Your minds are filthy, just like those other people.'

'Don't say that, Willie. Our minds are all right. Most clean....'

'Sorry, Walter. But the way you said that . . . She told me a week ago she'd be busy. She said she'd be re-arranging the Reverend Emmanuel's library.'

'There you are then. She's been putting his books in order for a week. Such a man with so many theories on why man is in the clay must have thousands of books. So don't worry.'

'I wasn't worrying for myself or Margaret. We've been going together for two years, steady. But if people start thinking these things about the Rev. Emmanuel, they might do him some wrong.'

'Don't worry about him, for God's sake. Think a bit less about that man, Willie. He got you a job, but that doesn't make him a god. Or does it? Have a talk with Margaret. See what she says. If her being under the same roof as Emmanuel is going to cause trouble of any sort, tell her she'd better get another job.'

'Yes. That's it. I'll talk to Margaret. I'll be glad to have a talk with her again. Listening to all those people . . . Made me ill . . . .'

His head bent low and his finger nails scratched thoughtfully along his scalp. We watched him with interest. His head jerked up suddenly and he stared at us as if he had gone crazy.

'You're thinking those things, too,' he shouted. 'I can feel you thinking those dirty, rotten things those people have been telling me.'

'You go and jump yourself, Willie,' said Ben, without pity.

'Tell me what you're thinking,' said Willie, in the hard tone of the Government man, who used to come around asking us questions about our means when we were on the Relief.

'Nothing,' said Walter. 'We never gave it a thought.'

'Do you think . . . ?' started Willie, quiet again. 'Do you really think the Reverend Emmanuel and . . . ?'

'Willie,' said Walter, speaking very slowly and calmly, drawing his chair close to Willie's and talking practically right into Willie's ear. 'On this subject of love, friend, we don't think anything. It is not a subject we ever thought fit to study. They do not run any classes about it at the Library and Institute, so it cannot be a subject of any great value. And from what we've seen of the general way in which this love caper works out among us, we can say that many of the voters would be better off if they were gelded or put in jail so as to be well away from it.'

'Oh Christ,' said Willie.

'That is about as much as you can say.'

During the days that passed between that last interview and the next time we saw Willie we were in a very curious state of mind indeed. First, we had great sympathy with this young Willie and for Margaret, too. We had seen too many voters having their prospects of happiness rolled over as regularly as railway lines not to want to see these two young elements emerge from this trouble and carry their lives forward on a reasonably peaceful basis. On the other hand, we had a great objection to things standing still. We were grateful even to disasters if they broke people of the habit of sitting down, stroking their own bellies and not giving a damn about whether the voter sitting next to them had a belly to stroke or not. Compared with that kind of selfishness, we have always considered freezing cold and drowning water to be good and kindly items.

We had seen, in our lifetimes, the whole of the Terraces, our community, sinking into a frost-bitten stupor through such things as poverty and unemployment. We had seen the slow decay that goes on when people become frozen and stupid and hopeless. We had hated, with the rapture of loud singing, the cruel silence and the witless indifference with which the outside world had surrounded us, and sometimes, when we had been driven nearly crazy by the feeling of shame and futility that had become like underwear to us, we could have gone down on our knees and prayed like fanatics for an earthquake, a thunderbolt, a plague of frogs, anything, provided it allowed us either to die with a sense of dignity or lashed us away from the jaws of the torpor into which we were sliding.

Our kindness, the sort of kindness you feel for individuals, the sort preachers extol, the sort that can make a man spend his whole life in the feeding of pigeons to relieve some part of the vast and maddening hunger he sees around him, had mostly evaporated. We had not the means to be kind, and what feeling can you experience for individuals whose features have been mostly eaten away by a disease that afflicts the mass? We had pity for our kind and hatred for those who had led our kind into wrong and dirty paths. We were not exactly cruel, but, having felt great hurt ourselves, we watched with the eye of expert amateurs the sight of any strange, bewildering tragedy that crashed down on the shoulders of anyone not as experienced in that field as we were.

We hoped, therefore, in our hearts, that some brutal nemesis might overtake this Rev. Emmanuel, for we would examine with interest any tragedy into which the being of this man entered as an ingredient. He had bloomed fairly and for long upon soil that our slow rotting had made rich, and we saw it as no more than the justice of history that the blossom might be made to wilt and die by the ugly, strangling weeds that took their life from the self-same earth.

Even about Willie we felt that an acute purge of suffering would make of him a voter less liable to error in the future, and if there is one thing this world needs even more than efficient drains, it is voters less liable to errors than the present specimens. We could see no harm in events that might cause Willie to forget those doctrines of the Rev. Emmanuel that had caused him to have such peculiar notions concerning the ways and means of pain and evil upon this planet.

When we next saw Willie we thought straightaway that he had swallowed the purge whole. Never had we seen any element look so shaken, if you count out two voters who stood for too long beneath a rocking chimney making bets on the direction in which it was going to fall, two such voters as would probably be improved by a fall of chimney.

When we got to Idomeneo's, there he was crouched up and looking even more like a curve in one of Idomeneo's stove pipes than he had on the previous Thursday evening. There were even windy noises coming from him, and by his side stood Idomeneo, running his hands restlessly over his brown shop coat and looking very upset by all this grief that was going on in Willie.

'I think he's bad,' said Idomeneo.

'He's not ill,' said Walter. 'For all his crouching and for all those windy noises which are certainly very windy, he's not ill. The facts of life are baying at his heels like hounds.'

When my friend Walter was very moved, either he shut up tight or he worked off his feelings by coming out with a touch of poetry like the one you have just heard about the hounds. We all thought it was a good touch and we nodded our heads in appreciation of this bardic quality that sometimes came to the top in Walter. But Idomeneo, who was still not as used to the English language as we were, stared down at Willie's legs as if he expected to see a couple of dogs there.

When Willie saw us he looked at us as if we were the first other dead people he had seen since he himself had passed over, and he did not seem to like the look of us. Dead for too long, no doubt. His eyes were red. That might have been due to crying or his work, which involved a lot of bending over things at great heat.

'Speak up, Willie,' said Walter.

Willie opened his mouth wide as if to tell us all, but as he opened it, two youths with coloured scarves wrapped around their necks and funny fancy ways of talking, which made them sound as if about a foot of the scarf might be between their teeth – social workers, maybe – came in, and Willie closed his mouth, put off his stride by the sudden entry of these unfamiliar elements.

'If you want to talk,' Idomeneo told us, 'if you want to talk, go right through to my kitchen.' Idomeneo was clever at stretching out his mind towards other people's and guessing their thoughts and feelings, however dark and dumb.

We marched from the back room into the kitchen, and as we went out we could see the two youths looking very disappointed at this departure, as if they had marked us down as very mature samples of social depression and had planned to keep us under close observation for an hour or so, and use our chattering as the first chapter of a book they might write on the submerged thirty million.

We got settled down in Idomeneo's kitchen. He did not have much in the way of furniture. Only one chair we found and that looked hard and stiff, like an electric chair without the coils. Idomeneo explained this by saying that the moneylending Italian in London had told him he would have to concentrate on the business and to hell with home comforts until the business was paying and the debt cleared.

We did not know if the business was paying, but we could see most clearly that the home comforts had gone to hell or somewhere. Most of us sat on old confectionery boxes. Ben sat on two biscuit tins and rattled like a phantom every time he stirred, which was often, these tins being insecure. We got Willie a cup of tea and we made him drink it very hot, because when a man has a scalded mouth he will talk if only to keep his gums cool and, anyway, the pain keeps his mind off outside troubles.

'It's true,' said Willie, just like Elijah saying, 'It is enough.'

'What's true, boy?'

'What they say about the Rev. Emmanuel. It's worse than true.'

'Steady now, Willie. Have you seen Margaret?'

'I saw her. I saw her last night. It was she who told me these things were true.'

'She told you?'

'Last night she told me everything about it. I'm glad I drunk that tea. Feel better now. I couldn't have believed it, the way she told me, so quiet and ordinary.'

'What did she say?'

'She said that the Reverend Emmanuel loves her.'

'Like a father, no doubt,' said Walter.

'No. Like a man. You know, Walter, like a man.'

'Oh, like a man.'

'I was right,' said Ben.

'She said,' went on Willie. 'She said she loved him, loved him more than anybody else she could think of, even me. She said she was sorry for me but she couldn't help it. And then she said . . . God, I can hardly believe she said those things.'

'Tell us,' said Walter. 'Boys like us can believe anything.'

Willie gulped some more of his tea and as the stuff stung down his throat he made a comical face that made Arthur laugh. Arthur was very moved by Willie's tale and this laugh was meant to relieve the moved, excited feeling he had.

'She said she didn't feel any shame any more about such things as her body. That's what she said. Her body. If the Reverend Emmanuel wants it he can have it, because he needs something after being cheated of true love for all these years. And she told me, straight to my face, that when the Reverend Emmanuel has stood up in his pulpit next Sunday and defended his right to true love against his followers, she will be there waiting for him when he comes back up the mountain, waiting ready to give him her all.'

'Did you ever hear such bloody nonsense?' asked Ben, staring fascinated at Willie, from whom all this nonsense had come, as if Willie were some kind of newly found ape with yellow stripes.

'Shut up, Ben,' said Walter. 'This is a very interesting story, Willie. So Margaret is waiting for Emmanuel to defend his right to true love against his followers, and then, later on Sunday evening, she will give her all.'

'All,' said Willie, in a voice that was like the wind crawling through a hill gap.

'I didn't know they ran this love caper on such time table lines.'

'She'd want to do it reverently,' whispered Willie, leaving the impression in our minds that these things were not so bad when done on a Sunday, but that he would have personally led a large riot down through the Terraces if Margaret had decided to give her all and the Rev. Emmanuel to take it on a Friday or a Saturday. Willie was going nearly black with grief so we did not take him up on this point.

'Or what might just as easily happen,' said Arthur, 'is that Emmanuel might decide not to defend the right to true love at all. He might not defend anything in particular except his own health, and he might show Margaret the door just as he showed the door to the poorer voters and the sympathy he once had with them twenty years ago.'

'Who knows?' said Walter in an undecided way, and we were surprised to hear him utter a short proverb like 'Who knows', for we considered all proverbs, short or long, to be backward and a great hindrance to the voters. 'What day is it today?'

'Wednesday,' said Willie, as if the least he could do now was keep track of the calendar which was most likely the only thing that would ever stay still and regular again in his whirling, weeping world.

'This is my time of trial,' said Willie, jerking the slogan out of his mouth, mechanically, like spittle, and the sound of that slogan made us all feel that it would have been a lot better for Willie's education if that wood-merchant element had not succeeded in dragging him away from his early interest in newts and the date of the world's beginning.

'Your what,' asked Walter.

'My time of trial.'

'Boy, you know so little of life, life must be hurt to find anybody knowing so little of it. Your trial began at birth, Willie. When you got a job they were only bringing you up from the cells. They've got as far now as reading some of the charges. Wait till they start packing the jury and doping the judge, and clapping your prosecuting counsel in jail for obstructing the highway.'

'But say what you like, it's a hell of a thing.'

Ben, rattling about on his biscuit tins, said it was that, most certainly.

The next night we sat down to write a letter. A letter to the Rev. Emmanuel. At first, Ben and I objected to this business of letter-writing. The last attempt we had made at joint letter-writing had been a long message to the local Council on the subject of an increase in the burial fees at the local cemetery, an increase so steep it had scared several of the local voters right off dying, and had left them in a jammed position between life and death that was very boring to them and, no doubt, an annoyance to their neighbours.

This letter had not made a scrap of difference to the burial fees but it had made such a parting in the hair of the local Long Live the Past Brigade that they took it up and got it printed in the County newspaper as an example of fluent blasphemy and sedition, with a very warm footnote from the editor saying that the pillory should be reintroduced for such letter-writers as we were.

'Why then, Walter,' asked Ben, 'should we be writing to the Rev. Emmanuel?'

Ben asked this question because he was the only one among us who had been to jail and who stood a good chance of spending the rest of his life in the pillory if this letter should turn out to be as wild in its tone as the last one, and if that editor should manage to find a pillory, which he most certainly would, because it is well known that the attics as well as the brains of these reactionary voters are full of old-fashioned equipment which they keep oiled up and ready for action against a day when events might invite them to stretch the limbs and otherwise maim the bodies of all elements who get more than two thoughts a year.

'I am against letter-writing,' added Ben.

'We are writing this letter just in case the Rev. Emmanuel should need a little boot behind him when he stands up next Sunday to take the plunge.'

'What plunge?'

'The plunge into defending true love.'

'That stuff about true love hurts me like toothache.'

'It is toothache, only people don't know that.'

'All right then,' said Ben, and he helped us to look for a pamphlet which Arthur had bought and put away in a cupboard which, said Arthur, was full of good statements on the rights of the individual. A few of these statements, we thought, would make just the right basis for a letter of encouragement to so unsteady and vacillating a character as Emmanuel, who had probably forgotten most of what he had known about such a subject as the individual and his rights, during the years he had spent keeping his hair snowy and his mind idle.

Arthur read over some of the statements in the pamphlet, and we agreed that they were very strong and good and struck a hopeful note for the future. Then we got down to the business of writing the letter, and the actual writing was done by my friend Walter who was the neatest handwriter that ever served as storesman to the local Council.

This was the letter we wrote:

'Dear Rev. Emmanuel. As socially conscious voters we take a keen interest in the issue that has arisen over your relations with our young friend, Margaret, of whom we think highly . . . . As you are well aware, we consider those who follow your teachings to be a lot duller about the head than any sledge, and consider such dullness in these voters to be a great obstacle on the road to whatever new world might emerge from the struggles of today's reformers. We consider that these voters have never done anything in their lives more stupid than to create all this bother about our young friend, Margaret, and to try to order your personal affairs as if you were their handmaiden. They have never done anything more stupid in their lives except follow you.

'We advise you to take a strong line with them, remind them that their wooden-headed antics are a menace to common health and civilized progress alike. Remind them that the girl you once wished to marry, having been abandoned by you on the request of the chapel's leading member, a sod, as ever was, lived a life of stark, killing unhappiness and poverty that should be a poison to your conscience as long as you live. Tell them that you are going to grasp your full quota of personal happiness however much our present arrangements of living might deny that happiness to people like Mrs Radnor. And remind them with all the passion that blazed in your heart when you were young, that if it were not for the block-headed slavishness of such as they who find contentment only when they are rolling in their own collective misery, that the winning of even the meanest happiness would not be the hazardous and toilsome venture it is today for the large majority. Sharpen your anger, defiance and hatred. Sharpen them and hurl them forward until their points pierce the bodies of your listeners and pin them to the benches they sit on.

'You owe this to Mrs Radnor. You owe it also to all the sick and harassed and disappointed people whose cause on this earth you abandoned and helped to destroy when you gave away the quite good mind you were born with and exchanged it for a canister through which spoke the voices of the mighty. Speak and we shall be with you. Yours, in the sacred cause of freedom for the individual and progress for the masses.'

Then we signed our names with the happy, important feeling that men will, no doubt, have when they sign the last treaty against greed and arrogance. We read over the letter carefully. We thought it a great improvement on that last one we had written on the subject of the burial fees, in which we had referred to at least half a dozen well-known figures as bastards, and finished off a portrait of the Council's chairman with the remark that this element struck us as being no better than a bloody hypocrite who went raising burial fees for the voters in the Terraces to a point where it would be far more profitable for these voters to place themselves in the middle of the road as soon as they felt the last spasm coming on, and roll down into the river, while this chairman himself had a family vault somewhere in North Wales where the burial fees were probably cheaper than they were anywhere else in the world, outside those countries where they left the dead about the place to vanish of their own accord. This new letter contained no such rough expressions, and my friend Arthur said it sounded soft as silk. We all agreed that we did seem to be getting very mellow with the years.

Then we went out. First to post the letter, then to the back room at Idomeneo's to tell Willie that we would be coming along to Emmanuel's chapel on the following Sunday.

The chapel had not started to fill when we got there. Willie led us into the front row of the gallery just above the clock, and we were watched closely by a large voter with a watch-chain, who was some kind of guard or sidesman and he most likely thought we had come with the single idea of going home with the clock, because anybody could see that our faces were dark with the valiant loneliness of disbelief, and pursuing an interest in nothing more supernatural than a minimum living wage.

We gave back some very fierce looks to this sidesman, Ben leading us in this, Ben being out of temper with some painful cramp he had in his back as the result of sitting around on cold stones whenever the rain put a stop to bricklaying, and the hard bench of the gallery seat did not agree with the cramp any more than Ben agreed with the sidesman. The sidesman dropped his inspection.

People swarmed in from all the entrances, and pretty soon the chapel was well on the way to having a double layer of voters which would have been cosy for all except the bottom layer, so we struggled to keep an open space between us and the roof. Seeing this open space we knew that we would always be able to breathe if we wanted to keep on living, and we would be able, if the worst came to the worst, to climb out through one of the fanlights if we wanted to keep on thinking.

When Emmanuel came in he was springy with excitement, and he hopped up the pulpit steps like a black and white goat. He was excited and happy so that his happiness could almost be seen like a fire burning around him. Being a virgin and having been a lonely man, no doubt, the prospect of a maiden waiting at home to give him her all had a very inflaming effect upon him and made his emotions very strong and fierce.

For the first half-hour there was a series of short items like hymns and prayers, and we stood up and down, off and on, following the majority in this like good democratic voters. Then came the sermon and we stretched our heads tensely over the gallery to catch every word, and with such a wild look that the sidesman with the watch-chain stood up and started to keep an eye on us again.

We watched the Rev. Emmanuel closely. We noticed that he had changed since the time he came in. We noticed that he was singling out clumps of hostile faces among the voters, and staring at them. We could see the fire draining out of him. We could see it so clearly we nearly wept, and we wished that at least the draining fire would do some damage to the light blue carpet in the pulpit on which Emmanuel stood.

He leaned forward, pale, trembling, uneasy. He read a text to which we gave no need, these texts being so numerous, we understand, that most of them must be out of date. His tongue fumbled about with some tame, trite axioms that he must have uttered a thousand times before, because we could feel the tenseness of the voters all around us relaxing as if they knew that Emmanuel had already hoisted the flag of defeat and we, who had seen defeat so often and felt the sting of it on our brains, our faces and our backs, and hated it as a man would hate his own mocking ghost which he sees for ever before him, pressed our foreheads into the varnished woodwork of the gallery to flatten the sadness that swelled behind them.

'Hear, hear,' said my friend Walter in a loud voice, so suddenly that Ben and Arthur and Willie and I all jumped, but seeing that Walter was on the right track, we, too, said 'Hear, her.'

All the people craned and twisted their heads to see who was making this noise, and the sidesman with the watch-chain would no doubt have advanced upon us there and then if Ben had not been looking at him with a cruel, hungry look that promised darkness for the sidesman and a spell in the County jail for Ben.

'Hear, hear,' we all said again, enthusiastically and more loudly this time, as if we had just heard the most passionate speech of all time.

In the lull, Emmanuel rallied. He stiffened himself. The mild, placatory, undecided look went from his face and contempt grew on it like a grey plaster mask as he surveyed the congregation from one end of the building to the other. He began to speak, quietly. He spoke of the folly of those who turn aside from the truth to find a temporary respite from their pain in dumb acceptance. He spoke of those who crawl like rats from the sight of a world that grows blacker and more bitter, to the holes of seclusion and stupidity. He spoke of the Terraces and of the myriad types of anguish that had been cradled there. He told of the coalowner deacon who had waxed rich and gross upon the wretchedness of those who sat before him, who had grown to such power he had laid before a pastor of God a set of rules that stated when he should speak and when be silent. He spoke of the chapel as an oasis of delusion and servility in a wilderness of failure, want and revolt.

And with each new item in his accusing catalogue, we hailed him with 'Hear, hear'. From this corner of the building and that came the sound of some new voice taking up the refrain 'Hear, hear', to urge Emmanuel to some higher step again of scorn and revelation, and the sound of each friendly, supporting voice was a wind that blew the burning anger of the man to a deeper and more hurting red.

He was aflame now, nearly drunk with the strong, wild strangeness of the truths beneath his tongue. His eyes were bright and so open now that the flesh around them must have been in pain. His hands were upstretched above his head as if he were dragging fresh stores of anger down from heaven itself. He spoke of himself, and it was then that his passion mounted, mounted until it bulged in his blood and pressed a web of dark veins on to his face. He spoke of the years he had lived, years of waste, loneliness, longing, stupid, stupid, hurtful, terrible, a ghastly, petty tragedy, the excreted, idiot filth of the violent fraudulent rich in their campaign to make a pounded cash-till of every human life not born with their stamp upon it, a brutal, damnable oppression to be destroyed if mankind were to live. Then he spoke of Mrs Radnor and here we had beauty of speech and feeling at its most rapturous. All the old caverns of our being filled with warm, fraternal tears. He began to describe the way in which he had seen her lying dead on that bed in the Terraces.

But Emmanuel never finished what he had to say about Mrs Radnor. His body twitched violently upward in the middle of a phrase and he crashed with the loudest bang we ever heard to the blue carpet. He grew still, with one hand clutched over his hair as the audience heaved to its feet and began to gabble.

They carried him outside to a waiting car. A doctor announced from inside the car that the Rev. Emmanuel was dead. The car proceeded slowly towards his home. We, and a large number of other people, fell in behind, for there was something like a magnet in the body of this man who had dropped dead with so much life going on in his mind.

The procession made its way up the tree-lined drive on the other side of the valley. Willie walked at my side, looking tight, bulging, as if someone had tied him tight with string from head to foot. I whistled the duet from *Tosca* that Willie liked and it acted on him straightaway as if a knife had flashed up from the ground to his head cutting every inch of the twine that bound him. He started to cry worse than a baby. We pushed him to the side of the roadway and for a minute after we could hear him crying among the trees like some new kind of bird that once lived among men.

As we reached the open space in front of Emmanuel's house, we saw a curtain lift in one of the windows and behind the curtain we saw the face of Margaret staring out at us, and the face was dark, dumb and beautiful as such faces sometimes are.

Then we walked home.

'You should have known,' said Ben, 'that if he got worked up he would die.'

'Why not?' asked Walter. 'How else would you want it? How else could it be?'

We shook our heads, saying neither yes nor no, but feeling that wisdom, though sweet, is hard as the hills.

SIMEON

We all looked upon Simeon with respect. The house of Simeon stood nearer the mountain top than any other in the valley. It was surrounded by some two acres of cultivated land. It was rich land and bore for Simeon many flowers and vegetables. Skirting the house was a narrow plantation of oaks through which a stream ran to feed the river in the valley.

We all thought it must be nice to have trees as near to the house as Simeon had them, and a stream that had white water and not black water like the river we had to spend most of our time staring at down in the valley. Simeon also had four goats. He had trained them well. They were gentle, sociable animals. It was a pleasure to sit down and watch the way they watched you. Simeon, whose taste, every so often, ran to fine phrases, called these goats his spirits of contemplation.

On summer evenings, when the mountains were very quiet, Simeon would send down the young lad he kept for odd jobs to fetch us. There was myself and my friends, Colenso and Emrys, and perhaps a few other young comrades who liked sitting about the mountain singing to the evening as it came down.

We were about sixteen years old at the time. No more than sixteen. Simeon would tell us to sit somewhere in the plantation of oaks and sing. We would never know right away what it was he expected us to sing. Simeon said he did not like hymns because he had broken with the chapel ever since the time he tried to argue with some preacher that sun worship was the only form of truth. People, Simeon had said, had managed to act so daftly without sunstroke, perhaps they would improve with sunstroke. So he had broken with the chapel after this bit of reasoning, and told us not to sing him any hymns till he lost his hearing. They smelled of dead men, that was the reason he gave. He'd say, sing any song you know that's got the long notes in it, notes you can harmonize on, sad notes that make a man want to cry.

As we sang, he would sit on a small knoll, five yards from the oak nearest the house. He would listen for about five minutes; then he'd send the farm boy over to us with a shilling and the farm boy would say Simeon had told him to tell us it was wonderful the way the notes we sang seemed to move about among the trees as if they were looking for something. That did not make sense to us or to the farm boy. But the shilling did. We would take it and thank him.

We all thought Simeon led a very lonely kind of life in that big house stuck so near the top of the mountain. His wife had died a long time before. He had three daughters. Two, Elsa and Bess, lived with him, and a third, whose name no one seemed to know, had been away about five years living with her grandmother on the mother's side. This third daughter was the youngest.

The people in the valley always wondered what sort of a life it was they lived in that house on the mountain. But they never found either Simeon or the daughters in the valley, so they had to keep on guessing. They knew Elsa had a little son and Bess had one, too. They also knew that neither Elsa nor Bess was married. We used to ask our parents how it was Bess and Elsa came to have these little sons if they were not married. We knew that nobody can just start keeping little sons like you can with goats or chickens.

Our parents would say they thought it was funny, too, because they had never seen the girls knocking about with anybody on a regular basis. But most people were united in saying that the father of both children was, in all likelihood, one Walter James Mathias, a sturdy fellow who had drifted into the valley looking for work a few years before, stamped about like a stallion for a year or two on account of his being sturdy and attractive in appearance when properly washed and turned out, then vanished, and some people said he had wound up in a sanatorium, which, said those same people, was the natural winding-up place for all subjects who go stamping about like stallions without being supported by those regular meals that steady work will bring. This Walter James Mathias had been seen many times loafing around Simeon's oak plantation, so the story held water. Our imagination played tenderly with the thought of that Walter James Mathias, who had slid into the valley like a comet, kindled fires here and there, then vanished into the dark.

One night, we wandered up the mountain, all three of us who liked walking and singing together. Simeon hadn't sent the farm boy down to fetch us for a long time. We were passing by the oak plantation and I said Simeon might be sick and it would be a good idea to sit down in the plantation and give our best in the singing line without being asked. A Christian act that Simeon would no doubt like and appreciate even though he had no truck with the chapels and held pagan views about the sunstroke. Colenso Lloyd, whose voice kept putting off breaking and who stood alone, for that reason, in the soprano section of our group, said it wasn't much use singing if Simeon wouldn't be there to listen, because if Simeon wasn't there to listen, there wouldn't be any shilling at the end of it.

Emrys Price, who was one of the darkest lads I ever knew, and a very rich alto, whose father was an agitator who had been in jail, said Colenso was talking like a cross between a crab and a cap'list, because it was singing for the sake of singing that mattered and not what you got out of it. Colenso looked ashamed when he heard that and told Emrys he'd show him who was a crab.

So we went under the oaks and I stroked the white head of one of Simeon's goats, which I called Bob because it looked nearly as silly as a fellow called that who taught me in the Sunday School, taught me some very mixed sort of doctrines that didn't seem to add up to much sense, as far as my own feelings about life went, these feelings being on the wondering and sombre side. While I stroked the goat, we sang 'All thro' the night', with trimmings on it, lingering over each note till we had stuck it about a mile deep into the rich, black earth of harmonies that lay in our throats. We always made a good job of 'All thro' the night'. Perhaps it was the title that got us into the mood for making beauty. That was the way we sometimes seemed to be travelling. All through the night.

We heard someone come towards us through the trees. We thought it might be the farm boy and Colenso said it might mean we'd have more than a shilling this time for having sung without being asked. Colenso always had a weakness for gain and, for all the arguments he had with me and Emrys on this very point, was a bit obstinate in believing that man is put on earth with the idea of making something for himself.

But it was not the farm boy coming through the trees. It was Simeon himself. He had a red, round face as a rule. But it was thin and pale that night. His eyes looked sunken in and there was black skin around his eyes that looked like the puckered black blouse my mother wore when she was burying a relative. Simeon was stooped a bit, too, and walked on a stick. His lower lip was fat and stuck out, and you noticed it more with the rest of his face all sunken like that. And his stomach stuck out as well in an upward sort of way. I never saw a stomach like Simeon's. It looked built on a slant. He wore a corduroy coat and thick tweed trousers, brown as October leaves.

We stopped singing as he came and stood before us. 'You kids sing all right,' he said. We moved our legs about to show we were glad to hear that. Simeon grinned to see the way we had plenty to say with our legs but nothing with our mouths.

'Must be all right to be like you. Must be very happy to be like you boys,' he said.

We looked at each other when he said that to give each other's mind a help. We did that because we were very puzzled by what Simeon had said. I will try to explain why we found his remark so puzzling. We were not boys who went around with the notion of being depressed for the sake of being depressed, but we were wide awake enough to know that there was nothing either all right or happy about the way we were.

There was Emrys to start with. He had just gone into the pit as a butty to his uncle, and this uncle was what Emrys called a mean sort of a sod who thought the race was to the fittest and the tightest, and never gave much to Emrys in the way of pay to take home at the end of the week.

Colenso had gone into the roofing business with his father who was, by all accounts, a very keen roofer and wanted Colenso to be just like him. So Colenso spent so much of his working day going up and down ladders, he got giddy and had to spend an hour or so each evening taking it easy before starting to walk at any speed along the flat in case he pitched forward on his face or fell over on his back.

As for me, all I did was earn a few shillings Fridays and Saturdays delivering packages for a grocer. I was thin and they said I was too light for pit work. They said I was so light I'd be able to float to the surface instead of taking the cage. A manager I saw about it told me to clear off home, because if he took me on as a miner, measuring no more than about seven and a half inches around the waist, one of those red papers would surely get hold of a photograph of me in my working clothes and stick me over the front page, as proof that, owing to the coalowners and other scheming subjects of that kind, the miners have been getting steadily thinner all the way down from that first day when somebody started using coal.

I told the manager that, as far as I could see in my young way, the miners had been getting thinner in the way described until they had reached a point where they had to go to work in pairs just to convince themselves and the wage givers that there was any work going on at all. When the manager heard this, he clipped me across the ear so hard I thought I'd have to do all my listening with my nose from then on, and he shouted he hoped I'd get a bit thinner so that they could put me away for giving the place an unhealthy look. I shouted back that I probably would, and I hoped to myself that I wouldn't because I was promising myself to give him that clip back sometime.

So I delivered groceries at the week-end. The people who couldn't pay the whole bill and wanted some of the stuff on tick, always gave me twopence or threepence to make it all right with the grocer. These little gifts always made the tick all right with me, but that grocer was a funny man, and talk as I might I never seemed to make it all right with him.

He was another of those who believed man was put on earth with the idea of making something. He tried to make out that I must be in league with the people who didn't pay up. I wasn't exactly in league with these people, but I did think more of them than I did of the grocer. I never told him that, of course, being at that time very discreet in my relations with other people. I took the curses he handed out to me with as good a heart as possible, because I could always buy a few fags out of the extra shilling or so I made in tips out of the people who were on the next-week and never-never system.

But it wasn't much of a job, all the same. Some of the people I delivered to ate a lot of groceries, and their packages were so heavy some Saturdays I thought they must be keeping a camel or two in the pantry to keep their nine or ten kids company during the long winter nights. I told Colenso and Emrys often enough that, as far as I could see, subjects like us wouldn't be much worse off dead. Colenso had seen somebody dead and he didn't agree at all with what I said because, he said, it was hellish being dead. But after a couple of months traipsing like an ape up and down his father's ladders, climbing on to roofs and not knowing what to do when he got there, and falling off sometimes because he got so puzzled standing on the height and staring at the backside of his father, who was leaning over the tiles in front of him, Colenso admitted that the chap he had seen dead might have taken the thing all the wrong way, might have been a poor sort of sample of dead man and that, up against such activities as tiling, there might be something in what I said after all. Emrys, of course, didn't need much persuading to come over to my way of thinking.

Emrys' father, as I said, was a brooding kind of man and most of this brooding was done by him because the coalowners were stopping him from working when they were not having him put in jail for creating trouble on account of being stopped from working. So life had got very confused for Emrys' father, and he had wondered more than once if he might not be doing the best thing all round if he forgot the mines and the miners and got some sort of a steady job in jail. And Emrys had caught on to a lot of his old man's outlook, and always swore in his more earnest moments that the dead seemed to be on to a very good thing indeed . . . .

Now there was this Simeon whom we took to be some kind of first-line god in his nice big roomy house on the mountain, as dark and cool with trees as the beer they used to sell in the valleys, telling us it would be all right to be as we were. Colenso looked perplexed when Simeon said that and Emrys said just, 'Oh,' to show he didn't hold with what Simeon said.

'Any of you boys out of work?' asked Simeon.

I told him that I did a bit of carrying out for Hicks the grocer, and added in a softer voice that that was a slender kind of a job, and that somebody'd have to be carrying me out if Hicks spent much more time cuffing me on the ears for delivering goods without getting the bill paid. Colenso said he was working with his old man. Emrys said he didn't exactly know what he was supposed to be doing, but he spent a lot of time in the pit trying to do it. Emrys was on the point of adding to this statement a few bitter words about that uncle of his who did queer things with Emrys' pay, but Simeon cut him short by turning to me and smiling.

'You seem to be the worst off of the lot,' he told me.

I took that as a compliment and smiled back at Simeon for all I was worth. There was a lot of fierce competition in the line of being worst-off where we lived. I was pleased by the judgement Simeon had passed on me. It was a kind of field day for me to have my wretchedness picked out from the common ruck by so shrewd and well-off a man as Simeon.

'I'm pretty bad off,' I said.

'How d'you like a job with me?'

'Oh, I'd like that. I'm fed up with Hicks. I'd like a job with you, Mr Simeon. I'd like that better than anything, honest.'

'All right, then. My farm boy's gone off to the factories somewhere. There's nobody to do odd jobs about the place and run down the valley for me. You'd do all right.'

'Thank you, Mr Simeon.'

'Come up Monday morning.'

'I'll be up like a flash.'

He turned as I said that. He walked slowly through the trees towards his house. As I watched him go out of sight, the rain started to fall as it often did among those hills, and in my ears there was a lot of glad, surprised silence, and in that silence the raindrops on the thick leaves around sounded like hoof-kicks on a drum.

My companions and I began to make our way down the mountain side. Colenso and Emrys began chaffing me about the funny jobs I'd probably have to do for a queer chap like Simeon. I could see that Colenso was jealous. He was being got down by all those ladders, so I was determined to have a lot of patience with him. My father always said patience dampened the ground at your feet so that your feet trod on it without a sound, and people never heard you as you passed on your way to the grave, and you weren't bothered as much by people then as you would be if you went stamping on the hard ground like a self-important horse, drawing attention to yourself.

'Simeon's not right,' said Colenso, with a lot of darkness on his brow that made him look like a man we had often seen taking the part of a rascally foreman in cowboy films.

'What's wrong with Simeon?' I asked.

'There's nothing wrong with anybody,' put in Emrys, who'd start talking about all men being free and equal even if what you were talking about was wooden legs or tadpoles or stiff necks.

'What's wrong with Simeon, Colenso?' I asked again.

'My old man says he's a witch.'

'A witch is a woman. So how in God's name can Simeon be a witch?'

'A sorcerer, then.'

'What the hell's that when it's at home?'

'A witch.'

'A witch is a woman. You're gettin' very obstinate to argue with, Colenso.'

'Simeon's that, a witch or something.'

'How'd your old man know that? He's a tiler.'

'He talked with the preacher.'

'That preacher's had it in for Simeon ever since Simeon started saying people ought to be baptized with sunstrokes or somethin'. How did the preacher say Simeon was a witch?'

'Those goats got something to do with it,' said Colenso.

'There's nothing wrong with goats. Is there, Emrys?'

'Goats are all right,' said Emrys. 'There's nothing wrong with anybody.'

'Depends on what you do with 'em,' said Colenso, shifting away from the stony path we were walking along as he said that, and giving a very deep look as if to say that we'd spend the rest of the evening working out what he meant with this reference to goats. But I had had enough of deep looks from Hicks the grocer when he was giving me his talks on the dangers of free trade so I didn't want any more of such looks from my own friend Colenso. I took him like a dose of salts.

'Colenso,' I said, 'there's only two things you can do with goats an' Simeon does 'em. Keep 'em an' milk 'em.'

'There's other things.'

'Your old man's been hearin' of brands of goats we haven't got around here. A goat is a goat, Colenso, an' your old man can do twice as much time on the tiles as he does now an' he won't make it any different. A goat is a goat.'

'Not if you're like Simeon it isn't.'

'What can Simeon do with goats that we can't?'

'He's a bad man, that's what.'

'He looks all right to me.'

'He's a ram.' Colenso stopped and looked at me wide-eyed as he said that.

'Everybody's rams,' said Emrys dourly. 'My old man was saying there'll be nothin' but rammin' all over the place till people take their minds off it with thinkin' and readin'.'

'That's fair enough,' I said, thinking that Emrys had pretty well summed up my own view of that problem.

'But Simeon's a terrible ram,' went on Colenso. 'The biggest of all, they say. A terrible sort of ram.'

'I thought that Walter James Mathias, who was about here a spell back, was the biggest ram. People made out that he was that, anyway. How do you square that with what you say about Simeon?'

'Up against Simeon,' said Colenso, trying to make this sound as if he had just had it from the prophet's mouth, 'Walter James Mathias was no more than a lamb, busy as he might have been, no more than a lamb.'

'What's goats got to do with this, Colenso?'

'You got animals on the brain, Colenso,' said Emrys in a discontented way, as if he thought it would be better all round if Colenso now left the animals and started to concentrate on the troubles of man, of which Emrys' father always went around with a stomachful.

'You'll see,' said Colenso. 'Oh, yes, you'll see.'

I answered by starting a song that was full of high, happy notes. Simeon was good enough for me. As I sang, Colenso, who was not finished with his jealousy yet, began some tale about me having to be on my guard with Simeon and having to wear a pair of steel underpants with a padlock on them, but this tale did not even stop me singing.

As we neared our homes, I heard Emrys telling Colenso that he would do his character a lot of good and get rid of such weaknesses as the desire for gain and being jealous of his comrades if he let himself go one day and kicked one of the ladders from under his old man. That would not do much harm anyway, said Emrys, with all the earnestness in the world in his still, dark eyes because the only people in the valley who could afford to get their roofs repaired were the very people who deserved to get their beds leaked on when it rained. Emrys said the roof in his house had leaked so much he had floated, during one rainy spell, from one bedroom to another and had been rowed back by his father.

'That's daft,' said Colenso.

'You mean you think my father can't row?'

'No. That about you floating. That's daft.'

'There's as much sense in that, Colenso, as in what you were saying about Simeon and the goats.'

On the following Monday my life in the house of Simeon began. The grocer Hicks was glad to see the back of me; so glad he would have been willing to make a long speech about this if I had been willing to stand still and listen, which I was not, being very indifferent to Hicks and his whole way of speaking. He had always said there was nothing to choose between me and the slump as a reason for the grey in his hair and the cruel look in his eye, and now with me gone and the slump getting worse, he said, at least he could settle down to going mad with the sure knowledge of which evil he owed his decline to. The last shaft I got in at Hicks was that if he had had difficulty in telling me from the slump, I had the same difficulty in telling him from the cheese. We parted with the hottest words on his side and the greatest speed on mine.

My mother said she was glad to see me getting a nice, healthy open-air job up on the mountain, and she lingered for a long time over the open-air part of it as if she were looking forward to the day when I would be earning enough playing the part of a bull in light opera to get her set of fifty Biblical prints out of pawn. I thought that was a black prospect because those prints had driven my father into becoming shortsighted, and I decided to give the system a hand in keeping down my wages for the sake of my father's eyes.

I promised to get my mother a pint of stolen goat's milk because she was never too strong, and when I saw my father looking down in the mouth because I was making no promises to him, I said I'd get him a whole stolen goat. That cheered him up and he said he might still live to see the day when he'd have a coalowner in the family. That was me he meant. A man of much faith, my father. Never got him much, however.

I settled down quickly into my work with Simeon. There were odd bits of cleaning to do in the outhouses. I did some hoeing in the vegetable plots and brought vegetables into the house when they were needed. Once a day I went down into the valley on errands for Simeon. Nearly always Simeon was by my side to give me a hand with any job I didn't get the hang of straight away. And always he was smiling.

I said before Simeon had a red round face with grey hair that made his face look even redder and kinder. I could have stood and stared at Simeon's face and enjoyed it. There was so very few faces like his down in the valley. The redness had usually gone when they left the shawl, and the kindness was usually eaten away slowly and painfully during the years they spent imploring somebody to take them back into the shawl, lull them to sleep in it or smother them in it, no great matter which. Looking at Simeon and seeing the way he smiled at me, I used to laugh inside myself when I thought of what that thick-headed Colenso had said about Simeon being a bad man.

There never was a cooler place on earth than the big flagged kitchen where Simeon and I would sit in the evenings. The whole house was quiet and that big, cool kitchen was the quietest part of it. It was as if, at one time, it might have been full of sound, and someone had caught up all the scraps of sound in his hand and tossed them to the last tiniest scrap out of the window. There I would sit with Simeon waiting for the dark. Colenso and Emrys would hang about some nights, but Simeon told me he didn't want them inside. So I kept them out, and Colenso took that as a reason for cooking up some new tales about Simeon that were sillier than ever. It was like Emrys said. That boy, Colenso, had animals on the brain.

Simeon seemed to like having me sit opposite him on the broad uncovered table in the kitchen. That table had the thickest legs I had ever seen, even including my Aunt Polly, who had got a job in a cake shop and had eaten her way back on to the Insurance. Simeon liked looking at me. As I've said, there was nothing in me that would ever want to make people look twice unless they were testing their eyes, or unless I had just stolen something from them and they were identifying me with a view to putting me in jail. He probably liked looking at me because I was thin-thin, maybe, in some new and wonderful way.

I had a lot of hair on my head that had a thick, gentle, shiny wave in it that I owed to years of brushing that had worn the bristles clean off a pair of brushes my father had had given him by the pigeon fanciers when my father had lost his first and last pair of birds in a race. His birds had taken so long to complete the course my old man had changed his dwelling twice before the birds tried to find the house they had departed from. Why the pigeon fanciers should have given my father a pair of hair brushes for such a bad start in the fancying business, I never could discover. Probably as a warning to him to keep as far away in future from the fancying business as he could. Anyway, the brushes had given me a wave in my hair that sometimes took people's mind off how thin I was, so they had served a purpose. . . .

Some evenings, Simeon got me to sing for him. I never knew a man like Simeon for wanting to hear the same song over and over again. I thought that perhaps it was only this same song that fitted his particular shape of ear. He taught me a little song he said was Spanish with English words fitted on not to make it too complicated for me. A love song, about two doves on a roof, waiting for a third dove that would never come back to them because it was dead on another roof, not a song's distance away. A sad song, especially when I had sung it over so often I started to feel I might be the one who had put that third dove to rest on the other roof.

I did a lot of thinking about those doves. I thought once they may have been relations of those pigeons of my father, coming back to get some satisfaction from the waves in my hair that had been made by the brushes my father had got in return for them. It was a sad song. The doves cried at the end of it, and during that bit of the song I went up into a kind of thin head voice that Simeon liked very much. I sang it so often I felt like a gramophone. When I got to the end of it, a little bit of the redness always went out of Simeon's face, and he would stare past me through the window.

One night, when he was staring like that, he twisted his face up suddenly as if he had put his teeth on a slice of lemon, and slapped both his hands down on the table-boards that were still dark and damp after the cleaning I had given them.

'God, Ben,' he said. 'It's a hell of a thing sometimes, this living.'

I stuck my tongue against my teeth and muttered that I supposed it was, this tongue sticking and muttering being part of my usual method when I was a bit puzzled about what I ought to say to somebody. I got part of the flavour of what Simeon had just said, but I did not get the whole sense of it.

Then, other nights, he would say that something would have to be done about my brain. He'd stand over me when he said that with a glimmer in his eyes that a man wears when he is on the point of getting really busy, as if he were going to start dragging my brain through my ears, raw and red like cow liver, and polish off with his sleeve all the mud he'd find on it, a lot of mud, no doubt. But all he'd do, after all this standing and glimmering, was read to me. Poetry. Simeon was strong on a man called Shelley. It was stuff as deep as any I'd ever heard. It had a fine beat, the way Simeon said it, like the shadow of a song that would be bigger than any other kind of song, if you could find the right music for it.

'You understand that?' Simeon would ask. 'That clear, Ben?'

'No.'

'One day you'll understand. Light grows, boy. Hellish funny, but it does, in all of us. You'll understand one day.'

'S'pose I will.'

So the days went by. I never saw much in the first weeks of Elsa and Bess, the daughters of Simeon. He seemed to keep them stowed away in some other part of the house. I thought that if Simeon did not like these daughters, he was very lucky to have a big enough house to be able to stow them away in some part of it where he didn't travel much. Most of the houses I knew, down in the valley, were so small you wouldn't have place to hide a mouse you didn't like, let alone big articles like daughters.

Once in a while I heard these daughters talking through the green, tall door that separated the kitchen from the passageway that led upstairs. I had been told that they had a child apiece, but I never heard the cry of a child more than once.

One night, when I was climbing up to the box-room that Simeon had given me to sleep in, I saw a door open on the landing and a girl's face pop out. It was very sudden, the way her face popped out, and gave me a stir. She stared at me for a few seconds. Her eyes were big. Her lips hung apart and were wet. Then the door slammed shut and when I got into my box-room I lay awake for a long time thinking of that.

Beyond my window was the oak plantation where I used to sing with my friends, Colenso and Emrys. I wondered what those two boys would have said to a face staring at them from a landing door and slamming the door shut. Colenso most probably would have been nimble-witted enough to get in a couple of remarks about the hard times he had on his father's ladders. Emrys would have said 'Jesus', and left it at that. Being much more like Emrys than I was like Colenso, that is what I did. I said, 'Jesus,' in a soft voice and closed my eyes to sleep, and the last thought before the sleep took me was that my brain must have been built on the same lines as the rest of my body. Many inches too thin for the kind of all weather work we have to do on this earth.

The next night I went up to my bed pretty early. It was autumn. Simeon had cut down a few trees. We were sawing and cutting them into logs. The work was heavy and made me tired. The doctor who used to come around examining us when I was at school used to say I was so underfed it was a wonder that my mouth hadn't closed up through lack of practice. The doctor would have been very surprised to see me spending a whole day cutting logs for Simeon, but his surprise would never have made his whole body ache like mine ached after all that wood-cutting. I kept at it and never let on to Simeon that if he took a chop at me with his axe in mistake for a log, I was too far gone to feel it. I could feel myself filling up with tiredness as a bucket under a tap fills with water. When it started to overflow at the top, I made my way to bed. I had a funny feeling that I was dead and the whole world was aching.

I took a book to bed with me. I always did that when I remembered because I had once heard Emrys' father saying that if men made a habit of never sleeping with anything but books, there'd be a lot more sleep and a lot less trouble in the world. This book I had was a cowboy tale with paper covers. The action of it kept moving all the time. There was some fresh character coming in on every page wanting to kill one of the old characters, and generally managing to. It was a hard book to keep abreast of, on account of this constant thinning out among all the old characters who had lived two pages or more.

You could almost feel the dead weight of bodies in the pages you'd just read, and this made the book very heavy to hold. So I put it down and lay on the pillow, thinking about the light that came in through the window about people and money and muscles. I thought about those things because there was an ache in my muscles; I wanted some money and I was starting to be puzzled by people.

I heard Simeon come up the stairs. His bedroom was further along the landing than mine. I waited to hear his steps pass my door. They did not pass. He turned into one of the other bedrooms. One of the girls' bedrooms, I supposed. Girls or women. I didn't know the difference.

I heard voices. Simeon's and a woman's. Simeon's voice seemed soft and wheedling. The woman was crying. Simeon's voice grew louder. Then I heard him shout:

'God damn, I'm your father, aren't I?'

And that set the woman screaming. Screaming does quaint things to me, makes me go cold. That screaming froze me. It was very loud. My blood is too thin. Can't stand screaming at any price. Another bedroom door opened. Then there was more noise than I could cope with. Simeon shouting away as if he wanted to show how easy it was to break all one's blood vessels at once, and I bent my ear forward to hear the popping of those vessels, two women screaming and there were hard, rapid slaps like hands coming down on flesh. Then kids screaming. Two kids, wailing on different keys and coming together on one key when they wanted to get deafening. Then some more rushing of feet and the kids' voices grew nearer, as if someone had dragged them on to the landing. Then a woman's voice, tearing out on a tone that made all the rest sound like silence, that struck me like being what it would feel like if you were dropped from the sky on a night of storm and landed on the sharp end of a weathercock.

'See yourself there, you pig! See yourself there, you pig! See yourself there, you pig!' That is what that woman's voice was saying, and she sounded as if she would have kept on saying it, but a hand came down over the woman's mouth, and I could hear a moaning muffle of her voice coming through the hand that was clamped over her face. Then doors shut and there was silence.

I threw the bedclothes from me, the silence seemed so thick. I heard Simeon pass across the landing to his bedroom. I picked up the cowboy tale at a page where forty or so people belonging to different tribes or families, who were working up a feud, were shooting at each other across a public square. Something, I thought, like Simeon's landing on a full night.

There was a knock on my door. I made up my mind as soon as I heard that knock that if it was anybody wanting to crawl under my bed to have a second round of screaming, I'd leave Simeon in the morning, first thing, and go back to the groceries if the grocer would have me, and not open fire on me across the public square like those subjects in the cowboy tale who kept going on the old feud basis. I couldn't stand screaming. My blood's too thin, as I said. But it was Simeon. He stuck his head around the door and asked if he could come in. That surprised me. I didn't think the fellow who gave you pay had to ask whether he could come into your bedroom. He could have come in, taken the bed and left me standing against the wall, and I would not have seen anything very wrong in that. There had been so many slaves in my family we got more pliable from father to son.

There was still enough daylight for me to see Simeon plainly. There was that glimmer in his eye. I thought there was more poetry coming, and I only hoped Simeon would make it some very easy stuff, because I was tired and a bit frightened with all the shouting I had heard. But he didn't have any book with him so it couldn't be poetry.

He sat down on the edge of the bed. He looked hard at me. I lifted up the collar of my pyjama coat which had fallen over my shoulder.

Simeon stretched out his arm and pulled the collar down to where it had been before. He pulled my arm from beneath the bedclothes, and I thought that if he was measuring me for a new suit of pyjamas he had chosen a funny time of day for it. His breath was heavy and his whole body was warm as a burning coke. I hated hot bodies. Mine was always cold.

I watched Simeon like a rabbit a weasel. I chuckled once, like an idiot, just to have something to do. Simeon chuckled back. He sounded like an idiot, too. Too many idiots in one small box-room was my way of looking at it. He edged into the bed and I thought that my mother had boiled cabbage on slower fires than the fires that were burning in Simeon. He was so hot. I was so cold. It was like mustard and ice-cream mixed. It made you sick. He put one hand on each of my shoulders, and then took his hands away to see the width of my shoulders.

'Thin,' he said softly. 'So thin. They starve the body. Then the brain. The wanton, wicked waste. And you're so bright, too, Ben. You should never be like this.'

He ran his hands over my bare chest. It was bare because my mother had taken the buttons off my pyjamas to keep my father's trousers up at a time when the old man was having all the trouble in the world keeping himself up. Simeon's thick, coarse fingernails tickled me. If he had been paying me ten shillings a week as odd-job boy, and not five, he would still have been tickling me. I am very sensitive to this tickling. As with screaming, I don't like it. I started to screech with laughter. He shushed me quiet.

'Oh, don't do that, Mr Simeon,' I gasped. 'For Chris' sake, don't do that. I'm ticklish.'

He did it again. Without meaning any offence, but only wanting to show Simeon I never bargained on being tickled to death after a hard day's work on the logs, I raised up my legs and kicked Simeon on to the floor. There was anger in his eyes for a second, but the anger went away sharply, as if it were a fly quick to answer the flick of a finger, but he laughed back at me when he saw that I making a great effort to do some laughing. He grew serious and, still sitting on the floor, he pointed his finger at me and said, very solemnly:

'Lonely, Ben. That's what I am, boy. I'm lonely and I'm trapped. There's no way I can turn. Anybody ever hate you, Ben, like they hate me?' He jerked his finger towards the girls' bedroom. 'See that nobody ever does. It's a hell of a nasty, messy feeling it gives you.'

I nodded with vigour, without understanding. He stood up and opened the door.

'Just like a trap,' he said. 'There's a path. You walk along it. Good. Path ends. Can't walk. Hell of a feeling. Ben. Got to find another path.'

I nodded again. Simeon was getting worse than the man Shelley for being deep. But the way I nodded must have been pretty bright, because Simeon looked pleased, even though his talk made him out to be stuck in the bend of a drain-pipe.

'You like goats, Ben?'

'Oh, they're all right.'

'Could you love goats?'

'What you want to love a goat for?'

'What you want to love anything for?'

'I don't know, Mr Simeon. I'm pretty young.'

'Goats are good. If goats could talk and answer to your love, a man wouldn't have to worry his soul.'

With that, he walked out and closed the door, leaving me with a lot of thinking going on in my head that stopped me sleeping.

The next day, Simeon went off on his own for a walk on the mountain. He told me to spend my time putting some black paint on the kitchen range. I dawdled over this job, sitting on my haunches and staring at the range for five minutes or so, between the strokes of the brush. The brush was a good new one and the paint was thick and syrupy, and I got a lot of pleasure fooling about with it. In the middle of one of my staring spells, the tall, green door that led to the stairs was thrown open. It opened so suddenly I lost my balance and I fell on my back.

A woman came in. She took a good look at me. She didn't seem much put out by the fact that I was on my back. Probably thought from the general look of me I spent most of my time like that, on my back, with a paint brush in my hand. I struggled up on to my feet as fast as I could and said hullo to this woman. She was a woman with a dark, heavy, miserable face. She looked like something that had been kept in the dark for a long time.

'Where is he?' she asked.

'Who?'

'My father.'

'Out. On the mountain.'

'Where's he gone?'

'Didn't say. For a walk, I think.'

The woman vanished. I heard her calling from the foot of the stairs.

'Come on down, Elsa. He's out for a spell.'

The two women, Bess and Elsa, came into the kitchen. Elsa looked a bit younger and prettier than Bess, but she had the same kind of kept-in-the-dark look, too. They both walked slowly about the kitchen, staring hard through the windows once in a while as if they were afraid of being caught there. They paid no more attention to me than if I had been a shade around the light.

'It's nice to get into this part of the house again for a change,' said Bess.

'It's nice and cool,' said Elsa.

'I'll get the kids down,' said Bess, and went upstairs.

Elsa sat down beside me and started to laugh right into my face, and rubbed against me. I thought at first she was a bit funny in the head, because there was a girl I had seen in the valley who did such things as that on a big scale, and she had the name for being funny in her ways. But I saw after that this Elsa did those things only because she hadn't had the chance to do them for a long time. There couldn't have been any other reason for her to do all this laughing and rubbing against a thin, young subject like myself.

Bess brought down the children. They were both boys. One would have been about four. The other three. They were not like the kids I had seen down in the valley. They were quiet and still in everything they did. The kids in the valley might have been a bit underweight on account of the many troubles that came upon their parents, but they were always ready to make a noise at any time of day, sometimes in the night as well. These two kids were like Simeon to look at, terribly like Simeon, and although they were kids their faces looked old, especially about the eyes, like Simeon. It was funny to see them. You expected to hear them start talking in deep voices, about wages or gardens or pigeons, like men of forty, and then they would babble something that made you realize they were no more than kids after all, could barely talk. As soon as they got into the kitchen, they walked over to the corner nearest to the door, sat down near each other and played with the long fringe of the mat on which they sat, as silent as if they were dead nearly.

'What have you got here to eat?' asked Bess, as soon as the two kids had settled down on that mat.

'Potatoes,' I said. 'A dish of cold potatoes.'

'Let's have some of those then.'

I fetched the potatoes out of the pantry. Elsa made a pot of tea. Bess cut up some bread. We sat around the table and ate and drank. They both stared at me right through the meal, which made me feel the potatoes against my lips colder than they really were. They looked at me as if I was something strange, as if I was one of those talking goats that Simeon had told me in the box-room he wouldn't mind having.

'What did he bring you here for?' asked Bess.

'To help him with the work,' I said.

'He needs no help. He's already done a lot more than he should have done without any help. The best thing you can do, boy, is go away from here.'

I was on the point of explaining that this job with Simeon was a much softer berth than the one I had had in the grocery business and, anyway, there was a great scarcity of jobs in the world at this period for ordinary subjects like myself, but there was a scowl on the face of the woman Bess that seemed to say she wasn't much interested in the state of the world or in the reason I might have for wanting to hang around the house of Simeon. In any case, as soon as she had eaten three potatoes and gulped one cup of tea she left the kitchen and walked quickly down into the garden.

'What's the matter with her?' I asked Elsa.

'She doesn't like my father.'

'Why?'

'I don't like him either.'

'Why?' Asking all these questions, I began to feel like one of those Government men who go around inquiring about people's means, and I didn't like feeling like that, so I decided to drop this questioning. Elsa shrugged her shoulders and I had the horse sense to realize that there was not much more that she could have done.

'Let me help you with the painting,' she said, as if painting were some sort of game, which is what it was the way I did it.

I gave her the brush, standing over her like a foreman and remembering what my father had said about having a coalowner in the family yet. Elsa started slapping the paint on as fast as it could go. She laughed as the thickness of the paint made the brush drag slowly over the smooth surface of the iron. I sat down near her, watching and wondering, in a mixed-up sort of way, what kind of life she must have had to let her laugh even at such things as painting grates, which didn't strike me as being very bright.

'You're thin,' she said suddenly, slewing around towards me.

'Never eat much,' I said, putting a lot of drama in my voice because I thought this weakness ought to be made use of.

'Oh,' she said, pityingly, and threw her arms around my neck, and I got some of the black varnish from her fingers on to my flesh. She kissed me hard on the lips to crown her pity. So hard it sickened me a bit because her teeth hurt my lips. It seemed to me that being thin, while it gave you a lowly status with finicky subjects like pit managers, was a sure way to be cuddled and made much of by everybody else, from Simeon downwards.

She fetched over one of the kids. The younger one. Its companion made no comment on being left alone. He kept playing with his mat fringe, as if somebody had peeled the world clean of everything but that. Elsa brought the kid to her knee, near me.

'Say "Hullo" to Ben,' she said. I had told her my name was Ben.

The kid said nothing, but turned his face in to his mother's breast and made a soft noise that wasn't talking or crying.

'Shy,' said Elsa, and I said kids were like that as a rule, and she nodded seriously when she heard that, as if there wasn't much Ben didn't know about kids.

'Who's he like?' she asked me eagerly.

'Couldn't say off hand.'

'Is he like me?' she asked.

'No.' I felt her face fall as I said that and was sorry I hadn't said yes, because I'm a believer in saying things that make people happy.

'Who's he like then, if he isn't like me?'

I took a long, hard look at the kid, even twisted my head about in a very busy way to get in a view from all angles.

'Simeon,' I said. 'He's the spittin' image of Simeon.'

Her head banged down on my shoulder sharp as a knife. I felt her crying torrents and I had her tears on my neck, and I thought that between her tears and the varnish, my neck would be in a rare mess by the time we finished with each other. I never bothered to wonder why she was crying, because the force of her head falling on my shoulder had knocked the wind out of me. There was not much to knock out, but I found it hard to get along without that little.

Elsa didn't cry for long. She wasn't like my mother who seemed to have her tear tank fitted in from the feet up, and never ran dry for many hours after she got started, always having had a lot of topics to practise her crying on.

'Oh, no need to cry,' I said, and Elsa looked up at me as if I had let her into a secret, and she stopped crying.

She wiped her eyes and sent the kid back to his corner. She made me talk about myself, and I told her all about me and Emrys and Colenso, and the work we did and the way we used to loaf about in the evenings. She didn't seem too interested in these themes and she cut me short as I was in the middle of a careful explanation of why Emrys' father was always running into trouble and jail and so on.

She asked what girls I knew and what I did to them. I didn't know any girls, having had a lot of other things to think of ever since I could remember, and I said so. She didn't believe me and almost pushed me off my chair with her disbelief, the way girls do, giving the idea that she was playful up to a point, but showing at the same time that she would be prepared to put the chair around my head if I continued to put her off with these denials.

So I told her the tale about the Sunday School picnic where Emrys found himself landed, after the eating had finished, with the girl who had won the scripture-recitation contest, and who had been driven so mad with such a load of scripture she was ripe for anything, even Emrys. I told this tale with myself in the place of Emrys, because I could see that no second-hand stuff would please this Elsa. I felt no qualms about that being a lie, because I had always thought that Emrys had made it all up out of his head, anyway.

'Tell me more,' she said. That stumped me. I didn't know any more true-life stories and I thought that Elsa, for a grown woman, didn't seem to know much more about these things than I did.

'Tell me more, Ben.'

'I don't know any more.'

She pushed me again, unbelievingly. She pushed me so hard I played for a minute with the idea of retelling the tale of the Sunday School picnic, with two scripture-reciting champions this time instead of one, but even so it would have meant covering too much of the same ground again, and a man gets sick of scripture-reciters even when he's only lying about them.

'Honest,' I said. 'I don't know any more. I'm very ignorant.'

I saw her hands moving towards me again, so I raised my hands in a peace gesture and moved my chair back to give my brain a bit more room to spring about. I told her a few of the stories, silly dirty stories, about married men and women and things like that, that I had heard chaps telling by the hour, in the little draughts room in the Free Library where somebody had mislaid the draughts years before so that the boys could really get going with their story telling.

Elsa laughed her head off with each fresh story I told, and that made me feel good and made me picture myself at a later age as a kind of king in the little draughts room, providing, of course, that I could get hold of a few fresh tales to ginger up the stock of old, stale ones I was telling Elsa. When I had pumped myself dry of dirt, she leaned back in her chair, tears of laughter in her eyes.

'How old are you, Ben?'

'Sixteen last.'

'Same age as Eleanor.'

'Who's Eleanor?'

'My sister.'

'Where's she?'

'She's not here.'

'How's that?'

'Bess sent her away.'

'Why's that?'

'Bess wanted to get Eleanor out of the old man's way.'

'What's wrong with the old man's way?'

'Oh, just the old man's way.'

'Oh.'

I was beginning to think there must be something wrong with Simeon to explain the way Bess and Elsa talked about him, but I couldn't see it. He was all right to me. I thought again that Bess and Elsa might be a bit touched. But after the way Simeon had carried on with me that night in the box-room, tickling my chest with his fingers and saying he was trapped and wanting goats to talk and all that, I thought Simeon might be a bit touched as well.

But I drew back at the thought, because with all the poor grub I had had to eat in my time, and hanging about for years on end with a subject like Emrys, whose father seemed to be attached to the jail door with a piece of elastic string, it was maybe I who was touched and all these other people who were all right. But all the same, there was some funny things being said in that house, and there was a funny look about those kids. You didn't have to be fat or rich to notice there was a funny look about those kids.

The night was beginning to fall. I asked Elsa if she'd want some more tea. She said yes, without turning her head from the fire. Ever since she had mentioned the girl Eleanor, she had been gazing into the fire, quietly and thoughtfully.

I walked to the tap, which was beneath the window that looked out on the garden. Right down at the bottom of the garden, beneath the tall, brick wall that separated the garden from the rough hillside, the woman Bess was on her knees in the soft, black soil, her hands clasped together and her shoulders heaving with big sobs that looked so painful they hurt me to see them, and I felt so hurt and pitying as I stood there watching her it made my ears sharp, and I thought I could hear the plain, distant rattle of her sobs even from where I stood inside the house, with the water from the tap pelting hard into the kettle in my hand.

Bess was kneeling among a plot of cabbages. I looked at those cabbages. It was not as good a crop of cabbages as they might have been. The summer had been tricky and false that year. But I couldn't see that a woman needed to cry over cabbages because they happened to be a bit backward. I shut off the tap and walked quickly with it to the fire, and said nothing to Elsa of what I had seen at the bottom of the garden.

Before the kettle had even started to sing, in walked Simeon. He was swinging his walking stick and smiling all over his face, which was red and broad with all the mountain air he had been breathing in. To me he looked so healthy it seemed he couldn't have left any unbreathed air on the mountain. As soon as he saw Elsa and the two children behind the door, the smile left his face as if his swinging stick had smashed it off.

'Who brought these down?' he asked, starting on a quiet tone.

'We did,' said Elsa, trying to stand up to him but looking so frightened I thought she'd faint.

'Get the bloody things out of my sight,' he said, roaring now, and banged on the table with the full length of his stick, and roaring a bit more when he found he had caught his fingers between his stick and the table. He stiffened suddenly, as if the thought that must have struck him was hard and cold and sharp, like an icicle.

'Where's that Bess?' he asked, very quietly now, as if he were as frightened as Elsa herself. She just stood there dumb, putting her whole weight on a chair, and Simeon turned to me for an answer. I jerked my finger towards the garden. He bounded to the window. He leaned over the sink, his body twitching a little as if he had a kind of hiccup in his throat. He put one hand on the handle of the tap, turned the water on and then turned it off again in an instant, as if he had to be doing something to stop him punching his hand through the window. Then, still bounding, he crossed the kitchen, made his way, running with all his strength, down the garden path.

I watched him from the window, screwing myself up to keep my eyes from shutting, afraid to see what Simeon might do, angry like that. From behind, Elsa's voice, gone small and thin, was asking me all the time what Simeon was doing. But her voice sounded like something in my own stomach, and not like a voice at all, so I paid no attention to her.

Bess looked up when Simeon was about a yard away from her. Her face went very white. I could see how very white it became, because of all the black earth and dark green cabbage leaves around it, framing it. She gave a little scream, like a short word without any letters in it. Simeon's stick came down on her shoulders, and I heard the hard grunt of wind from his mouth as his arm fell. The blow knocked Bess forward and her mouth landed full on the earth. He bawled on her to get up. She got up so slowly, I thought I was watching something die. Her face was savage. She rubbed from her mouth the bits of black earth that had stuck there when she fell. Simeon followed her up the garden path.

I dodged out of the kitchen and hid behind the house, to be out of Simeon's way. I was still near enough to the kitchen door to hear what was said and done plainly enough.

As soon as Simeon got back into the kitchen, he told Elsa to take herself and the children upstairs.

'And keep them out of my way,' he said. 'I go sick at the sight of them. You understand that? Sick.'

Elsa and the children went upstairs. When Bess started to go through the door after them, Simeon drew her back.

'And if I catch you down in that garden again,' he said, 'it'll be worse than the stick you'll get.'

'You can't hurt me any more,' said Bess, in a voice that was like the greyish, gravelly earth I stood on.

'Don't be too sure of that,' said Simeon.

'You're a bloody devil.'

'That's part of it.'

'Somebody'll kill you, maybe.'

'Who?'

'Somebody.'

'You?'

'I've got the baby to think of.'

'Keep on thinking of it and keep your mind off me.'

'You've made a pretty mess of us all with your bloody lust.'

'A man's got to love somebody. When he runs short of people to love, he mostly makes a mess. That's all.'

'Only a devil could stand there and grin about it. But there's one thing I'm thankful for, one thing that makes me happy even in this hell on earth you've given us here. My baby and Elsa's are boys. You'll never want them, will you? You'll never go mad after their bodies and hearts, will you? You'll never destroy the things they'll love, will you? They'll be men when they grow up and you'll be old and weak then. And sometimes I hope they'll be mad as you are when they grow, mad and cruel, so you'll be afraid of them like we're afraid of you. And you wanted Eleanor, too, didn't you? But you didn't have her. I sent her away. I'd have rather seen her dead than here with us, like we are. Rather seen her dead. But she's safe. I sent her away. I saw to that, didn't I? I was a bit cleverer than you there, wasn't I . . . ? What are you laughing at?'

'I'm laughing at you.'

'Why are you laughing at me?'

'Because Eleanor is coming back.'

'Coming back?'

'Her aunt's dead. They're sending Eleanor back to me, back to her home with me where she belongs.'

'Coming back, you say? Coming back here?'

'This week.'

'God help her.' I heard Bess start crying.

'No hope of that. That makes you look sad, doesn't it? Pity we got to tie all these knots in one another, but there you are. And let me warn you. When Eleanor comes, I don't want you or Elsa to speak a word to her. Not a word. If you do, you'll be very sorry.'

Then there was silence in the kitchen. I slipped across the garden towards the oak plantation where I thought I'd feel more at ease, because trees never seemed to cause as much trouble to one another as men and women.

When night fell altogether, I made my way back to the house. I found Simeon in the kitchen throwing coal on to the fire and then piling logs into the deep recess at the back of the chimney. He seemed to be preparing for a long, warm night. He looked cheerful and was humming that song about the doves in a high key, and I could not help feeling that Simeon must a rare sort of man to be able to lay about Bess with his stick one minute, and then sing a very tender song like that dove song the next.

'Get that barrel out of the pantry, Benny,' he said.

I got the barrel. It was not a big barrel, but full to the brim and heavy for me. I put it down on the table with a bang.

'Get two glasses, Ben.'

I fetched the glasses while Simeon opened the barrel. He filled the glasses and put his down on the fire hob.

'No need to light the lamp, Benny. This fire'll be giving more light than the sun soon. Wonderful things, flames.'

'Yes, Mr Simeon.'

'Drink that beer.'

'Don't like it.'

'Drink it.'

'Why?'

'Build you up. You're too thin. You got to have thick walls of strength inside of you, thick like castle walls, if you want to get any happiness out of living. Life's got sharp eyes, boy, and a nasty heart. If you're weak, whang, you get its foot right in your neck. Do you want life's foot in your neck, Benny?'

'No fear.'

'Drink then, boy, and be damned to the nonconformists and the conformists. Let's drink to Venus.'

I thought Venus was a brand of mineral water they sold up and down the valley. I drank to it and winced at the nastiness of the stuff I drank. Simeon opened his legs out wide on the fender and grinned into the mounting fire. He emptied his glasses quickly, and I was glad of that because I was kept so busy refilling I had no time to drink myself. The stuff gave me the willies. I didn't like the taste of it and, anyway, I had heard Emrys' father talking about it so often as standing next to rent, faith and charity as a chain on the leg of the nearly legless people.

After the seventh glass, Simeon wanted me to sing. I asked him what, knowing what the answer would be, but anxious to pass the time on with these questions.

'The doves, Benny. I don't want to hear about anything but the doves.'

'I'm wearing the wings off those doves, seems to me.'

'Don't answer me back, boy. If I want to hear a song about doves, you'll sing me a song about doves, and no lip.'

'That beer gave me the hiccups a bit.'

'The song won't suffer for a belch or two.'

Thinking that if the song would not suffer, I would, I started and hiccupped with concentrated force in the middle of one or two notes which must have given Simeon the notion that I had grown to dislike these doves very much, and was now trying to blow them on to a roof in some other town. But I got through it, and when I was finished Simeon stroked my hair in a tender way, and there were tears in his eyes nearly as big as my head if you took the hair off.

I felt like stroking his tears just to finish things off, but Simeon might have taken that the wrong way, and I had seen enough already of how Simeon had performed with that walking stick not to want to have him taking things the wrong way when he was alone with me. Then he said he felt like reciting, and I said that would be a nice change for the both of us.

He half stood up to do this reciting, in a crouching attitude that reminded me of wrestlers, and I thought the poem to be recited might be about wrestlers and I looked forward to it. But he recited a poem about a man who drank a phial or something and found he kept very young all the time as a result of this drinking, and managed to live about five hundred years and to love people in all sorts of ways during that span.

'Lucky sod,' said Simeon when he had finished the poem.

'What did he drink, this fellow?'

'Don't know, Benny. Something out of a phial, it says in the piece.'

'Does anybody know?'

'No. Not a soul. If anybody did know, I would, and I'd drink it.'

'You want to live five hundred years?'

'Nothing I'd like better.'

''S a long time, seems to me.'

'Not if you got passion.'

'P'raps it was beer the bloke drunk.'

'No. Not beer. Beer's good for about five minutes, not five hundred years.'

'My old man's only about forty an' he says he's sick of it already.'

'Sick of what, Benny?'

'Livin', I suppose. He didn't say in particular what he was sick of, but I suppose it was livin' he meant, 'cause that's all the old man does is live. He doesn't get much pleasure, the old man.'

'Your old man should never have been born.'

'Hadn't looked at it that way.'

'Tell your old man he should never have been born.'

'I'll tell him, Mr Simeon, but it's a bit late.'

'He'll know better in the future.'

'I'll tell him. He was only sayin' the last time I saw him, that what people need is more advice.'

Then Simeon drank for a spell in silence, and tears came down his cheeks as more crowded into his eyes.

'One day,' he said, 'I'm going to write a poem.'

'That's good,' I said, thinking that that kind of encouraging talk should stop any man from crying.

'A long poem.'

'What about, Mr Simeon?'

'Love.'

'That's very popular,' I said, with my mind full of doves.

'My love.'

'Which one?' I asked, thinking that men got fresh loves like they got suits, every so often. Simeon bent over and caught me a sudden, stinging blow over the ear.

'Don't joke with me, you wormy little sod,' he shouted.

'I wasn't jokin'.'

'My love. What a love that was. My wife, Benny. Whatever men have said about beauty, you could have said about her. And kindness, too. Christ, her kindness. A word from her and you felt as though you had a world in each pocket, and half the stars of heaven where your heart should be. She died. That was the end of it, boy. She died.'

'People do.'

'What you say?'

'People do. Very common around where I live.'

'Look how funny it is, Benny.' Simeon's voice kept dropping into a low drool, and I had to go close to him to hear what he was saying. 'Look how funny, boy. When she died, I said I'll keep on loving her. Not only the memory of her. That's daft and silly as a way of loving. No guts in it or beauty or sense. I said I'd love all the things she'd ever seen, touched, made. Dresses, curtains . . . and then I said even the kids. God, yes. Even the kids. She made them, didn't she? That was a cruel thing for me to do, Benny, a hell of a rotten, cruel thing to do, and sometimes when I think of it I could scream and tear my heart out and sink my teeth into it to punish myself for all the pain I've been causing, just for the sake of keeping on loving when death came along and said I'd have to get along without loving. I should have listened to what death said, Benny. I should have listened. I know now. Oh, Christ Jesus, yes, I know now. Death knows about these things because death takes, and look at all the wise men it's taken in its time, and it must have taken their wisdom, too, and made it its own. But I didn't listen. I said I'd love that woman till I died, love her with my body like

I'd always loved her. And I'll never change till I die . . . .' His head dropped drowsily on to his chest. His mouth was drivelling. 'I'll never change,' he whispered. He went to sleep.

I watched him sleeping. His body kept slumping over to one side and I kept pushing him upright, afraid he'd fall off the chair and on to the floor or into the fire. But I kept thinking, all the time I was dodging about on either side of him pushing him upright, that this man Simeon, judging from the way he talked, seemed to be in so much of a tangle and a mess, what with one thing and the other, that it wouldn't be such a bad waste of coal if he did fall into the fire.

After about five minutes, my arms got tired of propping him upright and I let him slide to the floor, where the only harm he could come to would be to the mice. His eyes didn't open for a second as I directed his downward slide. I stretched him out on the mat in front of the fire, and got an old raincoat from behind a door to put over him. I left him then to his dreams, in which he probably went chasing himself around the moon like mad just for the sake of being able to tell himself that being out of breath was a hell of a thing, and the moon was a hell of a thing for being there to tempt you to go chasing yourself around it. Simeon was getting a lot too deep for me.

I lit the candle in my bedroom. I hoped everybody in the house was as fast asleep as Simeon was. I wanted to read another page of that cowboy tale before going to sleep, so that I wouldn't find myself forgetting what started off the feud that kept the characters shooting at each other across the public square. I hadn't been in bed a minute before my door was knocked. I didn't bother to ask who was there, because I knew they'd come in anyway. About as private as the top of a mountain, that box-room.

It was Bess. She walked with her shoulders crouched as if the blow from Simeon still hurt.

'Where is he?' she asked.

'In the kitchen. On the mat.'

'Drunk?'

'I think so. He was queer.'

'He's a devil, that man.'

'Oh yes.' I still thought all drunken men were devils.

'You saw what he did to me?'

'The stick? Oh, yes. That was a whanger.'

'You've got to help us, Benny.'

'Who? Me?'

'Don't look so silly when you say something.'

'Oh, no. What can I do? I'm underweight. Everybody says that. I can't do anything. I can't help anybody.'

'Don't sit there and say you can't, boy, like an idiot.' She came to the side of the bed. 'You've got to help us.'

'All right. How?'

'You've got to help us against our father.'

'How can I do that? He's been all right to me, honest. Never met anybody better, taken all round. He gave me a flip tonight and he gave you that whanger with the stick, which I'll admit was a real whanger, but still he's better than the bloke I worked with before. You wouldn't believe what a bloke that was, that grocer . . . .'

'You're only a kid. You wouldn't understand.'

'I understand about the jobs I do.'

'And that's about all.'

'That's about enough, where I come from.'

'Listen and don't argue or I'll pull your ears off.'

'All right. I get trodden on. So I'll listen.'

'My sister's coming. My sister Eleanor.'

'I know.'

'Who told you?'

'Elsa. She told me down in the kitchen.'

'He wants her.'

'Who?'

'My father.'

'What for?'

'I said don't argue. He wants to ruin her like he ruined us.'

'What you mean, ruin?'

'Do what you're told. She's young, like you. Make her your friend. Be with her all the time. Whatever else you do, keep her away from my father as if he were a plague. Tell her to get away from this house. Make her listen to you. Tell her she can't stay here. Do you understand that? Tell her to get away from this house.'

'Oh, it's not such a bad place. I like it all right.'

'You like it! You like it! God in heaven!'

'Yes. I like it. Now with that grocer . . .'

'Don't chatter.' She moved towards the window. Her voice, when she spoke again, was low and cold and whispering, like the draught that came under the door. 'And once you've won Eleanor's friendship and made her like you, be careful. My father doesn't like men or boys who try to take his daughters away from him. You see . . . 's hard to explain to a kid like you . . . he wants his daughter, because he's mad. If he finds you trying to take Eleanor away, and that's what I want you to do, he'll hate you, he'll want to kill you.'

'Kill me? Now look . . .'

'You've been warned in advance so there'll be little danger. There was a man once who wanted to take me away. He was a fine lad. Thin like you, but taller and stronger. He would have done anything for me. He died because my father wanted him to die.' She stared down at the bottom of the garden. 'He would have lived if my father hadn't seen him. His name was Walter James Mathias.'

'I've heard of him.'

'He's dead now.'

'Did you say Simeon killed? . . .'

'I didn't say anything.'

'But shouldn't the police . . . or somebody . . . ?'

'What happened to Walter James Mathias is my business, my father's and Walter's. And where he sleeps, he's near to me. Very near to me and that's good.' For two or three minutes she looked out of the window towards the bottom of the garden where she had been kneeling in the cabbage plot. Then, without another word, with her lips sticking stiffly outward, she left the room.

I picked up the cowboy tale from force of habit. I laid it down without reading a line. The print had gone dim. Anyway, it couldn't compete with Simeon and his family. Not for a minute. I got out of bed. I stood by the window. I looked out into the darkness as Bess had done, in the direction in which she had looked, towards the cabbage bed at the bottom of the garden. I felt colder than I had ever felt before in my life. And often, I've felt very cold . . . .

Two days later Eleanor came. Simeon sent me down to meet the bus she was travelling by. I was to carry her bag up the hillside.

I'll tell you Eleanor was pretty but that would only be a tiny part of all I'd want to say. She must have been just like the woman Simeon tried to tell me about the night he got drunk by the fire. She was velvet, white, black and laughing. She was a girl you could love all over and all at once.

I hardly felt the weight of the bag I carried for her up the steep hillside that led to Simeon's house. The sound of her voice in my ear held in it more of music in a moment than had been uttered in my singing throat in a lifetime. I talked and laughed back at her when she laughed, and whatever I said always seemed to be the thing she'd been waiting to hear, and by the time we were half-way up the hillside we were friends. She clapped her hands when she came in sight of the house.

'I'm going to like being here again,' she said, and I forgot about Bess for a good many minutes and spent all my brains thanking God for Simeon, whose kindness had allowed me to see, for howsoever short a time, a girl like Eleanor.

Simeon had food waiting for her when we went in. I always had food with Simeon, so the three of us sat around the table and ate. Simeon only nibbled at his food. He stared at Eleanor and held one of her hands in his so tightly I felt like asking him how he expected her to eat anything with him trying out his grips on her like that. He was all smiles, and his voice was so gentle and soft and purring it was a wonder he didn't send himself off to sleep. He was like a clean-shaven Santa Claus as he sat there smiling at Eleanor, and I hoped he'd get stuck in the chimney on his next trip down.

Every word he said to Eleanor made me think of what Bess had said. In a far away, cloudy sort of fashion, I was beginning busily to water what was growing in my heart to be a first rate hatred of Simeon. I told myself, through every mouthful of food I ate, that I wouldn't be needing any more encouragement from Bess to stand between Eleanor and him. '. . . even if it means the bloody cabbage patch!' I heard my brain telling me, suddenly and distinctly, and when I heard those words inside me the food I had in my mouth took on a queer taste and I left the room quickly because I couldn't eat any more.

I was back in a minute. Not because I felt any better; I couldn't bear to be away from Eleanor.

'Make this house your little world, Eleanor,' Simeon was saying. 'The mountain above us is wild and ugly. The valley below is not so wild, but it's even uglier than the mountain. I want you to live for me, my dear. I'm very lonely now. I'm getting quite old, as you see. That was why I was so glad to know you could come. I wanted you so much to come back to me. You're so like your mother, Eleanor. It's as if she had come back. Your eyes, your hair. As if she had come back. Don't try to be too friendly with your sisters. They're jealous of you. You'll soon see that. You are so very beautiful, Eleanor. I can't blame them for not liking you, for being jealous. Whatever you want to say, say to your father. He'll always want to listen. And, of course, there's Benny here. Don't mind him. He's so thin you can just laugh at him. Benny has spent a lot of his time down in the valley being half starved, and it will make you laugh sometimes to watch him eat.' Simeon laughed, but Eleanor blushed, and my fingers tightened on the edge of the table.

The next week went by quickly. Each evening Simeon would keep Eleanor talking a long time in the kitchen. And when she went off into the parlour that led off from the kitchen, where Simeon had arranged for her to sleep, he would stare at the parlour door for a long, long time before he would think of saying anything to me. And whenever he talked to Eleanor during those evenings, he would ask her every so often:

'You're happy to be here, Eleanor? You wouldn't like to leave me again, would you, my dear?'

Eleanor would always say no to those questions and Simeon, when he heard her say that, would always rub his hands and smile. The pale, sad look he had worn on his face sometimes when I came to work for him first had vanished from his face altogether since Eleanor had come. When he and I went out of doors together, he would do things in front of me, throw logs about and smash them in two with one stroke of the axe, to show me how strong he was. He seemed to be very strong indeed, stronger than ever, and I was very impressed by the distance to which he could throw some of those logs, and that led me on to thinking that with me being something less than half the weight of some of these logs, and with more places for a man to get a good trip on, Simeon would probably be able to throw me right over the mountain and have me bounce right back again if the fancy ever took him to use me for such purposes. I got no joy from the sight of Simeon performing in this strong manner, and I began to hope that if I really did annoy Simeon by making a friend of Eleanor, as Bess had said, that either Simeon would start to weaken or I would start to put on some flesh.

The week that followed was a very happy week for me. Every day Eleanor and I were together a lot. Some business about Simeon's land had cropped up, and he had to go down to the valley every day to see about that, and he stayed down in the valley most of the day.

Eleanor and I were glad to see the back of Simeon. I took her away from the house as much as I could and up on the mountain, where the autumn ferns were thick and red and crisp. I was a fast walker and Eleanor liked walking with me, because she walked fast, too. Everything I liked Eleanor liked. During all that week I got a bit less dark about the mind, and I began to find things I liked that I hadn't even thought of liking before.

We played among the ferns like little kids do. We felt like little kids. Happy to be just there and free and as young as we'd ever be. When I ran after her and caught her, she'd give me a kiss and day by day, through all that long, sweet week the kisses she gave me grew longer and of purer gold. Then, on the sixth evening of that week, coming down from the mountain, we stopped near the toolshed, which was at the back of the house, and I gave Eleanor a last kiss before going into the house. I had grown very fond of this kissing. If I hadn't I would not have done it so near the house. I was pulling my lips away from Eleanor's when I heard her voice suddenly in my ear.

'He's looking.'

'Who?'

'My father.'

I saw Simeon's face watching us from the kitchen window. I only saw it for an instant, but I thought I noticed that all the red colour it had most often had drained away from it. When we went in he looked the same as usual. But he wore no smile upon his face, and he said not a word as he sat down at table. He sat hunched up on his chair and played about with his fingers in his coat pockets, as he waited for me to serve the cold meal. He kept silent throughout that evening, and Eleanor, who was as sick as I was of so much silence but not paid as I was to put up with it, went to bed early.

When she had gone Simeon sat down by the fire and told me to bring the beer. He drank in quiet sips for an hour or so. I sat in my usual place by the fireside.

'You like my daughter, Benny?' he asked, without turning his head towards me.

'Oh, yes,' I said.

'She's nice.'

'She's grand.'

He threw his glass hard against the bars of the grate as I said that. I jumped from my chair, but his foot came up behind my legs and he tossed me to the floor, his hand on my neck.

'You lean, miserable little bastard,' he said, and his voice was like a wooden rattle. 'I have laws for those who take my daughters. Good laws. They are my laws, just as my daughters are my daughters. Mine. Do you hear that? Mine. Every tiny, mortal, bloody scrap of them, mine. You must be made to stop loving, Benny. Nature didn't mean you for the glory of loving, little Benny. You must be made to stop, like that other lean and hungry ram was made to stop. And I'm the one to stop you. He died easy, that other. And so will you, Benny my boy.'

He got worked up with all this talking and he started to wave one of his arms about, and his eyes were big and strong like flares. The pressure of his body on mine relaxed. My legs felt freer. I kicked up like a salmon. My feet must have landed where they hurt because Simeon yowled and leaped away. I was through the door and out on the dark hillside, crouched behind a wall, before his yowl had properly drooped back again into silence.

I could see Simeon outlined against the kitchen door, his head moving this way and that in an effort to find me. Then the door shut and as soon as the light from the door had been shut off and I was left with no more light than starlight, I decided that I would kill Simeon. I decided it quickly, without finding any stones to trip over in my brain. Just like I would have decided to sing a song, but I had never wanted to sing any song as much as I wanted to kill Simeon. I crept along to the toolshed. I found a long-handled pick and the smooth feel of its thick wooden handle assured me that it was what I wanted. I made my way back to the house and stood at the side of the small kitchen window, peering in.

Inside the kitchen Simeon was standing still at the door of the parlour where Eleanor was sleeping. His hand would stretch for the knob of the door and then withdraw. Then he walked back towards the table in the middle of the room, scratching his head angrily with both hands.

I kept telling myself that now was the time to go in there, but my limbs were frozen, and I felt as daft as ever I'd felt, standing there in the dark with a pick in my hands as tall as myself, too afraid and sick inside me to move an inch. Even my eyelids wouldn't move. I noticed that because I wanted to blink and I couldn't.

I saw Simeon walk quickly towards the parlour door. This time he did no hand stretching or hesitating. He swung open the door and marched in. I shouted to myself that now was the time and I couldn't wait any longer, but my voice just laughed at itself in little echoes at the bottom of the garden, and I still couldn't move. I stared like an owl at the darkness of the parlour through the door that Simeon had left open.

I saw Eleanor flash out into the kitchen, white in a night robe and fast as a hare. After her came Simeon and he was moving pretty fast. It steadied me to see people moving, even people moving horribly like that. I watched them as if they were cinema people. I saw Eleanor pick up a bread knife from the table. She held it stiffly in front of her. I saw Simeon run towards it, his mouth moving like a fish's mouth, his eyes swollen with the crying he was doing and glued to her face, and not seeing the knife that was sticking out in front of Eleanor. I saw his body rush into the knife and I saw the knife slide into his body as if it had been waiting for nothing but that, glad to take it in to the hilt.

I heard a long, choking scream from Simeon. I saw the door leading to the stairs open. Bess came in running. She paid no attention to Eleanor. After Bess came Elsa and the two kids. Bess kneeled down at Simeon's side. And Elsa and the kids, as if they were in a mime, followed Bess in everything she did and kneeled down, too.

I found my limbs unlocked. I threw away my pick. I ran into the kitchen and took hold of Eleanor, who was swaying with her hands grasped on the table.

Bess had the breadknife in her hands.

'He's dead and I did it. He's dead and I did it. He's dead and I did it.' She was moaning and swaying in time with her words, and Elsa and the children did the same, and in all their faces as they kneeled there was a blank, startled look as if they had suddenly seen the world change before their eyes.

Through the kitchen door and out on to the dark hillside again, I started to run with Eleanor by my side, and running like that, with the free, clean, black air on our heads, was the only thing in our lives that mattered to either of us just then.

THE PERFECT STRANGER

P. J. Kavanagh

This celebrated autobiography, winner of the Richard Hillary Memorial Prize for 1966, is as readable and funny as it is hauntingly tender. It is P. J. Kavanagh's tribute to the memory of his first wife, Sally, the perfect stranger – and it is also the absorbing, amusing tale of his early years, from schooldays and undergraduate life to the time he spent in Korea as a soldier and his happy, but short-lived, marriage to Sally.

'A real book; human, tender, gentle, loving, intelligent' – *Sheffield Morning Telegraph*

'A love story beautifully told' – *Sunday Telegraph*

Autobiography 40p

MORTAL PASSION

George Mikes

A side-splitting novel by an author who has built up a huge, world-wide following with his alien's-eye view on national pride and prejudice *How to be an Alien*, which has sold over one and a half million copies. In *Mortal Passion*, George Mikes turns his delightful comic talents to the more universal lunacies of mankind.

'He produces funny sensations by sound good sense and by direct assault; by suddenly exposing a hidden but obvious truth he shocks us into laughter' – *Spectator*

Fiction 40p

THE SONS OF THE FALCON

David Garnett

'A rumbustious story of a blood feud in the Caucasus in the 1860s which is bound to satisfy the most exacting adventure lovers' – *Daily Mail*

'Apart from the excitements of battles and earthquakes, this gripping narrative draws tremendous power from the deeply researched and convincingly presented evocation of the manners, customs, food, dancing and whole life-style of the different Transcaucasian peoples' – *The Times*

'This novel must be welcomed as an achievement . . . fierce, scarlet and unforgettable' – *The Guardian*

Fiction 45p

THE LUCK OF GINGER COFFEY

Brian Moore

The Luck Of Ginger Coffey is a brilliant example of Brian Moore's shrewd observation. Ginger Coffey is a thoroughly likeable failure; his new life in a new land (from Ireland to Canada) is hardly off the ground before it starts to crumble around him. At his lowest ebb, Ginger suddenly decides to fight back against his fate, and armed only with the luck of the Irish and a lot of bravado, he starts running uphill in hope, into a hilarious series of misadventures, disasters – and victories. *The Luck of Ginger Coffey* is a superbly entertaining novel.

Fiction 35p

These books are obtainable from booksellers and newsagents or can be ordered direct from the publishers. Send a cheque or postal order for the purchase price plus 6p postage and packing to Quartet Books Limited, P.O. Box 11, Falmouth, Cornwall TR10 9EN